Land
Mammals

AND

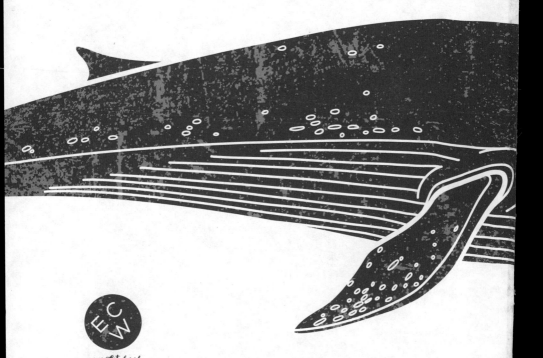

EC
W

a misfit book

Sea Creatures

A Novel

JEN NEALE

This is a work of fiction. Names, characters, places, and incidents either are the product of the author's imagination or are used fictitiously, and any resemblance to actual persons, living or dead, business establishments, events, or locales is entirely coincidental.

LIBRARY AND ARCHIVES CANADA
CATALOGUING IN PUBLICATION

Neale, Jennifer, 1984–, author
Land mammals and sea creatures : a novel / Jen Neale.

Issued in print and electronic formats.
ISBN 978-1-77041-414-3 (softcover)
ALSO ISSUED AS: 978-1-77305-183-3 (PDF),
978-1-77305-182-6 (EPUB)

I. TITLE.

PS8627.E219L36 2018   C813'.6
C2017-906186-0   C2017-906187-9

Editor for the press:
Michael Holmes/a misFit Book
Cover design: Michel Vrana
Author photo: Jackie Dives

The publication of *Land Mammals and Sea Creatures* has been generously supported by the Canada Council for the Arts which last year invested $153 million to bring the arts to Canadians throughout the country, and by the Government of Canada through the Canada Book Fund. *Nous remercions le Conseil des arts du Canada de son soutien. L'an dernier, le Conseil a investi 153 millions de dollars pour mettre de l'art dans la vie des Canadiennes et des Canadiens de tout le pays. Ce livre est financé en partie par le gouvernement du Canada.* We also acknowledge the Ontario Arts Council (OAC), an agency of the Government of Ontario, and the contribution of the Government of Ontario through the Ontario Book Publishing Tax Credit and the Ontario Media Development Corporation.

Ontario
Ontario Media Development
Corporation

ONTARIO ARTS COUNCIL
CONSEIL DES ARTS DE L'ONTARIO
an Ontario government agency
un organisme du gouvernement de l'Ontario

Canada Council
for the Arts

Conseil des Arts
du Canada

Canada

PRINTED AND BOUND IN CANADA   PRINTING: MARQUIS   5   4   3   2   1

RECYCLED
Paper made from
recycled material
FSC® C103567
www.fsc.org

For my family

PART I

Arrival

one

BLUE WHALE

Julie Bird closed her eyes and listened to water slap the hull. The tinny taste of lager coated the back of her tongue. She and her father, Marty, spread themselves over lawn chairs on the deck of the old troller. Waves rolled under the boat, and the strips of rainbow vinyl creaked under their weight. Ice sloshed rhythmically against the sides of the cooler.

Ian, Marty's best and only friend, emerged from the cabin and fished another beer from the ice. He called out to his two passengers. "Set?"

Julie's father had his beer jammed into his prosthesis—his Captain Hook—and held it in the air for Ian to see. With his good hand he held binoculars fast to his eyes.

For the last half hour, Marty had been watching a figure on shore and giving Julie updates. The details were still shady. The figure, of indeterminate age, gender and height, had been weighted like a pack mule when it'd arrived on the beach, and it was now setting up a bright orange A-frame tent that contrasted the navy water and dark conifers. Marty's eyebrows, or the fatty lumps where his eyebrows used to be, rose.

"Now they're stringing up a hammock in the trees. Looks like they're there for the long haul. I didn't think anyone camped on Tallicurn."

"Marty, please stop spying," Julie said.

"They just seem so familiar."

"You know a lot of faraway specks?"

By Marty's feet sat a small Tupperware container of herring pieces that were melting together in the heat. He'd set up a rod on the port side for some mooching, but so far, the line hadn't budged. Marty wouldn't have noticed anyway. Earlier, Ian had tossed a piece into the open water to "get the ocean's juices flowing."

"Hey," Marty said. "I think they're waving at me." He took off his bandana, scratched his bald head, and retied the fabric.

"Marty, you're a stick figure on a boat to them," Julie said.

"Look." Marty handed the binoculars to her. Through the viewfinder, she saw a crowd of gulls circling above the orange tent. Farther down the beach, the backlit figure appeared with a blond puff of hair catching the light and shining like an anglerfish lure. The person stood in the water, looking in their direction. The waves crashed against their shins. They were gesturing with their arms, but it didn't seem like a wave. More of a *come hither*.

Ian barged into the middle of their assembly and pointed starboard. "Hey, you two. Whale."

Plumes of mist were approaching the troller. With a bird's-eye view, one could trace a straight line between the puff-topped shadow, the fishing boat and the whale.

"Think it's an orca?" Julie asked.

"Nah. No pod—it's solo." Ian hoisted himself up and took the binoculars from Julie's hand. He stood on the deck with one leg propped on the railing. His white shorts flapped in the breeze, revealing a vast expanse of untanned thigh. "Too big, too," he said.

"Grey?" Julie asked.

"Maybe. Look at it." Ian passed the binoculars back.

All she could see was sun bouncing off waves and a flash of black and white as a flock of murres glided above the surface, but then the whale's rolling back filled the viewing area. A burst of mist shot into the air and dissipated. Julie adjusted the sight. A group of fat barnacles pocked the skin around its blowhole, but otherwise the whale's complexion was uninterrupted slate, like a blackboard wiped clean with a damp cloth. It was smoother than the greys Julie had seen.

"Fuck, yeah," she whispered.

The back of the whale rolled over the surface until the flukes broke free and heaved into the air. The whale dipped below the waves.

Ian's voice came from behind them, somewhere between a prayer and a curse. "It's coming toward us."

Julie imagined the whale as a submarine designed to look like a biological being, but with two soldiers sitting behind the eyes. If they could build a camera the size of a housefly, why not this? The submarine theory seemed so much more likely than a living being double the length of the Greyhound she rode from Port Braid to Vancouver. Fifty-five people could sit inside that Greyhound on a busy holiday, meaning that 110 humans could be comfortably hidden within the whale's blubber, with leg and luggage room to spare.

Julie zipped her life vest and shoved one at her father as the whale got closer to the boat. As usual, Marty wouldn't think of his welfare, so she'd have to do it for him. She watched him slide the life vest on and struggle to do it up. When the zipper wouldn't go past his belly, he visited the cooler for another beer. Julie counted this as his fourth, still within safe limits for a calm day.

The list of events that could disrupt a calm day had shape-shifted since she was last home in Port Braid. Once again the rules had to be relearned. Marty's triggers developed like allergies. Some were long-term—bird bangers, air brakes, metal-tinged smoke—and others came and went in a matter of years—the smell of Julie's hair straightener, the rattle of Boggle.

She stood up for a better look, binoculars pressed to her cheekbones.

The whale broke the surface again, much closer to the boat. Its blowhole looked like a nose thieved from an Easter Island statue. It let out another giant breath, and this time Julie could hear the sound—a bucket of ice water hitting a campfire. Julie brought the binoculars down and turned to her father. "It's a blue, you know."

Marty scoffed.

Blues migrated by Port Braid but weren't typically interested in stopping. They were half-starved from raising their young at the equator. Up north, all they'd have to do to be full was open their mouths.

So much of Port Braid's aesthetic was based on the idea that whale spirits permeated the air: a metallic statue stood proud outside the bank, a badly constructed orca mural graced the side of the pharmacy, and of course, all of the T-shirts in the town's single gift shop were a blend of semi-transparent moons, whales, wolves, eagles and feathers.

"I'm serious," Julie said. "It's a blue."

Marty brought his beer to his lips and held it there, waiting for the beast to reappear.

A bulge of water appeared a few boat-lengths away. Julie's breath caught. The whale's nose pushed through the centre of this water mountain. Its body rose up to its pectoral fins. Columns of water fell away. The animal lunged and sent a boat-rocking wave.

The force of its leap propelled it forward and downward. Its head and body slapped the water in one massive parallel line. At the sound of the collision, the three dropped back to their seats.

Ian started laughing. "Jesus," he said. "It's a blue." He grabbed Marty's shoulders and planted a kiss on his cheek.

This was a game they played. Julie said something that was true; Marty claimed it couldn't be true; Ian proclaimed it as truth and thus it became an axiom of their shared reality.

Marty started laughing too. A strange smell wafted through the air—something like sewage combined with the taste of a wet Tylenol tab.

Julie saw the whale's shadow coming in their direction. "Marty!" Julie gripped the railing with white knuckles.

The whale's smooth skin surfed above the waves, its torpedo-shaped face just under the surface. The whale exhaled again, sending flecks of mist against their faces and filling their nostrils with the medicinal stench of its breath.

Ian looked to Marty for help. Save his poor baby boat. The whale's back grazed the farthest reach of their fishing lines and their bobbers were swallowed by the waves.

The three of them held tight to the railing and rope ties. Julie looked over at her father. He had a wet sheen along his lower lids. Under his breath, Ian said, "Not my boat, not my boat." They all fell silent and waited for the impact. Julie stared down and counted the splashes against the hull. One . . . two . . . three . . . four. The world was devoid of sound except for the slap of waves and the gurgle of upturned water that followed the whale's progress.

Julie had the urge to jump over the railing and ride the whale to the bottom of the sea, swinging a seaweed cowboy hat over her head.

Just before its nose reached the hull, it began to dive. As the whale slid down, Julie held her breath and closed her eyes. The boat leaned starboard as the great mass passed underneath. Her daily life, being home in Marty's half-dilapidated bungalow, had consisted of grey mornings eating cold eggs out of a pan and day-time television marathons. *Even if I die . . .* she thought.

Julie opened her eyes and watched as the mast returned to centre.

"Where's she going?" Ian's grip on the railing had released but the parental look of concern stayed.

Julie tasted blood in her spit. She turned to her father. "Marty, I think she's beaching."

"I don't think so, kiddo."

Another massive plume rose from the whale as it accelerated toward the shoreline. Rocks jutted from the water around the beach at Tallicurn.

The figure on the beach had waded farther out. One of their hands held a cigarette.

The smell of gasoline flooded the air as Ian started the engine and manoeuvered the boat to pursue the whale.

The individual shapes of the spruce and shore pines came into focus as the boat chugged closer to the shore. A bald eagle soared out from the evergreens with two ravens attacking its tail feathers.

Ian yelled over the sound of the engine. "She's beaching!"

Marty nodded. "Maybe we can steer her back."

"In this piece of shit?" Julie asked.

A look of hurt crossed Ian's face.

A stirred line of silt illuminated the whale's route from boat to beach. Julie begged the blue to come to its senses. She pictured herself on her knees at the bottom, an air traffic—water traffic—controller, waving an orange flag. *It's all death and seagulls this way, Whale. Here's a card for a suicide prevention hotline.* But she spoke in a high-pitched language incompatible with the whale's low drumming pulses.

The beast came up for another breath, its tail now too weak to rise above the waves. The sandbars came one after another and brought the whale closer to the dry summer air.

Ian killed the engine and came back onto the deck. The boat bobbed and swayed.

Marty voice was a child's. "She'll turn back."

Seagulls screamed louder. The blue's breaths came more frequently but shot lower into the air. Finally its back was forced to stay above the surface.

Ian stood like a Renaissance-era navigator at the front of his boat, hand shielding his eyes.

"It's happening," he said, and Marty nodded. The whale had somehow disappointed Ian by beelining for shore. Marty rose and put his prosthesis on Ian's shoulder.

The whale, with a last push, reached the shallows. It emerged from the water past its eyes and slid along the sand until finally, as its last motion, it rolled sixty degrees onto its right side, its tail still curled into deeper water. A freight train derailing, it folded in on itself, crumpled by its own mass and speed. Waves lapped around the whale's bottom fin. Its length took up half the shoreline and blocked the view of the orange tent and the spruce. Out of the water, its form flattened against the sand. A deflated inner tube.

The two men stood in a silent vigil, their shoulders dropped low, while Julie flopped down on the lawn chair.

Marty broke away and picked up the on-board radio to call the coast guard.

Ian started the engine back up and chugged toward shore. They anchored as close as they could and lowered themselves into the little rubber dinghy, bringing along the essentials: the binoculars and the remaining beer.

The sun's effects were catching up to Julie. Her nausea went beyond seasickness, augmented by the sun and swells of emotion and probably the beer, and she was unsure if she wanted a glass of ice water or a toilet to puke in.

The sides of the behemoth rose in quick starts. Its graceless fin grasped at the air.

They dragged the boat onto the sand and walked to the whale's eye, dark and glossy, which somehow didn't seem that much bigger than Julie's. It was, of course. It was half the size of her fist, but it shrank in proportion to the animal. The design of the whale's eye was meant to make out images in the deep pressure of the ocean, so Julie imagined that now the whale saw only a collection of colours standing in front of it. It made her regret her neon tank top. She reached out a hand and felt the whale's rubbery skin. The coolness of it startled her. Julie turned to Marty. "Feel that."

"Nah." Marty stood with his arms crossed over his chest the same way he did when trying to end a conversation. He rubbed under his bandana, a nervous twitch predicting his next bout of psoriasis. His eyes darted in the direction of the orange tent. Julie followed his gaze and saw the figure from the shore, now fully fleshed in contour and colour.

The blond flop of curls bounced over her eyes as she strode toward them. There was tightness to her face, as though strings pulled back from her cheekbones and from the sides of her mouth. A cigarette hung from her lips, and she carried a bucket that bounced against her legs. She stopped in front of them and scratched at some crud on her rolled-up jeans. Her eyes locked on to Marty. Marty stared back. The seagulls screamed over their heads.

The woman rubbed the shaved sides of her head and hooked the bucket onto Marty's prosthesis. "For you. You can try to keep it wet for a while, if that makes you feel better." She touched a barnacle on the beast's side. "Every dying whale has a story to tell."

The woman flicked Marty's arm, turned and walked to the back of the beach, kicking sand as she went. She disappeared into the trees.

Julie inspected the bucket. "What the fuck was that?"

Marty stared in the direction that his spying victim had gone. He ducked his head and visited the ocean for the first bucket of seawater. His body was weighted to the left as he heaved the bucked across the beach. The splash barely reached the top of the whale. They'd need twenty people passing twenty buckets if they wanted to keep its body from drying out.

Julie and Ian sat side by side in the sand and inspected the whale. Along its throat were deep parallel grooves highlighted by a lighter grey–hued skin.

When Julie was young, during a competition to rid the local lake of undesirable catches, she did her best to keep a school of junk fish alive in a bucket. She couldn't bring herself to smash the heads of the sunfish and spiny dogfish, even though the organizers told her she couldn't win the grand prize gift certificate with a bucket of live ones. So she left them in her pail. Until they suffocated. Probably killed more than anyone else, in fact. Buckets of water would only prolong the whale's suffering. But it was something to keep Marty busy. The whale would be crushed under its own weight on land, and it wouldn't take long. The whale fin shook hands with the air, blocking and unblocking the stream of sunshine.

The blue's mouth gaped to reveal the hair-like baleen plates. Shallow breaths, like panting, moved the whale's sides. Julie gagged at the whale's breath, but she couldn't move away from the animal.

The sun moved lower in the sky and the tide retreated. The fingertips of the waves stopped reaching the whale's mass, and finally Marty gave up his efforts and sat in the sand. Julie reached out occasionally to feel the whale's skin, which radiated hotter each time. The skin grew tacky. Julie scanned the horizon for the coast guard but no ships came into sight, and at this point that was for the best. What would they do? Drag the animal by its tail into the ocean? Would it tear in two on the sand? Or, if they got it out to sea, wouldn't it come back?

Ian turned to Marty. "Maybe you can sell deep-fried blubber." He announced he wanted his photo with the whale, for posterity. He jogged up to the little orange tent and grabbed something resting on the far side.

"Ian," Julie said. "You dipshit."

"She's long gone. Thought I spotted something. Here." Ian came back with a fishing rod in his hand. He knelt by the whale's mouth with his back blocking their view. When he stepped away, Julie saw that he had pushed the hook through a small section of the whale's bottom lip. "Where's your camera?" he asked Julie.

"Fuck you, Ian. It's still alive."

"Come on, Julie, it can't feel that."

"Take it out, shit wad."

"Julie." Marty turned to her—to her—to stop the fight. His hand shook.

"Tell him to take it out, Marty."

Ian slumped his shoulders. "Marty, for Christ's sake, I just want a photo. You can hang it at the bar."

Marty rose to his feet and fumbled with Ian's phone. He asked Julie for a hand.

"Figure it out yourself." She got up and moved to the other side of the whale. It still laboured for breath and they were taking photos. *Har, har, you caught a blue whale.*

She watched her father aim the screen and snap a shot of Ian reeling in the blue.

Just before the sun buried itself below the ocean, the whale's breath became shallower until, anticlimactically, it stopped.

"That's it," Marty said.

They prepped the dinghy for the ride back to the boat. There was still light enough to see the whale's full frame.

Marty gazed back at the trees. "Something familiar about her."

The seagulls overhead couldn't wait to tear the whale apart. A few began to land close by, shrieking at the deathbed. Above the seagulls, an eagle coasted in slow circles, pestered again by ravens.

Julie, Ian and Marty said cheers to the whale's life. They tipped their beers and drained the last few drops. Before Julie climbed into the dinghy, though, she saw a quick movement in the sky.

The bald eagle, with its wings tucked in, plummeted toward earth. Julie shook Marty's arm. "It's falling."

"It's just diving," Marty said. They stared up.

It fell in a straight line, with the ravens still chasing its tail. If Julie hadn't seen it circling a moment ago, she would have thought it was a piece of luggage dropped from a plane.

"Holy shit," Ian whispered, and Marty nodded.

The bald eagle hit the rocks headfirst and left a streak of gore and feathers. The two ravens hit the rocks on either side and bounced. Their crumbled bodies lay less than twenty metres from the whale's deflated form, some feathers scattered across the rocks and sand.

two

SALMON SHARK

Marty tacked the whale photo above the cash register at The Halibut and started his morning routine. Neither he nor Julie got much rest the night the whale died, instead watching reruns of *The Golden Girls* until it started to get light, and since then the late nights had become regular.

His coffee steamed on the counter. Only coffee could keep him alive. He lined ketchup bottles along the bar and pulled the bulk container from the fridge. Part of his routine was to see which table had gone through the most ketchup. The table by the window frequently won, claiming tourists who wanted to admire the harbour and green peaks. The ketchup bottles along the bar usually did well too, with the lunch breakers that sat with heads bowed, piles of crispy fish and mid-afternoon pints. The all-time champion, though, was the table tucked around the side of the bar. This is where Ian—and Ian alone—sat. His table looked onto the bathroom and the liquor selection. Ian came in once per day and made ketchup soup of his French fries. Marty considered charging extra for the excessive use, but that would only make Ian's tab bigger.

With the ketchup bottles full, he mopped the floor.

The Halibut would have its twenty-year anniversary this August. Every year, more photos and knick-knacks climbed the walls. The first year, the restaurant had only five stools, a couple of plywood tables and a deep fryer. Now, even the rafters had dangling articles, like the mounted codfish that sang Willie Nelson songs.

Marty wrung the mop so no extra water dripped around the legs of the upright piano that belonged to Brenda—Julie's mom. It was the last relic from her life and the only piece that Julie refused to let him toss. He dusted the lid and ran a layer of orange polish over its body. He wiped clean the framed photo of his old dog Midge, which hung above the instrument.

The night the whale died, in the couple hours he did sleep in the La-Z-Boy in front of the TV, Marty had that old dream about Midge. The small space, the field of mice. First time he'd had it in a long time.

They had been walking together. Nubs of her spine waved like a sea monster's spikes, but her tongue lolled and she grinned. The path got smaller and led into a dark place. Midge rolled over for a belly rub and then curled into a letter *c*. The air had gotten tight and Marty woke up. Julie was still by his side, snoring loud enough to drown out the reruns.

He dried the ground around the piano legs. When he was finished, he set the mop back in the closet. He took two sips of coffee every time he got something done. Ketchup, mopping, dusting, empty the tip jar if necessary, clean the deep fryer and sit down with the newspaper until someone came in. These were the daily routines. There were bigger cycles—annual ones. He sold tickets for the Halibut anniversary dinner. He booked a Christmas party for a rotating cast of local businesses. Julie came home for the odd summer visit. She asked him, regularly, why he was open for breakfast. Has anyone ever come in for breakfast? Well, no, kiddo. But this was where he wanted to be.

He checked the phone to see if the Centre for Disease Control had left a message. He didn't know if they would. The town went on like normal. Across the street, people sat outside Nantucket Café and sipped their overpriced Americanos. Marty sipped on his black brew.

He saw the photo of the whale in the paper. Their aerial shot missed the point. They got the whole body in the frame, but with no perspective—he could be looking at a mackerel drying on a sidewalk. The article mentioned the bickering between the town's people and the coast guard. "It's not our problem. It's private land," the coast guard said. The townspeople retorted, "Hell if we know who owns it." Some good Samaritan, or maybe the coast guard, roped off the whale with police tape. Don't eat whale meat, the article said. A few gastro-freaks in Alaska nearly died after they served up a beached whale. Whale bodies stay hot for a long time. They're plus-sized petri dishes.

The bird bodies were taken away quickly by the CDC. That doesn't cost as much as disposing of a whale.

Someone tapped on the glass door. Fran Tucker held Marty's daily order wrapped in a Walmart bag. "I've got some treats for you today," she said when he opened the door.

"Oh?"

She lifted out a bloody newspaper package. "Some halibut for the Halibut."

"Thanks, Franny."

"And. I got you some salmon shark."

"Oh yeah?"

"You want it? It was by-catch. Bill almost tossed it, but you might as well take the steaks. I know it's not a usual on the menu, but I thought . . ."

"It can be our special." He slapped her on the back.

"Bill was gillnetting, so it shouldn't be too big a shock he got one, but he says he threw it back three times. Kept coming back for more."

"Sure it was the same one?"

"Said he saw this same cut from the netting. Just under the pectoral fin."

"Must have been hungry for his catch, then."

"No doubt. Still strange. Kept sliding its head through the net and tangling its fins up. Finally it got so tangled he had to kill it. Or so he said. Honest, doesn't seem that cut-up to me. I think he was pissed it ruined his net, or he was tired of throwing it back. Anyway, sliced it open and its gut was empty. No salmon. Nothing. The meat seems fine, though."

She pulled out the rest of the day's catch—some sole, some cod, some salmon—and flopped the packages on the bar. Marty poured her daily cup of coffee.

"Salmon shark heart is a real delicacy," she told him. "Served raw. I'm trying it tonight. You think I'm crazy?"

"Yup." He swirled his coffee and looked down at the copasetic package of shark. "So, what do you think of all this, Franny?" He gestured at the newspaper.

"Such a shame."

"A shame is when you spill milk."

She rolled her eyes. "My cousin works on the *Queen Mary* going up to Alaska, and he thought she might have been hit by a ship. That happens."

He shook his head. "Not a scratch on her."

"Well, my sister thought maybe she was just old."

"Maybe. There are the birds too."

"I just hope they drag that thing away. Hey, how's your kid?"

"Ah, she didn't have to come."

"Yeah. No, no." Fran looked up at the clock. "Shoot. I gotta get moving. Thanks for the brew." She downed her coffee and sauntered out of the restaurant.

Marty unwrapped the shark and breathed the aroma. It was properly bled out and gutted. Sharks piss through their skin, so improper butchering means the meat will smell like ammonia. But Fran never delivered subpar meat. Even if the fish has strange tendencies. He was feeling funny about it—the shark reentering the net, the birds, the whale.

Marty unwrapped the coho salmon. The flesh smelled sweet and had a neon orange hue. A few of the recently arrived yuppies, the ones from the new Gregion Lake development, thought it was a shame to deep-fry fish. They wanted them pan-fried and served on a bear-shaped cedar plank. To Marty, the deep fryer was the greatest respect you could pay a fish. Nothing else packed so much juice in the flakes. His dishes were crispy and soft, and the fish were always caught that day.

Part of the yuppies' problem was his liberal use of the fryer for other food items. On Wild Card Wednesdays, for a $5 "corkage" fee, patrons could bring in their own produce for the deep fryer. The health authority would shit themselves if they knew, but the town hadn't given him up so far. He had to change the oil once a week anyway, so it might as well be Wednesdays.

Just like the yuppies didn't embrace him, neither did other fish and chip shop owners. He'd met a few in other towns, and their cooking philosophy stopped at "frozen fish is cheap."

The entrance bell rang. Standing in the doorway was the girl from Tallicurn. A seeping heat rose in his gut. He put down the salmon. She wore the same outfit as on the day the whale died—a cut-up sleeveless tee and rolled-up jeans. She carried a bursting bag of groceries.

"Hullo," Marty said.

"Hi." She looked him up and down and let out a big breath. "So, you own this place?"

"Yes."

She toured the interior of The Halibut, picked a stuffed kangaroo off the shelf of knick-knacks and gave it a squeeze. She looked Marty in the eye. "You know who I am?"

Marty swallowed. More so these days, his brain felt like a loose stack of paper. Drafts came in and carried away vital pages of names and faces. But no, Ian and Julie hadn't known her either, so she wasn't a Port Braider. He couldn't know her. It was impossible. He told her he had no idea.

The girl nodded slowly. She gazed at the whale photo over the register. "I've got a sort of proposition for you."

"Lay it on me."

The girl walked over and swung a leg over a barstool. The blond flop of curls hung over her eyes. She placed the kangaroo on the bar.

"Well?" he asked. His heart pounded.

She reached for the coffee pot and pulled it in for a hug. "Just wanted to make sure you were the right guy for this. Mug, please." He passed one to her. "I'm a Jerry Lee Lewis impersonator." She sniffed.

"Fine. Go on."

"Jennie Lee Lewis. I go by JLL." She stuck her hand out for a shake. Her grip surprised him.

She filled her mug with a flourish, raising the pot higher and higher as the black liquid poured out. Every movement JLL made was sharp—a clear beginning, middle and end to each gesture. She lowered her eyebrows. "You have a stage here?"

"Nope, afraid not. Not really that kind of place."

Her eyes narrowed. "What kind of place are you?"

Marty pointed up at the menu. "Fish. Chips. Some beer. There's a bar on Lilac Street. The Lion's Den."

JLL pointed at the piano in the corner and raised her eyebrows.

Marty laughed and shook his head. "Who are you?"

"I told you. Jennie Lee Lewis. I'm a Jerry Lee Lewis impersonator."

"So, I don't know you?"

"Yeah, I guess you don't." She shrugged. "Some people have heard of me."

"And why Jerry Lee Lewis?"

"Why do you have a fish and chip shop with a piano in the corner?"

"Fair question." He scratched under his bandana. "Aren't we going to talk about how we both saw a whale beach the other day?"

"I'd rather not. Listen, let me play here in the evenings."

"No."

"Six shows." She sipped her coffee.

"No."

"Screw you." JLL hopped off the bar stool and hoisted her grocery bag over her shoulder. She made toward the door.

"Where were you when the whale died?" He felt that his question sounded too large. It occurred to him that it sounded like "where were you during the moon landing" or "what were you doing when you heard about 9/11," like the event had some great historical significance. Like everyone's brains should be etched with what they ate for dinner that night, and whether it tasted bad because of the tragedy.

"Why?"

"You just left."

JLL put her hand on the door. "How long have you wanted to die?"

The heat turned to acid in Marty's stomach. "I don't want to die."

"You don't have to bullshit me. There's this look that suicidal people get around death. Maybe your two friends are blind to it, but I could see that green jealousy in your eyes." JLL scrunched her face. "I didn't feel like watching anymore."

Marty picked up the stuffed kangaroo and turned it over in his hand. There was a compartment for batteries on the bottom, and he wondered what the toy used to do.

JLL continued. "You don't have too long left. So don't worry."

She opened the door. Marty could hear the tap in the bathroom drip water onto the porcelain.

"Hold on." He set the toy down. "I want to let you play here."

"Good."

"I'm just not good with change."

The handles on JLL's grocery bag were stretched to thin strings, but somehow the plastic held on. "You'll see. I'm going to bring this place to life."

She walked out, looked both ways and headed west.

Marty tried to keep his mind off the encounter with Jennie Lee Lewis as he took orders from the lunch breakers and the tourists. His hand shook as he lowered fish into the fryer.

The tourists ate their food without speaking to him or each other. He set the price of the salmon shark low, at $8 with fries and slaw, and still nobody ordered it. "You won't find this every day," he told tourists. "Local legend: if you don't eat shark, shark might eat you."

The salmon went first. People from out of town ordered the salmon, thinking it was the BC thing to do, when really it was one of the worst meats for fish and chips—too wet. Next went the halibut, then the cod, then the lowly sole.

At the end of the workday, Marty packaged up the salmon shark to take to Fran's. He could grill steaks on the barbecue; Fran eating raw heart might be something he needed to see.

three

CAT

In the bungalow on Sequoia Street, while she waited for her father to come back from Fran's, Julie embarked on the next item on her list. She stood in the entrance to Marty's room. The rice vinegar scent of sweaty sheets crept under the door. She pushed in.

Everything about his bedroom screamed 1970s. Actually, it was the entire bungalow. The wood-panelled walls, the harvest gold tiles, the avocado green appliances, the pass-throughs and neon lights that linked rooms. All of it someone's dusty and faded version of the future. The carpets and curtains, smelling of smoke and mildew, were remnants of the previous owners, who now must be decades dead.

This bungalow ate time. In Vancouver, she arrived at her land-scaping job at 7 a.m. She went to shows. She called friends. She headed up a field hockey team. But here there seemed to be time for only one chore each day.

Marty's sheets formed a coil in the corner of his king-sized bed. He wasn't sleeping these days. A stack of *Scientific American*s stood on his bedside table, all of them worn at the corners. The tube of psoriasis cream was squeezed flat. The label told Julie he hadn't picked up a refill since February.

Earlier that day, she picked up the rotary dialler to call The Halibut and was met with silence. She spent an hour with the phone company getting Marty's house phone reconnected. It has to be the old number, she told them. At very least, don't give him that new area code. She had to put his four months of unpaid bills onto her credit card. She realized that through the last year, she had only ever called him at The Halibut. She'd missed another warning sign. *This number cannot be completed as dialled.*

The thinned fabric in the centre of the fitted sheet showed the exact diameter of Marty's nighttime flailing. The sheets pulled off the mattress with ease, the elastic corroded after decades of use. She nearly gagged at the sight of the sweat-stained and sunken mattress. And yet, for all these years since she moved away, he'd left the king-sized mattress in her childhood bedroom unused. Why hadn't he swapped the beds?

She gathered the sheets in a ball and hauled them to the laundry room. At the last second, she tossed them in the garbage bin instead.

As she was hiding the disposed sheets under a layer of loose trash, her cell rang. Lucy. The roommate. The ex-roommate. Calling from that perfect heritage suite in Vancouver, with the neighbour's tuxedo cat and the dusty houseplants.

Lucy's voice seemed to echo through the receiver. "What am I supposed to do with this couch?"

Two days remained in the month. Two days before move-out. Julie heard the croak of a spray bottle.

"Why does your voice sound strange?" Julie asked.

"I'm cleaning the oven."

"You're calling me from inside an oven."

"Yeah, Julie, it seemed fitting." More frantic spraying. A bang. "Fuck."

"I thought you wanted the couch."

"Your couch doesn't fit through the door."

Julie sank to the laundry room floor. She spotted a lone tube sock hidden amongst lint under the dryer. "Why are you cleaning? We're not getting the damage deposit."

"Because you didn't give enough notice." Paper towel being torn. A tap going at full blast.

"I'm paying you back. Stop cleaning. Leave the couch."

"I just think you could have vacuumed."

"I apologize." She wondered if she'd see this human again, how worthwhile it was to salvage this relationship. Julie would return to the city when Marty was improved, but despite six months living together, Lucy was only a peripheral friend.

Lucy sighed. The tap water stopped. "You left some things. I need to know what to do." Lucy listed off the items. A spider plant, Halloween face paint, a Teflon pan, a sequin-coated dress and an envelope with her grad photos, which Lucy found in a bathroom cupboard.

Julie retrieved the sock from under the dryer. It carried with it long, matted strands of lint. "Just toss it all."

"I can't toss it."

"You want the dress?"

"Listen." The oven door slammed. "I'll pack the photos with my stuff. You can pick them up when you're back."

"OK. Thank you."

After the phone call with Lucy, Julie heard Marty's key turn in the front door. The distinctive one-two thump of his boots landing in the closet. His heavy steps carrying him to the kitchen and the click as he turned on the burner for tea.

She found him sitting on the counter beside the stove. The burner glowed red under the kettle. A Ziploc bag of fish steaks sat by his other side.

"Do you actually never get tired of eating fish?" she asked. He looked down at the bag as though it had the answer. "Marty, wake up."

He shook his head. "Sorry, kiddo. Fran talked my ear off. CDC call?"

"When was the last time you picked up your house phone?"

Marty rubbed his forehead. "Your father's getting old."

She declined to point out that forgetting was a substandard excuse for four months of missed payments. "At least you're not as old as you look."

He punched her arm.

The kettle started to sing and Marty lifted it from the glowing rings and made the tea in the Brown Betty pot. He set their tea up on the TV tray between their two La-Z-Boys in the living room. Carton of milk, pot of tea, two mugs. Steam looped from the spout.

"The show's on soon, isn't it?" Marty asked.

"That's the best part of that channel. *Golden Girls* is always on soon."

The TV tray and the two rocking La-Z-Boys served as the only furniture in the living room. The ficus and the aloe plant in the corner had to sit on the hardwood. The leather on Marty's chair was worn, but Julie's looked almost new.

Julie struck a match and lit the two tea lights on the TV tray. The ceiling fan sliced air above their heads.

Marty lowered himself into his chair, poured milk in Julie's mug and then his own. They leaned back in their chairs, and Marty picked up the remote. He started playing with the buttons.

"It's two minutes to. You can turn it on," she said.

Marty picked at the buttons, lowered the remote.

"Jules, have I ever told you the story about Midge?"

"Your old dog?"

Marty tapped the remote against his leg. "Yeah."

"You know that you haven't. I know that you have a full photo album dedicated to Midge. I know that you sit around looking at them sometimes. I know you've avoided every question I've ever asked. And I know we're now missing the intro theme song."

"I want to tell you this story."

"Right now?"

"Tonight's episode is the one where they think Blanche murdered someone."

"But I like that one," she said.

Marty looked at Julie. "I thought you'd want to hear this."

Julie watched her father's face. His cheeks were flushed. "I didn't think you were being serious."

Marty shifted in his chair. The leather creaked under him. "I am."

It was a strange thing to watch, this tomb of information, stored without incident in his lower intestines, starting to bubble from his lips. Julie stared at the ceiling so she wouldn't have to watch his face. There was always danger in his reminiscences. Visceral details can damage his mental health. But interrupting him now was no good either. Julie closed her eyes.

1992

Another big rig whined past Marty's Astro van on the I-54 and a missile screamed through his cranium. He shook his head to get it out. *Man up. Man up, man up.*

He squinted and concentrated on individual items on the road. This is a big rig in America. This is an empty soda cup on the gravel shoulder. That is a mountain ridge in New Mexico.

If Marty was going to make it, he needed quiet.

The southwest was supposed to cure all this. No more of Ontario's 400-series highways and no more shock jock morning radio pouring from his parents' kitchen, from where they watched him as he watched a blank TV screen.

Smoke snaked from the hood of his van and curled ribbons into the air. It'd been getting thicker for the last twenty miles, but this was the last-ditch attempt to get to White Sands National

Monument. Some old hippie told him over a shared beer that despite the missile testing range behind, this was the quietest place a man could sleep. You could camp if you asked.

Midge shuffled around in the back and lay back down. Her tail scooped around her nose like a fake moustache.

A cloud of the smoke billowed over the windshield and Marty lost sight of the road. He was transported into a faraway burning car and panicked. Rocks and sand pinged off the undercarriage as the van swerved to the side. The smell of burning car gave him another flash. Midge's body thudded against the van wall. The smoke cleared. This is sagebrush in America. This is the exit sign for Route 70.

Marty looked in the rearview mirror. Midge panted back at him, unfazed, still lying down despite the tumult. *God bless this silent dog*, he thought.

A sign for White Sands National Monument appeared on the right. It was a good place to finally break down. The van rolled to a stop. Relieved to die, it spewed out a final dark cloud.

He sat in the driver's seat and looked at the ridge of white sand starting in front of the van. He glanced over his shoulder to see Midge with her head between her paws and looking up at him, brows raised.

"Well, Midgey, we're here."

Midge thumped her tail against the bare metal floor.

Marty's phantom hand started to throb again, like someone clamped his fingernails. This came with stress—mostly at night-time while forcing sleep. He rubbed around the perimeter of the bandaged stump.

He swung open the back of the van and pulled out his sack. The dry air whisked sweat off his skin. Midge hopped through the open doors and sniffed at some long-gone roadkill stain. The shape suggested a snake. Midge—a true hound, except for never baying—always had her nose pressed against the earth. If she couldn't see, she'd still be able to sniff out the shape of him. She once jumped from the back of a pickup to retrieve a dried-up baguette on the other side of a rural highway in Ontario. Might have had essence of salami on it.

"Midgey, leave it alone."

Midge snuffled her way over and prodded his foot, trying to lick something off the bottom of his sneaker. The two of them started toward the entrance of the park. Marty's bag, a one-pocket piece of crap, rubbed against his shoulders as he made his way to the visitor centre. *Just got to ask about camping. In and out.* White grains blew in patterns across the road and travelled through wormholes in his brain.

The visitor centre was a low building with an unwelcoming blast of air conditioning. Midge trotted inside after Marty. A woman in a parks uniform half untucked came toward Marty. She braided a dark coil of hair as she walked and let it unravel when she reached him. Marty's chest clenched when their eyes met. A physical sensation that broke through the haze.

The woman pointed at Midge. "He's gotta be outside." She spoke from somewhere faraway. Her expression reminded Marty of himself when he looked in the mirror. The parks woman signalled for Marty to follow her to the parking lot. Her hair fell in a direct line from her scalp to her hips and swayed at the ends. She took Midge by the collar and used a piece of twine from her pocket to tie her to a parking pole. Marty let her do it.

"You always carry around twine?" he asked. She shrugged.

She knelt and scratched under Midge's chin, who relaxed into a panting grin. The ends of the woman's hair graced the pavement. She stood and touched Marty on the back. He recoiled.

"Thinking of some backcountry?" She might have been looking

behind him instead of into his eyes. A tick of pause separated her actions, like she was subtly doing the robot.

"Sure, why not," he said.

Midge sniffed something on the woman's pant leg.

"I have to tell you a few rules," the woman said. She scratched Midge's ear. "Walk at least a mile off the road before you set down. Make sure you've got enough water. Finally, be careful of snakes. And no taking sand with you, but that's mostly the kiddies. The backcountry forms are back in here."

The woman led Marty inside past glass cases containing taxidermied wonders of the area: rattlers, roadrunners, a mangy kit fox. The bass line of a song in the background made Marty's heart thump. Marty stopped in front of a cow-shaped animal with spiral horns the length of his own torso jutting from its head. A black patch marred its white face, with two stripes vertically crossing its eyes.

The parks woman pointed and smiled like she created it. "They introduced the African oryx around here in '69 because people wanted to hunt big things. They still do, every year. But we try to keep the oryx out of the park. Non-native species."

When he picked up the pen to sign his name, Marty spotted a set of small fingers reaching up the other side of the desk. He peered over the ledge and saw a girl. Little gnat of a thing.

"Hello, kiddo."

The girl squinted at him.

"My daughter," the parks woman said. "She's stuck doing filing for me today." The woman patted her daughter's hair and then extended her hand to Marty. "Nancy Shipton." He took her hand with his left. Nancy's eyes shot over to his missing right. Her hand lay like a warm slug in his.

"Marty Bird. Nice meeting you both." He turned to face the exit.

"Victoria, you should say hello."

"Hel-lo."

Marty looked back. A left hand wrapped around Nancy's body for a shake. She shook his hand up and down like a dog killing a rat. "I'll tell you about the park."

Marty looked to the door. Nancy didn't indicate that she would save him. She tore off his backcountry form and handed him a copy.

. Victoria led him to the first in a series of wall plaques. "This one talks about President Hoover starting the park. Tell me when you're done."

"Aren't you going to tell me about it?"

"Why? It's on the wall."

Marty dropped his sack and pretended to read the words. Out of the corner of his eye, he saw Victoria looking up at him.

"You know, I was scared of you," she said.

"Yeah?"

"But then I decided not to be. What happened to your hand?"

"I lost it in the Gulf."

"You're a soldier?"

"Combat engineer."

"Was it a gun or a bomb?"

"A car."

"Someone ran over your hand?"

"Something like that."

Victoria paused. "Once mom ran over a rabbit and it kept twitching." Victoria scrunched her face and brought Marty over to the next plaque. "This one talks about gypsum. And a white lizard. Where are you from?"

"Canada."

"You must be cold."

"No, I must be hot. Here. By comparison."

"No. It's cold in Canada. Are you sad about your hand?"

Marty stared at the words in front of him. The letters blurred because he didn't care. He held the stump in the direction of the girl. "Wanna touch it?"

"No. It'll hurt."

"Maybe, but go ahead."

Victoria ran a single finger along the bandages. She started at the wrist and moved over the end. It felt like she was tracing lines on his palm, along his thumb, across his tendons, but like his hand was half the size it should have been. A cartoon version of itself. Then there were the dead-numb patches.

"Yes," he said. "It makes me feel sad. I gotta get going."

Marty stepped away from the girl and filled up his water jug in the bathroom. He exited into the heat. A car idled in the parking lot and its rumbles made his heart do more flips. *Man the hell up.* Midge climbed to her feet and jumped up on him when he untied the leash. "Let's go."

They walked along the side of the single road, family vans passing them by. All these people had been driving around the whole time, unaware.

On either side of the road, white dunes rose up. This was a different country. Texas was brown—he could drive for a day seeing only stunted sagebrush to break up the monotony. Here, the dunes were clean. In Texas, and much of New Mexico, everything struggled to survive. Here nothing bothered at all. What a relief to not witness thirst. The Persian Gulf was like Texas until you got into the dunes, and then finally everything was dead.

If anything did break through the gypsum dunes at White Sands—like the soaptree yucca—it did it confidently. The yucca exploded from the gypsum, its pointed leaves surrounding a single tall stalk, a firework launched and bursting. Soaptree yucca didn't pitifully cling to the dust like the sagebrush did. Marty needed the lushness of the coast or the dryness of the desert.

He turned ninety degrees to get the legal one mile from the

road and unclipped Midge so she could go ahead. Instead of crunching and moving to the side like beach sand or brushing aside like the Gulf dirt, the gypsum compressed under his weight. Midge left perfect indents as she trotted. The x-shaped footprints of a roadrunner ascended the next dune over and disappeared.

The sun was moving lower in the sky, and an early evening wind blew across the gypsum. They trudged along until they found a spot where the sand sat perfectly flat and a dune blocked sound from the road. Finally, the palpitations faded. He breathed.

He pulled his tent from the sack and erected it. He opened a couple of cans: wet dog food for Midge and baked beans for himself. They ate their food cold. Midge sat in front of her meal panting and looking around the campsite with her look of worried joy.

"What's the matter, you? Not hungry?"

Midge cocked her head and came to join him in the shade of the tent's awning. She put a paw on his leg and flexed her toes.

"Too hot, huh?"

The silence cradled him. He was wrapped in the long arms of the last afternoon heat, and his physical form, finally, left. His was a viscous liquid, maybe melted wax, spreading out. His lungs turned from hard knobs to sludge. *I'm OK.*

Midge crawled halfway onto his lap, and Marty massaged the fur down her spine. He closed his eyes. Drool from Midge's tongue made its way through the fabric of his shorts.

A small *whoosh* penetrated his ear. He looked around, but couldn't see where it came from. He let his eyelids fall again. The *whoosh* reentered, as though a small bird beat its wings by his eardrum. After that, it was gone.

The two of them waited for the night.

Their food disappeared bit by bit as the sun dipped below the horizon. Marty reveled in breathing. With each breath, he could fill his chest further, until the relaxation hit his knees. The sunset reflected off the white sand and shot reds and oranges across the landscape.

He kicked off his shoes and lay back against the tent poles. It was almost dark now and the full moon crawled over the mountains to the east. Small stars poked out from the dusk. Midge's paws twitched with some dog dream and she didn't wake when Marty stroked her ears. Not even crickets here.

Hours later, with the memory of sun embedded in his thoughts, a metal clanging broke his meditation. He jumped to his feet, searching the horizon for movement. His heart pounded. He stepped back and tripped over a body, which leapt up and spun. Marty scrambled back and dove behind the nearest cover. He crouched and waited for another sound. Low voices sounded and a moment later he saw the beam of a flashlight bouncing across the sand. He felt the sand for his rifle.

"Marty Bird, are you out there?"

Marty flopped back. It was Nancy. Midge came around the tent and sniffed his face.

"Mar-ty!" And her daughter. Midge gave a low woof but didn't bother to investigate. Marty's heart slowed and finally he was able to call out to them.

When they got close, Marty saw that Nancy Shipton had two sleeping bags tucked under her arms, and Victoria dragged a tent sack through the gypsum. They stopped in front of him.

"We're joining you," Nancy said.

He could feel individual hairs standing on end.

"Victoria's idea. She said it was of 'life or death importance,' and I never doubt my kid when she uses words like that. I've got to be back in the morning anyways, so unless it's a problem for you . . ."

"It's not the best time."

Nancy's smile dropped. She massaged her upper arm and

looked to a point over the next dune. Victoria looked up at her mother.

Midge walked in lazy circles around their feet and nuzzled Victoria's free hand onto the top of her head for a scratch. Marty swore at himself.

"My mistake. Looks like you're invited." He forced a smile. Nancy looked over her shoulder, regret at having come here obvious, but she dropped her bag.

The two of them set up the tent expertly. They'd done this before. Victoria assembled the tent rods while Nancy fed them through the loops and pinned them to the earth. Lost for something to do, Marty tried to make his camping spot more livable. He put the dinner cans in his tent, out of sight, and pulled out his sleeping bag so they'd have a place to sit. The two of them walked back once the tent was up. Nancy looked down at the sleeping bag in the gypsum.

"You shouldn't have done that."

"Ah, well, you know."

"You'll have this space dust in your bag for months. Put that away."

Marty dusted off his bag and rolled it. Victoria and Nancy plopped themselves down and unwrapped tuna sandwiches. The plastic crinkled with each bite. He tried to focus on the silence that lay just outside of his campsite.

Marty had never seen a night as bright as the one at White Sands. The full moon reflected off the gypsum and made the whole area glow. It was like snow on the ground, and no trees or debris to smudge the canvas. Colours were easily discernible in the landscape. He wanted to jog over the smooth surface of the dunes and leap over snakes emerging from their daytime dens. He was here.

Marty pulled two beers from his bag and offered one to Nancy.

Without saying anything, she took them both and popped the tabs. Foam gurgled from the mouth and they slurped it away.

Marty liked the way Nancy looked. Now that he wasn't trying to escape the visitor's centre, he could see that. Her cheeks had a bluish tinge in the nighttime, but in the neon light of the visitor's centre, the tops of her cheekbones had shone red, like some snow-suited kid. Her upper and lower eyelashes nearly touched even with her eyes open. Reminiscent of Snuffleupagus.

Beside them, Victoria built mountains of sand and ploughed them down. After a while, she came over to her mother and laid her head in her lap. She closed her eyes and her breathing slowed.

Marty retrieved two more beers from his bag and handed them to Nancy to open. They cheersed.

"So——" Nancy raised her eyebrows at him "——you on some sort of voyage of self-discovery?"

"Just escaping for a while."

"Same shit." Nancy scratched her arm. "There are maybe three types of people who come through here. Families. Self-explanatory. Usually end up tobogganing down the dunes. There are the nature types who come to hike but spend too much time reading plaques. Then there are self-discovery folks. They often come without cars, somehow . . ." She reached over and poked his arm. "Some kind of trouble brewing in their eyes, and mostly unprepared for the desert. This is the desert, you know."

"I do actually have a car." Marty kept his eyes trained on Midge and shut his mouth. He dreaded this conversation.

"Oh, and there are conspiracy junkies who come hoping to spot something from the range next door. I caught one guy trying to hike in that direction with one bottle of Pepsi. Anyway, self-discovery folks are wont to come here on a full moon and they tend to wear bad sneakers. I talk to them in the morning, if I can, and sometimes their shoulders have relaxed a good two inches. Reformative place, I guess. You're a bit older than most, though."

Terrible fucking idea. The whole thing. Marty leaned back and considered how to worm into his tent without another word. A flash of a burnt leg and arm showed up along his sleeping bag and were gone.

Over his shoulder, he saw a shadow moving across the top of a nearby dune. An imaginary Iraqi. Marty breathed in and out. But the shape was too irregular and moving too quickly. He whispered without meaning to. "Look over there."

"Where?"

"Never mind."

Nancy inspected his face. The shape got closer.

"Listen," he said. "I know I sound rude, but could we just sit here quietly? I'm happy to drink beer with you, but . . ." His eyes shifted up to the shape again, and Nancy followed his gaze.

"Tell me what it is."

Please, he thought, *let it be there*. He pointed at the figure. It moved toward them now, and Marty could see its antenna horns rising up to the sky.

Nancy moved Victoria off her lap and stood up. The oryx stopped and lifted its head high.

"Ha!" Marty yelled, rising to his feet. Midge stood beside him with her nose raised and her tail stuck out behind her in a straight line. A growl rumbled from her stomach.

"Midge, sit." Her lips curled up, and she took a step forward. Marty pressed on her hind end so she'd lay off, but she didn't even know he was there. She moved her haunches to avoid his touch. Marty reached over and took her by the collar. She turned her head and nipped at his arm. Marty slapped her nose, but Midge again didn't seem to notice.

When Marty looked over, Victoria was standing by his other

side. She reached out her hand like she wanted to give the oryx a sugar lump. It started plodding toward them, totally unfazed by the dog. Victoria took a step forward as well. Midge exploded into sound. Her barks were high pitched and sent flashes of white pain through Marty. His pulse beat against his trachea. "Midge!"

The oryx's horns—chopsticks from its skull—were at least as long as its legs. Marty tackled Midge and held her under his elbow, but still she snarled and barked. Her skin shook. He clamped her mouth shut and she scurried back, pulling loose from his grasp. He reached out and grabbed her collar again. He yanked her close and stared into her eyes.

"Quiet! Quiet!" He slapped the dog's face but she machined on. Flashes moved across Marty's vision and a pain shot down his arm. He knew Nancy and the girl were looking at him with horror. His heart might come out.

The oryx's hunched back swayed as it moved down the slope. It moved at a steady pace, with the black bands across its upper leg marking its rhythm. Its tail swung behind it.

"Why's it getting so close?" Nancy asked.

The oryx was in full view now, its brown coat visible in contrast to the white sand. Marty imagined crushing Midge's skull. He couldn't take the barking anymore. He released Midge and she lunged forward. Regret came fast and he tried to grab her by the back legs, but she was gone.

The oryx spun on its hooves and galloped in the direction it came from. Midge's manic barking had a high-pitched overtone that Marty had never heard before. The oryx cleared the apex of the dune with Midge close behind and they were both gone from sight, but their path was traceable by Midge's screeching. Screeching, that's what it sounded like.

"What do we do?" Nancy asked.

"She'll come back." Marty rubbed his chest. Besides his time away, when Midge spent her time in his parents' suburban back-yard, she'd never strayed from eyeshot.

"At least she'll be easy to see on this backdrop." Nancy was right. It wasn't like Midge would get lost in the trees.

Victoria shook her head. "I don't think she's coming back."

"Victoria." Nancy shook her head at her daughter. The barking faded into a distant drone and died. The three of them stood silent, the warm air brushing their necks.

"I wish you two would leave," Marty said.

Nancy looked him in the eyes, put her arm around Victoria. "I don't think my beer is empty."

They sat back in the sand, and Nancy tried to bring the conversation to normalcy, but Marty couldn't concentrate on her words. He admired her for keeping this up for her daughter. He watched Nancy's mouth. In the darkness, it looked more like it was growing and shrinking instead of opening and closing.

A few metres away, Victoria crouched under the tent's awning and watched them talk.

"Marty," she said.

"Yes, kiddo?"

"You should come live with us for a while." She dragged her finger through the gypsum.

"Honey . . ." Nancy shook her head at Victoria.

"Mama, I think he should." The moon sat above their heads and shone down like an interrogation light.

"Victoria, we can't ask a stranger—no offence, Marty—to come home. This isn't a starling with a broken wing."

"Sure I am." He lifted his stump. He meant it like a joke, but Nancy's face dropped. She sprinkled the last few drops of her drink into the gypsum.

"Did you really want us to pick up and camp elsewhere, or should we just go to bed?"

"Bed sounds great."

"Victoria, time for bed." She rose and stretched. Marty watched the two of them move through the bedtime routine. Nancy squidged some toothpaste on their brushes and they each took a swig from the water canteen. They both brushed their teeth the wrong way—the freight train method—scrubbing horizontally with fervour across gums and teeth and letting foam drip to the ground. Nancy emptied some water onto a washcloth and wiped off Victoria's face.

"In ya get, toots," she said. Victoria ran over and hugged Marty around the neck, then crawled inside their tent and zipped up. Nancy turned to Marty. "I'm turning in too." But then she came and sat next to him. She stared at him a long time. Marty looked down.

"So, what's your story? Why the experimental road trip?"

"No story."

"We'll be gone in the morning."

They watched a snake slither over the sand a dozen yards from the tent. It left a zagged trail behind.

"You got a good kid there," he said.

"Scares the shit out of me sometimes."

"Why's that?"

"I'm a mercurial type. Victoria knows that." She stared at his beer can. "Doesn't mix well with parenting."

"You seem solid enough to me."

"My kid is more of a long-burning star." Nancy rubbed her hands along her shins and dusted gypsum back to the earth. "But I have a way of sorting it out."

"What's that?"

"I'm filling my kid's head with contingency plans." Nancy laughed into her chest. "If I self-destruct, I've got it set so she'll be better for it."

Marty focused on Nancy's face to see what was going on there. She moved closer to him.

"You remind me of me." Nancy fingered the tab on the can. "You can stay with us until your dog comes back."

"I appreciate it. I do. But I can't do that."

"Just an offer."

She stood up, dusted herself off and stepped into her tent. Marty was alone again, and silence overtook the desert. He stared up at the stars. Only a few of them were visible near where the horizon met the sky. All the others were drowned by the halogen moon.

Marty hadn't slept more than an hour a night since his return, so he sat back and hoped for the sound of paws on sand. He went into his tent with the first hint of blue sky, and he slept during the hour before dawn.

In the morning, Marty unzipped his tent and looked outside. Ripples of gypsum had long shadows from the angled morning light. Nancy and Victoria's tent was already gone. When the slightest noise made him sit up, how had they managed to sneak out during his interlude of sleep? The sky showcased swirls of orange and pink, more pastel and welcoming than the sunset had been. Marty reached out and touched the soft dirt. Midge was not back.

In his bag, he had two apples, a small bag of instant coffee and three cans of dog food. There was half a jug remaining of water. He polished off the fruits for breakfast and sprinkled coffee crystals on his tongue. As the day began to heat, he took his water jug and traced the path the oryx and Midge had left. A few tracks littered the dune, but a light wind had dusted the trail over. Before long, hoof and paw prints marked only the backside of dunes, the fronts wiped clean.

At the bottom of a large ridge, Marty lost the trail. He turned back to the tent.

In the shrinking triangle of shade the tent provided, Marty waited for his dog to come back to him. He sipped the water slowly.

At noon, the breeze and the triangle of shade disappeared and Marty was returned to silent heat. A thick paste coated his tongue. He closed his eyes and listened for faraway howls. Instead, the persistent *whoosh* found him. With his fingers blocking his ear canals, the *whoosh* retained the same volume and tone, irregular and frequent. The bird's wing beat whenever it wanted and pulsed air into his eardrum. *Whoosh*. *Whoosh*. Marty stood and whipped his head down, fighting to remove the pulse, but the whoosh made no concessions. Marty collapsed into his tent and made the realization that no matter where he went, he would never have his silence. That made Midge his last refuge. He scanned the horizon for his dog once more, and then packed his things and walked to the visitor centre. As he walked, he searched every dune for signs of a dog. He inspected the gypsum for yellow spots. *Don't eat the yellow gypsum.*

The air conditioning still blasted inside.

She must have seen him coming. Nancy stood with her arms by her sides. Marty placed his bags at her feet. "I could use a place to stay until my dog's back."

five

ELEPHANT

Late the following afternoon, Julie walked toward The Halibut to deliver a fruit salad and chicken sandwich for Marty's dinner. If she didn't arrive before five, she'd find Marty hunched over a pile of fries. If she was punctual, he ate what was prescribed.

When Marty had finished telling his story the night before, the tea lights had melted to clear puddles, small flames licked up the dregs of wax. The first thing she'd asked was *Who the hell is Nancy?* All he responded was that she wasn't a long-lost love, not Julie's secret mom. And that he wasn't capable of feeling that sort of thing then. Julie had changed the subject by asking about the details of the dog. What breed. How old. But Marty had transformed back to his silent self. The conversation was over. As usual, there had been no negotiation.

When she arrived at The Halibut, the *Closed* sign hung in

the window. Marty moved around inside, looking for something behind the counter. His movement was laboured these days, each action a concentrated effort of coordination. It made her angry, that natural aging was masking ailments earned in the Gulf. She would never know what was genetics-plus-time and what resulted from inhaling burnt oil and dregs of chemical weapons. For the Canadian government, Julie was sure, this grey area was a godsend.

She tapped on the glass. Marty shuffled over and unlocked the door. As soon as she was in, he went behind the counter and resumed the search. The smell of batter was still thick in the air. A mostly empty pint of ale sat at the window table.

Julie seated herself at the bar, pushed Marty's dinner across the counter. "Why are you closed?"

Marty grunted as he straightened up. "It was quiet. Ian might come in a bit, though. What's this?"

"They call them fruits." She eyed the large stack of dishes in the sink, wondered how many people he had kicked out to make it quiet. Marty dropped back below the counter. She asked what he was looking for.

"This." He hoisted the regional phone book onto the bar.

"Oh God." Julie appreciated Marty's refusal to modernize, but the phone book drove her crazy. That he had a rotary dialler in the restaurant was cute. Flipping through thousands of pages of wasted paper was not as quaint.

"Marty," she said. "Just tell me what you're looking for. I have my phone right here."

"Piano tuner."

Julie fingers froze on the screen. The piano was the only relic of her mother's existence that Marty had hung on to—it was a shrine without candles or photographs, except for the one of his old dead dog hanging above it.

When she was younger, a lot younger, Julie thought of the

piano as being her mother—an aloof surrogate whom she could see but was not allowed to touch. At night, when the piano still resided in the bungalow, Julie would sneak over to play dinky tunes. Her mother's only physical remnant was the worn-away groove in the centre of the bench. Her mother's ass.

Julie cleared her throat and asked why Marty suddenly had to tune the piano, since neither of them could play, and Marty told her about the woman from Tallicurn—Jennie Lee Lewis.

"You never let anyone touch the piano," Julie said.

"That's you. Anyway, I think she'll bring in some business."

"Remember when I sat on that piano bench, when I was like three, and you brushed me to the floor?"

He looked genuinely perplexed.

He folded and unfolded the cover of the phone book. Soon after her mother's accident, Marty had thrown away everything that belonged to her, except for that piano. In the weeks after Brenda's death, trash bags lined the end of the driveway. "There are no photos," he always said. "Quit snooping."

"I don't think her playing here is a good idea," Julie said.

"Sorry, kiddo, but tough shit." Marty slid the phone book back under the counter. "Can't find anything in this damn thing. Tea?"

"No."

He filled the electric kettle. They waited in silence. Over the cash register, a stuffed owl stared at Julie, its face molted down to the felt base. Julie took it and straightened its crooked wing. The water in the kettle bubbled. Marty tapped his fingers on the bar. He fidgeted with a loose thread on his button-up.

"Julie, I want to tell you the next part about Midge."

At first glance, he looked relaxed, but the side of his mouth twitched and he jangled his keys in his pocket.

"Marty, this is not what we're talking about right now."

"Just listen to the damn story. Or do you need your tea first?"

Julie shook her head.

"Good," he said. He took the owl from her, set it back on the register. Everything in its place at The Halibut. "I'd moved into Nancy's bungalow, and she had me sleeping on a cot by her bed."

"Marty, seriously. We're talking about the piano."

Marty yanked the tail of the thread from his shirt. "I decided one night that I couldn't sleep on that cot again."

"I'm worried about you." She reached for the owl but Marty beat her to it, moved it out of her reach. "Your neighbour called me in Vancouver. The guy across the street from you. They tried to be nice about it, but they said you'd been yelling. Again. Marty."

"People yell."

"On the front lawn."

"So you quit your job and took a twenty-hour bus ride north because of a neighbour complaint."

The kettle started to scream.

"It's not exactly a noise complaint."

Steam began pouring along the edges of the ceiling, around the corner toward the bathroom. Marty reached up and retrieved the mixed box of teas. "What kind do you want?"

"None."

Marty selected mint and dunked the tea bag, stirred until the water tinted green, pushed the mug toward her. She wrapped her hands around the hot mug.

She spoke slowly. "I'm trying to understand how after a quarter of a century you've suddenly gone from seeing the piano as a holy place to an ordinary instrument." She sipped the tea. The liquid scalded her tongue.

Marty crossed his arms. Said nothing.

She dropped her head onto her arms. "Oh my God. I'm talking to a wall."

"Same to you, kiddo."

"Just tell me what's changed."

"Time has passed. Can I continue with the story now?"

Julie lifted her head, blew on the tea. "No. I don't want to hear about your stupid dog."

He glanced out the window. "It's nice out. Let's go sit on the bench."

Julie shrugged, carried her mug out front of The Halibut, waiting for Marty to prepare his own drink. Angled afternoon sunshine warmed the sidewalk. Port Braid was at peak liveliness. Old women with tiny knapsacks moved between the two bookstores on the main drag. A group of chattering kids—first-time campers, judging by their pristine boots and floppy hats—ran to the frozen yogurt window, sure to be baffled by the local flavours of salal, choke and salmon berries. In the breeze, the cypresses threw scattered shadows over the street.

She heard a click behind her.

"Marty? Jesus."

Marty stood on the other side of the door, no mug in his hand.

She tried the handle but the door was locked. She knocked. "Let's not be children."

"Time to go, kiddo," he said. His voice had softened.

She looked at his face. Marty's sudden mood swings were hard to distinguish from his humour. Jokes and meltdowns both came on with no warning.

"Marty! What does that mean?" She could be humourless and safe, or she could let his emotional paroxysms progress to their conclusion. She kicked her mug into the scraggly bush by the front door. Tea splattered over the leaves.

He mouthed "go," turned and walked to The Halibut's back room. She tried the side door and the windows. Locked.

The police station was three blocks away. She was overreacting. She knew she was overreacting. But she was speed-walking toward it. Ravens filled the branches of a Garry oak, and they cackled at her as she passed.

A couple blocks later, her phone buzzed. Her lungs pulsed as she checked. A text from Ian, who'd just arrived at the restaurant. Conveying a message that Julie could come back.

She breathed. No, she did not feel like going back. Instead she walked down the main street, massaging the muscles in her shoulders, tightened into braided rope. The chatter of pedestrians passed her on either side, but her focus stayed on the lines of the sidewalk, the moss that grew between the slabs.

Someone grabbed her upper arm and spun her into an embrace. Alan Cheung stepped back, shook her shoulder, patted the side of her head. He put his beaming face inches from hers.

"Julie the Unruly. Jules of Fools. I knew you'd be home." He kissed her cheek.

She tried to muster the enthusiasm to greet an old pseudo parent. Alan was about Marty's age. In a lot of her childhood memories—ones at the beach, at school—Alan was beside her. He was always calling to see if there were any parenting duties Marty was willing to pass on.

Today he wore a Boy George T-shirt. His hair was chopped into a crew cut. He threw an arm around her and led her in the direction of his electronics store. She focused on slowing the rate of air entering and leaving her lungs to forget the encounter with Marty and be able to give Alan the catch-up he needed.

In the display window of Alan's store sat TVs from different eras. Three or four rear-projection TVs—one of them big enough to fill half her living room in Vancouver—lined up in order of their production year. They went from smallest to biggest, and then, beside the largest one, was the first of the flat screens. The flat screens got bigger from there. Alan's business plan for his store had always been a mystery. Julie wondered if Alan hoped to sell the rear-projection ones, or if he was slowly transforming his shop into a museum.

He gestured into his store. "I have a six pack. You're old enough to drink now, right? I ran out to buy it when your dad came by."

"Marty came by?"

"To rent the microphone."

"For that woman's shows?"

Alan shrugged. "I just thought it was some party."

He wandered into his store. Julie followed him. He leaned over the glass counter filled with disposable cameras and analog watches. An industrial-style lamp lit them from above. Alan uncapped a beer and handed it to her.

"No thanks, Alan."

"Come on. We're celebrating your return." He opened his own bottle and held it out for a cheers until she complied. They both took baby sips.

"How's he been, anyway?" Julie asked.

"Your dad? Fine, I assume." He picked at the label on the bottle. "You know, huh, I guess I don't pay so much attention to that when you're not around."

"But the restaurant's always open?"

"Oh, yeah, yeah. I think so. I think people go there a lot."

A couple more TVs sat at the back of the store, all playing the same movie, albeit with vastly different tints. The sound was off, but it had something to do with bathing suits and guns. One of the screens was so snowy it was hard to make out the action.

Julie asked Alan what he thought of the whale.

"I went down there yesterday. You know Liam Parks?"

Julie nodded. Liam Parks used to drive her to school sometimes. He was almost as bald as Marty, and somehow always smelled of cloves.

Alan sipped his beer and put it down. "I go down to check out the whale, and there's Liam Parks with a hacksaw."

"A hacksaw?"

Alan held his hands up. "I swear. A hacksaw. And I see him lining it up against the whale's fin. And you know what he asks me? He asks me if whales have blubber in their fins too, because he couldn't get a saw stroke going on its side. Angles were all wrong. And I tell him, 'Liam Parks, you can't eat that blubber,' and he tells me, 'I'm not going to eat it, I'm going to render it.' And you know how Liam Parks is. He doesn't elaborate on anything. So we just stand there, waiting for the other one to say something."

"And?"

"And finally it comes out that he's looking to make some lamp oil. Like he's freaking Ahab."

"I don't think Captain Ahab was known for his rendering."

Alan started shaking his head, incredulous of his own story-telling. "I tell him he can't do that. He can't melt the whale down."

"Why not, though?"

"Why not!" He stared at her. "It's a mystical creature of the deep. That's why."

"That chose to wash up like an old tire. Melt it down."

"Julie Bird." Alan rotated his bottle. "That whale gifted you with its final moment."

"I prefer living whales."

Alan shook his head. "Anyway. I told him not to do it. I told him it was a shame. And he left. Then, after I did a couple of laps of the beast, paid my respects, I left too. And guess who's trying to hide behind the Tallicurn sign, waiting for me to leave, holding his saw like it's a newborn?" Alan watched her face. The watches under the glass counted the seconds.

"Liam Parks," she said.

"Liam Parks!"

"Unbelievable." She passed her beer bottle back and forth between her hands, leaving a slick track of dew. "So, my father came in here to rent a microphone. You bought a six pack of beer." Sweat ran down the bottle and onto her hand. "What's your profit margin on that?"

"Ah. You forget that I get Julie Bird in my store as part of the deal."

"Sounds like a shit deal to me." She took another sip. "How long did he rent the microphone for?"

"He'll bring it back when he brings it back."

"And then you'll share another beer?"

He beamed. "Why not?"

She shook her head and pushed the beer back to him. "I gotta get going." With The Halibut already closed, she worried that Marty would be walking by Alan's store. She had an urge to be far away from him. Just for a while.

"And what do I do with these?" Alan asked.

"Save them for the next customers, I guess."

Outside Alan's store, Julie dialled the number of Billy Poole, the high school acquaintance she had the best chance of getting fucked up with on short notice. When he arrived in his pickup, a cloud of pot smoke flowed out the passenger side window, and between his index finger and thumb he pinched a spent roach like it was a nugget of gold. His hair was grown long now, dangling past his ears in strands. There was always a canine quality to Billy. A coyote, not a wolf. His eye teeth protruded farther than his other teeth. He howled a lot.

"Big city!" Billy slammed the truck into park and leapt out to greet her. He lifted her off the ground. It felt like her guts were going to bust out.

"Jesus, Billy. Put me down, get me out of here."

His truck door squeaked as he opened it. "Climb in, lady."

They picked up his friends Marjory and Lisa and drove around as dusk set in. Marjory and Lisa sat in the truck bed, leaning against opposite sides, their ponytails whipping in the summer wind while Julie reclined the passenger seat, watching the mosquitos drift through the open windows. Billy flicked on the headlights as they passed under a dark canopy of Douglas firs. Moths flitted into the light stream.

At some point they drove past the bungalow on Sequoia Street. Marty had all the lights on, and Julie glimpsed his head illuminated by the flashes of television. Good. She could stop thinking about him for the night.

In the glovebox of Billy's truck she found a plastic bottle of vodka. She waved it at him. "Really?"

He shrugged. Julie unscrewed the cap and nursed it as they drove.

six

RACCOONS

Julie opened her eyes and realized she was still in Billy Poole's basement suite. *Shit.* She meant to leave before it got light outside, to prove a point, but here she was with a single beam of light fighting through the dusty half-windows and the sour smell of unwashed boy blankets wrapped around her.

All right. She'd slept with him. She looked over at Billy, who slept on his back with his arms crossed over his chest, like a fucking teenage vampire. He wasn't a teenager anymore, obviously, but his inability to grow facial hair or chest hair combined with a general ignorance of the world outside hunting made him teenager enough. His mom still packed him sandwiches for lunch. When she'd gone to the fridge for juice the night before, she'd found the same Molson lunchbox he'd used in high school. Inside, peanut butter and fucking jelly.

Julie massaged her shoulders and stretched her neck. She climbed from the mattress on the floor, trying not to wake the slumbering vampire. It was a scavenger hunt to find all the pieces of her clothing in the folds of the blanket, but she eventually assembled her outfit from the night before. Her phone was the last piece to be found, in an empty mug on the coffee table. She checked her texts and saw one from Marty asking for a hand at The Halibut. Sent an hour ago, at 10 a.m. *Shit.*

Her mouth was a puddle of cigarettes. She squeezed some toothpaste onto her tongue and swished it around. Last night's underwear she stuffed in her pocket. She said goodbye to the mould haven.

As she turned the doorknob, Billy spoke. "Where ya going, Bourgeoisie?"

"Home. Go back to sleep."

He grinned so that his oversized canines hung over his lip. "Nice of you to drop by." He was trying to be triumphant.

"Sure thing, wiggles." Hungover, that was as belittling as she could get.

Julie stepped out of the Pooles' house and contemplated what to do. The rural road stretched in both directions. The day was grey, with a low milky ceiling of cloud. The walk to The Halibut would take an hour or more. She peered through the window of Billy's truck, saw the keys dangling from the ignition. She climbed in and rested her head on the steering wheel. Her head pounded with drink and smoke.

She turned the key and the truck chugged to life.

Billy came out a second later, blankets tied around his hips. "Are you stealing my truck?"

"Give me a lift, then."

He shook his head. "Still drunk." He waved her off. "Go, just go. I'll bike down later."

She knocked the truck into reverse. "I'll be parked at The Halibut."

Sitka spruce lined the narrow road that led back to town. It ran in a straight line, never pretending to be anything but a utilitarian A to B route. Like a lot of the roads around Port Braid, it was originally a logging path designed to strip this area of the only thing that made it worth living in.

Julie's eyelids drooped as she drove. She slapped her face, lowered the windows.

Up ahead she saw the hunched form of a raccoon and a couple of its babies standing on the shoulder by marker 34. She knew marker 34 well. If you walked a few metres past it, a thin trail led into the bush. She and her father called this area the Cold Forest. A chilled current ran through it. The trees there were different. The Cold Forest was all deciduous—oaks, maples and a few walnuts. Almost no light broke through. In the heart of the Cold Forest was a small pond. Marty used to take her swimming there when she was still too terrible to swim in the ocean or Gregion Lake. Her father often recounted how she refused to swim if other kids were around. She wouldn't do it in public until she was perfect. Retreating to this dingy pond in an abandoned forest was the only way to get her to practise the front crawl. He would take a beer, or two, and make sure the submerged vines didn't grab her ankles.

Julie heard rumours that the deciduous trees in the Cold Forest marked the ancient driveway of a farm. It seemed plausible. Either that, or a long-forgotten forest fire had cleared the evergreens. But near the path, you could find apple trees mixed in with more common species, bolstering the farm theory. The apples they produced were small and didn't seem like they could belong to a viable farm, but maybe things got smaller if you let them alone long enough.

The raccoons loved the Cold Forest. Julie hated raccoons. She readjusted the steering wheel so that she'd breeze close to them.

The mother raccoon's thief eyes came into view. It watched her intently, unflinching in its spot. The two babies hid behind their mother. One of them grabbed at her fur.

As Julie guided the truck onto the gravel shoulder, small rocks pinged the undercarriage. The raccoons weren't moving—her second game of chicken that day.

"Fine, fine, you little shits." She pulled the truck back into the centre of the road and refocused on the horizon. At the last moment, she saw a flash. She felt the distinct double thump as the animal went under the wheels.

Julie pulled off the road and put on the hazards.

The raccoon was dead. Super, super dead. The tires passed over its neck and stomach—who knows which tire did what damage—and the thing had torn open. Intestines were flattened onto the pavement. One of the two babies was gone too—its head smashed into the mess of its mother. The second baby paced along the length of the victims, touching them with its paws. It grasped its mother's tail and ears.

"Jesus. Why didn't you follow your momma?"

Julie considered stomping it with her boot. Maybe the mother had rabies. That would explain running at the pickup. But the baby had no foam spouting from its mouth, and if the mother had rabies, it wouldn't be carting around two helpless babies.

"Well, shit, little guy. I don't know."

She stood on the road. The sun peeked over the top of the evergreens and warmed the top of her scalp. Her head throbbed from the adrenalin and the hangover. The baby's paws were covered in blood. She couldn't leave it there to wallow with the corpse of its mother. If it wandered into the woods to find starvation or predators, she would let it, but she wouldn't let it hang out on the road deepening its psychological trauma.

Julie found an old blanket rolled up in the truck bed. When she returned to the crime scene, the raccoon gazed up at her. She slammed her boot into the pavement to scare it away from its mother. It retreated a few steps. She threw the blanket over the baby raccoon and scooped the package up. It squirmed. Its muffled screams escaped the fabric. She tossed the whole lot into the passenger seat and headed to the pet store, where she picked up a small crate and some wet dog food.

When she got to Marty's house, she pushed the little body into the crate and shut the door. The raccoon made laps and felt each surface with its paws. It clung on to the bars at the front, climbing up and down imaginary ladders.

When she was sure that the raccoon was safely enclosed, Julie went into the kitchen. The burner on the stove glowed red, an empty pot sitting on its coils. Its bottom was warped to shit. Marty must have abandoned making oatmeal and forgotten the stove. She turned it off and undressed on her way to the shower.

The water felt fantastic. Globs of shampoo ran down her body. The memory of Billy Poole's canine smile flashed into her mind, hanging above her head, and a simultaneous shot of pleasure came with it. Like Pavlov's dog down south. The canine smile somehow equated to that feeling. And that feeling was somewhere between *holy shit that was hot* and *holy shit that was disgusting*. Looking at her high school yearbook was forever marred.

When she turned off the nozzle, she could hear the phone ringing. Water dripped behind her as she sprinted for the rotary.

"Hello?"

"Julie, kiddo, I need your help."

"Congratulations on calling the house phone."

"It's busy here. Come down?"

"Really?"

"Just come help."

"On my way, pops."

"Hungover?"

"Hells yes."

So everything was back to normal. She checked on the raccoon one more time and hid the crate out back under her bedroom window.

When Julie got to The Halibut, it was anything but busy. Ian sat at his usual table and a couple with a screaming child occupied the window table. Marty stood behind the bar doing the crossword puzzle. He looked up as she walked in. "It lives."

"Shut up."

Julie leaned over the bar and inspected Marty's work thus far. She pointed at 34-down. "Male."

"What?"

"Cold water alligator young. Warm water makes for little female gators."

"Doesn't fit with spies."

"That's because that should be cabal." She smiled at him.

"Damn it."

Ian chuckled to himself in the corner. The screaming child, however, was nonplussed by her performance and was about to put its foot into a bowl of coleslaw on the table.

"Why did you make me come here?" Julie asked. Marty made her sit down. She sat at the piano bench to watch her father's reaction. His brow tensed for a moment and then relaxed. She pressed on a couple of keys.

"Still out of tune, Marty."

Julie inspected the instrument. The wood reflected her face. The piano smelled of oranges.

"I've got a guy coming later," Marty said.

She sighed. "OK."

Her most vivid memory of the piano was from her first night of drinking. Filled with schnapps, with a circle of vomit on her sweater, she had snuck into the bungalow. But it was empty. Marty's bedroom door hung open, all the lights in the house were on, but no one was around. She searched the town, still wearing the soiled top. Rain poured down and she remembered tasting conditioner from her soaked hair. She spotted him through the windows of The Halibut, hunched over the piano. A clipped newspaper article sat on the ledge in front of him, like a piece of ready sheet music. Julie couldn't make out the headline, but a black and white photo of three women was big enough to see. The water streamed down the window and distorted the image. Eyeballs and cheeks grew and shrank as droplets travelled in front of her vision, making gruesome trolls out of the women. She'd stayed there for a long time, holding herself back from knocking. Never sure if he was conscious. She never knocked, and he never moved. Eventually, she went home. But the newspaper clipping had stayed in her mind. She'd never seen it since but knew it was around.

Julie glanced over at her father. "So? Why am I here?"

He cleared his throat. "I'm going to tell you the next part about Midge now." Julie opened her mouth to protest, say he really didn't have to do that, but he shushed her. Listening would have to be her peace offering for the previous night.

Ian dropped his napkin on the table. "Fun as that sounds, family Bird, I'm out. Marty, pay you next time, yeah?" Marty shrugged and kept his eyes trained on Julie, potential absconder.

"All right," she said. Julie leaned back against the keys. Out of the corner of her eye, she saw the dad cleaning food off his child's feet.

1992

Nancy had dictated the sleeping arrangements while Marty stayed in her bungalow. He lay awake for long nights on a cot beside her bed. Each morning, when she turned on her hair dryer, he would hear the sound of a Humvee rolling by. Shifting, the springs creaking under him. Muddled thoughts telling him he was on a cot at the back of an M728 as it rumbled toward the next location for burial duty. His heart seizing before his day began.

Images accompanied the sounds, a video in his mind on an infinite loop. The driver didn't see it, or maybe he did. The arm of a corpse caught in the tread, the body pulled under the tank, squirting across the sand like a ketchup pack.

He'd open his eyes. His heart pounded back to life, pumping double speed for the time it lost. Nancy buttoning her parks uniform. He could only sit up from his cot beside the queen-size, rub his face and let the image of her, a person who lived in the United States, soak into his mind. People like her had been in the U.S. this entire time. Living lives like these.

One of these mornings, he decided he couldn't sleep on that cot for another night. He added cots to his list of must-avoids. The hour of sleep had done nothing for him. His quiet hell every night was watching the stages of dawn on the white ceiling.

Nancy stared at the mirror, her reflection looking as always like a person he should love. She ran a brush through her hair. That day marked the beginning of his second month in the Shipton bungalow, not that he was expecting flowers. Nancy took a small sip from the flask that lived on the dresser and turned to him.

"I left oatmeal in the pot for Victoria and Rose. Send Rose home after she has breakfast. And don't forget Victoria's piano lesson."

Marty nodded and wiped sleep out of his eyes. Rose, Victoria's best friend, seemed to spend more nights on Victoria's bedroom floor than in her own house.

Marty slid himself onto the bed. Nancy looked at him through the mirror. "You said you wouldn't push it."

Marty picked her hairs off the pillow. "I'm not."

Nancy picked at a scab on her hand. "I gotta run."

Marty grabbed Nancy's arm and pulled her close. She sank into a kneel by the bed and he brushed his lips against hers. He knew he was sticky with morning breath, but he pushed his tongue into her mouth. She scrunched her face at him. Smiled.

"All right, all right, big guy, I have to go." She went back to the mirror and gave her hair another couple of brushes. "You're on the cot tonight. Nice try, though."

When he heard the front door slam, Marty swung his feet onto the cold linoleum. Flooring an entire house with linoleum was a contractor's cruel joke, but Nancy said it didn't get as grotty as carpet. Bullshit. The linoleum curled up around the edges and a brown film grew from the creases. The only square of carpet in the house lay in the closet.

Marty pulled on his shirt and buttoned it one-handed. He learned this skill a week after surgery, but his learning curve had since levelled out. Using the bedroom phone he called the Las Cruces SPCA. A recording reminded him they didn't open until eight thirty.

Marty went to the kitchen to enjoy a quiet cup of coffee, but the kids emerged from their room at the same time, already talking.

The girls shared a love of things not meant for children. Victoria grabbed her friend's arm to emphasize her point as they wobbled down the hall to the kitchen.

"Bessie Smith and a man got in a car accident together and a doctor found them, and it took a really long time for an ambulance to come from the Black hospital, because they had other hospitals for white people . . ."

Rose bounced as she replied. "The Super Sports are like really, really, really good, but sometimes they're not real ones? My dad bought a '72 SS and he was so excited."

"And so the doctor that found them was going to drive her to the hospital in his car, but then another car drove down the highway and crashed into the doctor's car and wrecked it."

Victoria obsessed over dead blues singers. Black-and-white posters of long-gone blues heroes lined her bedroom walls.

"Then he found out that you have to look at the VIN? The fifth thing has to be a W, but there wasn't one, so the guy who sold it faked everything? And he did it to make the Malibu look like an SS."

Rose loved El Caminos. Her father was a keen collector. She was his spotter when he worked on the engines, his sounding board when his friends were tired of listening. Marty marvelled at how the two girls could talk endlessly about their passions, never having to listen to the other.

"So then two ambulances came—one for Black people and one for white people—and the Black people one took Bessie Smith. They took her arm off, and then she died anyway, which was messed up. But a million people came to the funeral."

"Some people think that there are more fake ones that real ones. Victoria, you have to, have to be, really careful? My dad keeps the fake one in the backyard to remind us. Same reason I have to put bad spelling tests on the fridge."

They sat at the table. When there was a break in their steam-train conversation, they stared at Marty. He looked up from the curled linoleum. "Yes?"

"What's for breakfast?"

"Cold oatmeal."

The girls groaned. Marty cracked enough eggs in a pan for all three of them. He reserved half of the pan for scrambling for the girls and fried his sunny-side-up eggs on the other side. The girls scattered smelly markers across the table and started colouring the morning funnies. Dilbert's face was a healthy green.

He scooped out his eggs while there was still a layer of transparent goop around the yolk. The girls' eggs he cooked to rubber.

Rose filled in Marmaduke with red stripes and blue stars. Real Amurican dog.

Victoria dug into the scrambled eggs. "Marty, do you know who Blind Lemon Jefferson is?"

"Blues guy?" This conversation exhausted him. *Marty, do you know who such-and-such is?* This always followed by the legend of their birth or the tragedy of their death.

"He was born blind and later his girlfriend killed him."

"Oh?"

"She poisoned his coffee. Or he died in a snowstorm when he got lost because he was blind. Or a dog attacked him in a snowstorm."

"I see. Snowstorm dogs are dangerous." Marty cut around the

yolk and lifted the whole thing into his mouth. He swished the viscous liquid around.

"Snowstorm dogs?"

"Oh yeah. We got those in Canada. Big dogs. Ten times bigger than anything here. They're white and they only come out during blizzards. You can't see them until they split your throat. It's your own blood that finally colours them in."

A smile grew across her face. "That's not true." She loved the morbid stuff and he had the material.

Marty leaned in close to Victoria. "But it *is*. Right, Rose? You've been to Canada."

Rose put on a serious face and nodded at Victoria.

Victoria glanced down at Marmaduke. "But Blind Lemon Jefferson wasn't a Canadian. Nobody really knows how he died."

"Victoria?" Marty held his throat and wheezed. "Did you poison my coffee?"

She grinned. "No."

Marty finished his eggs and started on the dishes. Out the window, heat waves already rose off the pavement.

His fog caught up as he looked out the window. The girls' voices faded away. He welcomed the numbness that blew through his arteries and swept out the pain in his hand. The light level in the kitchen dropped by degrees and the yapping of the neighbour's Pomeranian filtered out. It was a kind of silence. Pins and needles started along the back of his calves and coaxed relief into his knees.

The plate he was holding clattered into the sink. Panic pierced his chest and the hairs on the back of his neck stood erect. He cleared his throat and snatched up the plate, shoving it in the dish rack with soap bubbles running down its back.

He turned around to see Victoria staring at him.

"Yes?" He scratched at his scalp.

"I want a cool story."

He tried to remember what they were talking about. "You want me to read to you?"

"No, stupid." She chewed on a strand of hair. "Blues guys have to have a good story. I want one."

"You have a great story, kiddo." Marty went over to her chair and scooped her into a fireman's hold. She laughed and her body squirmed on his shoulder. He plopped her down on the couch in the living room. "Your mom loves you. You get to have sleepovers on white sand dunes during the full moon. You're from a town called Truth or Consequences. You're a legend already."

"But nothing sad has happened."

Marty felt like reassuring her about all the sad things in her life. *Don't worry, honey. Your dad doesn't love you. You live in a shit hole. There's red ink in your college fund.* "Let's keep it that way, nugget."

"Mom says that tragedies make people interesting."

"Uh huh."

Marty hustled Victoria out of the kitchen to get ready for her lesson. Rose stayed behind picking at her breakfast.

"You don't have anywhere to be, Rose?"

She shook her head.

"Let's at least get your teeth brushed."

Again, a head shake. "I don't have to until night."

"Suit yourself." Marty pulled his shoe polish kit out of the cupboard and put his boots on the black-crusted sheet.

"Marty?"

"Yes, kiddo?" Silence. Marty shrugged. He scooped a dab of polish out of the tin and spread it across the toe of his boot. He heard the sound of Victoria pounding on piano keys from her room. Any spare moment she had. He stuck his stump into the boot's opening to hold it in place. Rose looked down at the ground. "Yes, Rose? You may speak."

"Did you know?" She crinkled the newspaper between her hands.

"Know what?"

"Did you know that Victoria thinks you're going to die?"

Marty's chest imploded. Rose moved over to the ground beside him.

"What did she say, Rose?"

"I don't know."

"Think back."

"Well, just that in a couple of months, probably? You were going to die."

Marty massaged the polish into the leather using his circular brush. He spent extra time in the cracked areas around the laces to make sure they were saturated.

"Are you?" she asked.

Marty picked up the soft brush to give the boots their final shine. He swept it back and forth, changing angles to match the contours of the broken-in leather. He pictured slamming Rose's head into the floor and walking out. "Not that I know of, Rose. How did she say that I would die?"

"I don't think she really knows."

"Do you believe her?"

Rose whispered her answer. "Yes. Maybe. I don't know."

Marty finished his boots and put the supplies away. As he exited the kitchen, a high-pitched roar erupted behind him. A weight pounded onto his back and clung there. Marty's vision filled with light and he spun around and shoved. A body thumped against the doorframe. Blind, Marty stepped forward with fist out. Victoria lay on the ground. Marty's pulse echoed in his ears.

Victoria looked at him and laughed. "I scared you."

Marty sat down and closed his eyes.

"Come on," Victoria said. "We're late."

In the dry heat of Truth or Consequences, Marty walked Victoria to her piano lesson. They walked two extra blocks to avoid the stretch of road he didn't like, the one with the burned-out Chevy. He made this a game with Victoria, told her they had to change routes to avoid spies and hit men.

It was hot enough that snakes of hot gas rose off the hoods of parked cars. Most buildings in Truth or Consequences were single-storey beige cubes. The surrounding landscape was beige too, which made T or C feel like a Wild West town fast-forwarded to the '90s. Instead of whiskey bars, you went to little cafés. Instead of sheriffs, you got drawling cops. Instead of radical gunslingers, conservative gunslingers. Storefronts stood as the narrow divide between civilization and the desert.

As they walked past town residents, Marty could see the clear split between Conservatives and Liberals, good ol' folks and hippies. Most of the real homegrown Conservatives stayed at a safe distance in the next town, Elephant Butte, where they could drive their oversized RVs up to the shoreline of the reservoir, using ATVs to get to the toilets and back.

In 1950, Ralph Edwards, host of the famous game show *Truth or Consequences*, announced that the first town in America to rename itself in the show's honour would receive an annual celebration. Hot Springs, New Mexico, had nothing to lose and acted fast. Forty years later and Edwards was staying true to his word. The seventy-seven-year-old still came once a year to T or C for a May festival. A small contingent of residents was fighting for the town to change its name back to Hot Springs. For some people it's embarrassing to be interesting. However, most of these humans lived in Elephant Butte, like they should be the ones to talk.

As they waited for a light to change, Marty knelt beside Victoria.

"I talked to Rose today," he said. Victoria stared at a daddy-long-legs bumbling across the sidewalk. "Kiddo?"

Victoria shook her head. "So what?"

"So, she told me something you said."

"Rose is crazy."

"Yes. Rose is crazy." Marty ran his hand over his head. When he pulled it back, a nest of hair came with it. "You told her I was going to die."

Victoria hovered her foot over the spider.

"Why?" he asked. Victoria pushed down on the spider with her toe so its knees buckled. The light turned green and Victoria started to walk. Marty pulled her back. He held her chin. Her cheeks squeezed out between his fingers.

"What made you say that?"

Victoria buckled to the ground, like one of those wooden push puppets, her body completely limp. He tried to lift her up but her legs were jelly.

A couple of teenagers looked on from across the street. A black flash shot across Marty's vision. He grabbed a handful of Victoria's hair and lifted her to her feet. She shrieked. He let go just as the light turned yellow. Victoria sprinted across the street. A car turning right braked hard to avoid her. Marty darted behind the car and ran after her. He grabbed her shoulder.

"Kiddo, kiddo. You're fine." She was crying. The teens stared. A lollipop hung out of one of their mouths. Marty sighed. "Just tell me what you said."

"Both of you are gonna."

"Both of who?" he asked.

Victoria shook and spittle escaped from her lips. "You and my mom."

"Where are you getting this from?"

She sank to the ground again, hugged her knees. "That's the way I get to be special."

"What?"

She buried her face. He realized he wasn't getting anything else from her. He hoisted Victoria up, under her arms this time, and gave a thumbs-up to the teens. They shrugged and turned away. Marty let Victoria walk in front of him the rest of the way to the lesson. He followed ten paces behind until she turned into the music school. Then he sat on the curb until the buzzing in his brain stopped.

Back at Nancy's, he began to pack his things. He tried the Las Cruces SPCA again. A man picked up on the third ring. Still no impounded hounds. Midge hadn't turned herself in to the branch saying, *Sorry, Dad, I'm done playing with the oryx now.*

"You want to come take a look around?" the man on the phone asked. "We got a Rottie and a Chihuahua available."

"My van's impounded."

"Tough break, man."

It was nighttime when Nancy got home. Marty was on the front stoop, polishing her high-heeled boots. The street lamps lit his workspace. Nancy fetched a bottle of merlot from the pantry and joined him. He had five pairs of her shoes strewn around him, all with new luster. He tapped his previous project—her black stilettos—against the concrete to show them off. They shone.

Nancy's Snuffleupagus eyelashes joined and separated. She picked up one of the stilettos. "Those don't need polish, dumb-dumb." Nancy sucked on the wine. A bead of red escaped the corner of her mouth.

He grabbed the bottle from her and took a long drink. "Nance. It's time for me to go."

"Go?"

She stood and wandered inside, not waiting for the next thing he had to say. Marty hoped the girl was asleep. Her piano teacher had dropped her off when Marty failed to show up, and Victoria had gone straight to her room.

Inside, he found Nancy at the table, picking at some cold spaghetti.

A gossamer breeze came through the window and explored the room. The only clock in the house—a hand-me-down grandfather clock from Nancy's mother—sent a parade of ticks into the night.

"Nancy, I'm bad with Victoria."

Nancy stared at him. "Did you hit her?"

"No."

Nancy poised a coil of noodles by her lips and stared at him. Marty searched for fear or anger in her.

"But I don't know. Things are strange," he said.

Nancy squeezed Marty's hand and stood up. "You won't do anything to her."

"I should leave."

Nancy walked toward her bedroom. Just before she disappeared into darkness, she looked over her shoulder at him. He waited a minute, then followed. His bare feet suctioned to the linoleum. A tick from the grandfather clock accompanied each step. He passed by the framed photographs that graced the wood-panelled walls: photographs of fishing trips and birthday parties. In one of them, an infant Victoria lay in her father's arms.

Marty stepped into the black room and waited for his eyes to adjust. He could just make out Nancy's figure in her bed. Her bottom half was covered by the sheets, but her breasts were exposed. Marty always thought that Nancy would have small, practical nipples, but even in this light he could tell that they were large and dark. The faint sound of Victoria pressing piano keys came through the wall.

"Nancy, not now." He felt nothing. For a year, he hadn't felt anything but panic or rage.

Her hair fanned away from her head and covered both pillows. Her clothes were folded in a neat pile. The corner of the quilt was folded down, leaving an open space by her side.

"What am I supposed to do with this?" he asked her.

"Come on, then. You wanted in the bed."

Marty slid between the sheets and ran his good hand along the cavern between Nancy's hips and ribcage. Her skin was tight, stretched over a drum, nothing inside her torso. Only ribs and hipbones to hold everything taut. Her eyelashes cast a long shadow over her face and hid her expression. He was in bed with a copy of Nancy, a shadow on the cave wall. All he wanted to do was sleep, but he ran his tongue over her nipples. She did nothing to stop him, but also did nothing to encourage him. She placed a limp hand on the small of his back.

He rolled off her and slithered out of his pants.

Nancy turned to him. "You have to be quiet. Have you done this silent before?"

"Nope."

"Welcome to hell."

Sounded good to Marty. He moved down under the covers and positioned his face between Nancy's legs. He ran his tongue up and down.

Her thighs tensed around his head and boxed in his ears. He fought to keep himself here. Nancy pulled him up and on top of her. Her mouth hung agape and the sound of her breathing bounced around the dark room. He was soft.

Flash of the car on the Highway of Death, those flames licking out of eyeholes, reaching for a human bomb.

"Can we turn on the lights?" he asked.

But she kept moving against him. Her belly, her chest and long hair becoming one churning mass. It made him seasick.

"I can't," he said. Panic rose in his chest. He pushed Nancy away from his face. She hung over him, resting on her arms, her body still gently heaving, maybe waiting for him to come back. Then she flopped on her back and cleared her throat. The room hung in silence. Only the sound of their heavy breathing broke the air.

"You wanted me that bad, huh?" Nancy said. Red patches decorated her cheeks and chin. "Well, at least there's no harm in letting you graduate from the cot."

"Sorry." He wasn't a man anymore. He had to come to terms with that. Elsewhere.

"I'm not sad." She sat up and bundled her hair into a bun. She tied it in a knot using no elastics or pins. Marty traced his finger over the bumps of her spine. Near the centre, three or four vertebrae stuck out farther than the others, and he gave them an extra poke to send them back into place. "Nancy. It's for her sake that I should go."

"It's not her first rodeo. Trust me."

Nancy rose from the bed and stood in front of the mirror. She took a wad of tissue and wiped herself before sliding underwear back on.

"I've got to tell you something," she said.

Marty closed his eyes. He didn't want to know what she had to say about Victoria's history.

"Somebody saw Midge today."

eight

CAMOUFLAGING
CUTTLEFISH

When he finished telling his story, Marty stood at the bar in front of Julie, polishing one of the crystal wineglasses he kept on the top shelf. Julie realized she had her hands partly over her ears, protecting herself from Marty's verbal dalliances, which in the past had always led to dramatic breakdowns.

"That's it?" she asked.

From the base of one of the glasses Marty scooped the dusted carcass of a fruit fly. He nodded. "That's it for today."

"Who saw Midge?"

"Not now, Jules."

"That wasn't a story about Midge."

He could be intentionally obtuse, her father, but this was beyond his norm. At some point in the story, the family at the window table had walked out. Probably around the time her father mentioned his flaccid penis. Julie looked for signs of embarrassment on Marty's face, but there were none. Why was he telling this story now, in all its lurid detail? These days their lives were safe—the routines, the modes of conversation, the sights and sounds to avoid, these had all been cemented. It had been hard work. It seemed now that Marty was prodding at some sleeping dog, hoping it would rise and attack.

Marty returned the wineglass and took down a dusty bottle of Scotch, rotated it in his hand, inspected the label. Julie watched his face.

"Marty, it's great you want to tell me this stuff, but maybe you can cut back on the details. Stick to the dog stuff."

Marty sniffed the Scotch, set it down. "What's the point without the details?" He shrugged. "Without the details, the story is that Midge dies. That's the end."

"So I'm listening to your story, just waiting for Midge to die."

"You know the facts, Jules. Midge isn't popping out of a box at Christmas. It's the stuff in the middle. JLL and I talked about this."

"What? When?"

Marty looked bewildered. "After you left last night."

Someone tapped on the glass. A man stood there with his shirt buttoned to the top, holding a small leather briefcase. The tuner. Marty gestured for him to come in, showed him to the piano. The man lifted the lid and opened an app on his phone, began tapping keys one by one.

"What did you two talk about?" Julie asked Marty.

Marty stood over the piano tuner's shoulder, watching as he tightened and loosened the bolts. "Just a few things, kiddo."

The man shifted the tenor of notes from flat to sharp and back to the middle. Julie listened to the change.

It was becoming obvious now that the woman on Tallicurn had something to do with Marty's sudden change in behaviour. The only logical thing to do next was find this Jennie Lee Lewis character and possibly beat the shit out of her.

Julie bought herself a litre bottle of water at Orca Convenience and started the three-kilometre trek to Tallicurn Beach. As she trudged along the path, the pounding of her hangover displaced her anger. Her job was to make it to Tallicurn without succumbing to a nap in one of the sunspots on cedar-cushioned dirt.

Red cedars lined the trail, their string-cheese bark extending to the faraway canopy. Cedars meant a lack of underbrush. They sapped up the moisture around them. Even more arid were areas of shore pine. They drank every drop of water and coated the ground with a thick layer of acidic needles that no life ever seemed to push through, except for more pines. Coniferous forests were Julie's favourite for this reason. You could wander off the path in any direction. You could wear shorts in cedar forests. Occasionally, you would pass through a grove of arbutus trees, with their twisted arms and red peeling bark, and then the path became more distinct. A worn line of brown through the ferns.

Overhead, a few Steller's jays swooped lines of blue through the canopy. A downy woodpecker clung to a tree trunk, the distinct square of red adorning the back of its head looking like an injury, as though another bird had tried to bash in its skull.

Patches of sunlight broke through the canopy and heated the dead foliage, released the dry scent of cedar. The smell of dead fish mingled in the background, but as Julie got closer, the fog of chemical sea life became more distinct. She chugged water to wash the nausea away.

A brief field of reeds separated the beach from the trees, but finally she stumbled onto the sand. The water lapped up on shore and reached the washed-up old growth logs. There was the whale, still surrounded in police tape. No observers today. The beast looked like a water bladder, carried on the hips of early European explorers as they traipsed across the plains. Or like someone had inflated a harbour seal with a bicycle pump. The whale's mouth gaped. Its lower jaw had curled downward and the baleen plates had shrunk to wispy teeth.

Julie spotted the orange tent farther west, proud and alone on the expanse of sand. Julie stripped off her shirt and bundled it over her mouth and nose.

A turkey vulture, with its naked red head, cantered along the whale's head and tried to reach down to the eye.

As she approached the tent, Julie listened for signs of the woman. The tent sides flapped in the breeze. Flecks of sand pinged off the nylon. The fishing pole that Ian used for his sick photo balanced on the frame.

"Anyone there?" She tapped the zippered tent doors. No answer.

Julie pulled back the tent flaps and looked inside. In one corner lay a rolled-up sleeping bag and in the other was the woman's travelling backpack. The tent smelled of cigarettes. It was a relief compared to the whale smell. Julie spotted a few books poking out of the top of the backpack and grabbed the first one she saw, a journal with a red leather cover. She knelt in the tent and flipped to a random page. The writing was small, like the journal itself. She read from the top of the page.

that Aboriginal hunters in Chukotka don't eat the meat of "stinky whales" because it gives them numb-tongue as well as tied stomach . . . if they manage to get it down. Even their dogs won't eat the meat. Ten percent of the whale population, but also seals, walruses, birds, have breath and meat like penicillin. The whales might be eating stomachs-full

of seaweed out of food desperation, or they could be
swallowing biotoxins. Stinky whales don't count toward
hunting quotas, so if you get a stinky one, try try again.

Beside this section, parallel to the text, was a pencil-drawn grey whale with endotherm stink lines coming from its blowhole. It winked. A trail of seaweed spiralled from its mouth. She flipped through more pages. The short texts seemed to have one of two topics. Musicians she admired or some shit about suicidal animals. Julie slipped the journal into her pocket.

A shadow crossed the tent fabric. Julie hopped to her feet. Spots of black speckled her vision. There stood the woman, JLL, sporting that perfect blond pompadour, carrying a carton of eggs under her arm.

"Any good stuff in there?"

Julie waited for the dizzies to go away, afraid to apologize for being in the tent because of the bile threatening to creep up her throat.

The woman shrugged, held up the carton of eggs. "Breakfast."

She was a bit uglier than Julie remembered. Jerry Lee Lewis seemed like the right choice. Not that he was unattractive—Jennie wasn't exactly unattractive either—but there was something of a sneer, or a tensed muscle somewhere under the eyes, making the face contort into a look or superiority, or pissed-off-ness, or general disgruntletude.

"I don't think I introduced myself. Julie."

The woman narrowed her eyes. "Jennie Lee Lewis. I go by JLL."

"Nice to meet you, Jennie."

"JLL." She crawled into the tent and pulled out a two-burner camp stove, lit it up.

Julie rolled her eyes. "JLL."

"Breakfast or no breakfast?" JLL held an egg poised over her frying pan.

"More like lunch, isn't it?"

"Fine. Can I offer you some lunch?" The eggs sizzled and spat when JLL cracked them into the pan. Their edges turned transparent and curled away from the hot surface. JLL placed a small pot of water on the other burner.

"Listen," Julie said. "I'm just here to discuss a couple of things with you. Then I'll leave you to eat."

"You'll have coffee with me." JLL slid her eggs onto a plate, sliced around one of the yolks and lifted the entire thing on a fork into her mouth. Julie smiled.

"Funny. My father does that."

"Ah." A dribble of yolk emerged from the corner of her mouth. "What?"

"So Marty's your father." JLL chewed her eggs like they were cud. "I didn't know if you belonged to him or that other man on the boat."

"You've watched my father eat eggs?"

JLL gargled the yolk.

"All right," Julie continued. "Marty is my father. That's why I . . ."

JLL looked agitated. She tore the transparent edges from her eggs and tossed them into the sand.

The tide was retreating down the beach. Small geysers of salt water sprang from the sand as butter clams dug their way deeper below the surface. JLL sat her plate down. "I didn't know Marty had a child."

Julie knelt in front of JLL, picked her fork off the plate and inspected its tines. "I'm not a child."

Dried yolk connected the top of the arcs like yellow spider

webbing. She twirled the fork in her hand and tried to remain cool at all costs.

"So, you know Marty. Yes?" Julie asked.

"Yes, I know Marty. He asked me to play in his dinky restaurant."

"I'm not sure that's settled yet." Julie bit at the inside of her lip. "I meant, you knew Marty before coming here?"

JLL eyed Julie. Nodded.

"How well do you know him?" Julie asked.

JLL took her plate back on her lap, continued eating without the aid of her fork, tearing off strips of egg and shoving them in her mouth. Steam started rising from the pot on the stove.

"I bet he never let you have a dog." JLL's lips smacked as she chewed. "Right?"

Julie spun the fork through imaginary spaghetti. "No. I wasn't allowed a goldfish either. Why?"

"I know him pretty fucking well. I knew him when I was a kid."

"And he knows who you are?"

"Actually he seems to have no clue." JLL's eyes followed the crabs sidling across the beach. "It's been a long time. Listen, Julia . . ."

"Jesus. Jul*ie*."

JLL lowered her voice. "*Jesus Julie.* I'm here to help Marty sort through some stuff," she said. JLL reached over and grabbed Julie's hand. Her palms were greasy from the eggs. "It'll make him happier."

Julie scoffed. She tried to pull away but JLL held tight. Her grip was warm. Julie looked down at their doppelgänger fingers. Even their wrists were the same width.

"How old are you?" Julie asked.

JLL released her grip. "You're forward." She lifted the bubbling water from the camp stove. She scooped instant coffee into two mugs, began to pour the water.

A pulse of adrenaline hit Julie's bloodstream.

"You're Victoria." She watched as JLL tried to keep pouring. How the stream wavered. "That stupid story . . . You're that girl. You are."

JLL set the pot down and put her hands up. "I've been identified."

Julie rubbed her forehead. She thought about how Marty jittered every time he told a piece of the story. Marty did best when his history could be kept in a tidy, untouched package. It was magic, how his brain could maintain these separate compartments, that he could indulge in this story about Midge and never connect Victoria with the woman on Tallicurn. JLL seemed to read Julie's thoughts.

"Maybe he doesn't want to recognize me," she said. "Though I have forgiven him."

"Forgiven him?"

"He hasn't told you much, huh?" JLL passed Julie the stainless-steel mug of coffee. Steam that rose from the liquid was whipped away by wind. "Julia, I'd like to be straight with you."

Despite her best intentions, Julie took a sip of the coffee. It tasted of battery acid and burnt her tongue. JLL looked at her expectantly.

"Go on," Julie said.

"I'm here to help your father die."

Julie's muscles locked in place.

Down the beach, near the whale, a couple of seagulls fought over a catch. Their wings beat against one another, beaks poised like daggers at the other's throat.

Julie spoke slowly. "My father isn't sick."

JLL laughed out loud. She sipped her coffee. "His skin is flaking off his body, his chest aches, his organs are barely soldiering on, and none of them are paying attention to the system at large, and every time he hears a car door slam, he's dropped into a time period twenty-five years passed, and then his heart beats so hard that he confuses it with hate. You know, like that feeling after you stub your toe, but every hour, on the hour." She swirled her coffee. "Maybe you haven't been around a lot of healthy people?"

"Hey. Fuck you." Julie tossed her coffee in the sand. The liquid sank between the granules. "Maybe he's worse because you're making him talk about all kinds of old garbage."

JLL smiled, shook her head. "I'm not forcing him to talk about anything."

When Julie was a teenager, she'd believed she could pull life details out of Marty, draw out the full story, heal the segments one by one. She would be his counsellor when he wouldn't see one. She'd weather the flashbacks until they faded. Her tactic landed Marty at the vets' hospital in Prince Rupert for a full week. It had careened from her grasp so fast, her failure commemorated on the scarred door of their Toyota, the paint scraped off in one of Marty's midnight episodes.

"What do you mean you're going to help him die?" Julie asked.

"I plan to make him feel good about his choice." JLL got to her feet. "I need to chop a couple of logs for tonight." She grabbed a camping axe from beside the tent and began walking away. "Come with me."

Julie followed her. "His choice? Like, killing himself?"

The fighting seagulls resolved their dispute, ripping the morsel in two. They took off as JLL approached. She called over her shoulder. "Whatever you want to call it. Suicide, passing away at will, letting go."

JLL lit a cigarette as she walked and the smoke trailed behind her. They approached the whale. This close, Julie could see that the skin was stretched tight over its slug-like form, inflated more with the days that had passed. The chemical rot filled the air. A rush of thick saliva flooded her mouth. She spat on the ground, ran to catch up to JLL. She grabbed hold of the axe, brandished it like a weapon. "My father would never do that."

JLL licked her teeth. "Look. I know this is a hard thing to wrap your mind around, but give the idea a chance. And, listen, don't worry, I haven't told him who I am. I don't need to. I'm not planning on breaking his heart."

"Just killing him."

"Stopping his suffering. God. I can't believe Marty has a daughter. Shit." JLL reached to take her axe back.

A wave of anger passed through Julie. She turned and threw the axe. It flew end-over-end. The sharpened tip embedded in the side of the whale, just behind the eye. It made a satisfying smack. JLL walked to retrieve her tool, but Julie got there first and shoved her away. The whale's eye was sunken and pocked with holes from bird beaks, the gloss replaced by a muddy film.

Julie coughed as the chemical stench filled her mouth, nose, pores. She walked along the whale looking for the right spot. Fuck this girl and her camping axe. The deep grooves of the whale's neck faded into smoother skin. She let the weapon fall again against the whale's blubber. The tip landed just behind the pectoral fin, which jutted straight up, forced upright by bloat. An indent formed and exposed the pale fat beneath. She wasn't sure of her motivations, but it felt good.

She touched the exposed blubber with her finger. It was still warm. Incredibly, still warm. It felt soft, like fat on any cut of meat.

She heard JLL come up behind her. "Come on, Julia. You're being a kid. You're going to ruin my little beach home."

"Julie. You're calling my father a suicide risk."

JLL put a hand on the axe handle. "It's not like he hasn't tried. He just hasn't followed through."

The axe nearly slipped from Julie's grip.

"Oh," JLL said. "Didn't tell you that either, huh? Right before he abandoned my mom in favour of his dog."

"He wouldn't do that."

"Try to kill himself or abandon someone at their time of greatest need? Well, trust me, he's cool with both. But like I said, I've forgiven him."

The flood of anger rushed back. Julie ripped the axe from JLL's grip. She swung the hatchet at the pink sliver of blubber. Julie hacked again, and again, swore under her breath.

The blubber parted further with each swing. Seagulls overhead screeched their approval.

Julie landed a final hard blow.

"Woo! Here it comes." JLL said. She backed away and looked up as though expecting a rocket to launch.

The whale's blubber opened like a blossom. A bubble of exhumed insides appeared in the centre of the gash, its split mouth widening. The opening hissed. Blood emerged not as liquid but as mist. A spray of gas slapped Julie and painted her face. She scrambled back, shielded her eyes, the taste of aspirin and iron infecting her mouth. The whale's intestines crowned in the opening, then spooled out of its body, looped in the air. Snakes of it twisted and spun. The seagulls screamed louder. Whale guts slapped the beach in coils. The intestines piled out in impossible masses, blood and thick muck carving new paths in the sand, digging trenches of decay down to the lapping water. Julie's hands slid into the ditches. Tears flooded her eyes and she yelled for help.

Insides throttled out and the gash smiled wider. A waterfall of mass to be spilled. The guts poured out in thickening waves. A wall of blood as the whale's interior became exterior. Finally, the flow slackened. Blood pooled on the sand, some sinking into the earth.

Julie got on her knees and heaved. Brownish blood soaked her clothes. It dripped from her eyelashes.

A seagull landed near her, perched on the piled intestines and cried. Remaining blood trickled around Julie's ankles.

JLL called to her, the voice faraway. "You're like Carrie."

Julie clambered through the guts, tried to rise to her feet, tripped over a thick cord, slipped on the waste. The smell of rot and death everywhere, a taste in her mouth.

A towel was wrapped around her shoulders and a voice said in her ear, "My camping spot is fucked, isn't it? Your father asked me to stay with you. I wasn't going to, but I have a show to get ready for tonight."

Nausea filled Julie like bath water.

JLL led Julie through the fatty whale detritus. They waded into the ocean, walked until the water reached their hips, to where blood from the detonation dissipated. The red syrup spiralled off Julie's skin and clothes. She sobbed into the water, tried to push JLL away. But JLL stayed nearby, ready to exit the beach with her when she was ready.

PART II

The Whale Has Exploded

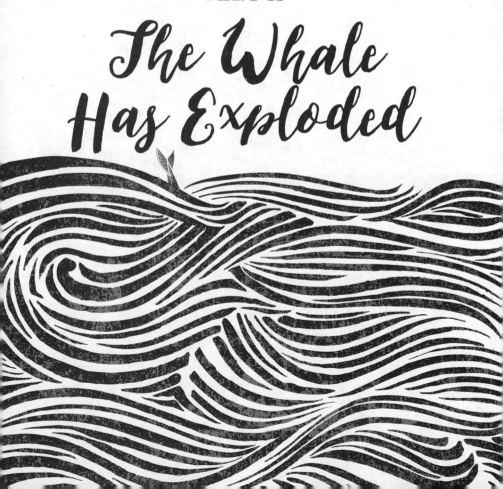

nine

ARCTIC HARE

On the path back from town, when the inertia of shock halted Julie's progress, JLL guided her forward. And when Julie stumbled off the trail to throw up behind a fern, JLL dropped her tent, backpack and fishing pole and gathered Julie's hair as she heaved. Her stomach was empty. Only yellow foam trickled on the fern spears. Though her clothes were acid death, she couldn't take them off. Stained a new shade of mauve, they clung to every crease of skin. She felt something rubbing against her chest and reached into her bra to pull out a filament of blubber. More dry heaves. She leaned over and waited, looking at the path ahead through crusted eyelashes. JLL hooked her fingers and pulled her forward.

Back in town, early evening light cast long angled shadows of fences and houses down the street. Despite the heat, the windows of homes were shut.

JLL held her T-shirt over her nose. "God. It's following us."

When they turned up the front path of the bungalow, Marty's face appeared in the window. He came outside, his eyes wide, his fists balled. For a moment, he looked ready to take JLL out.

Then came the indignity of being hosed off in her clothes by her father before being allowed inside. Marty hoisted JLL's bag on his shoulder, carried her belongings into their house. Julie heaved one more time in the rhododendron before following them, wrapped in JLL's sodden towel.

By the front entranceway, there was a stack of lights. Bedside lamps, a coil of Christmas lights from the patio, the under-the-counter pot lights. Every transportable light from the bungalow.

A trail of drips followed behind Julie as she walked to the kitchen. JLL was already in there, perched on the counter like she'd done it a hundred times before. Marty had the kettle on for coffee. The two of them chatted easily, JLL describing in excited detail how the whale came unravelled. It made Julie wonder how many times the two of them had talked in the time since JLL arrived, and whether JLL had been pursuing her quest, whether her father was in danger from her influence. Her stomach seized again. She couldn't consider the question now. Shower first.

In the bathroom, she stripped her clothing and cranked the hot water in the shower until steam blocked the view of the sink, her lonely toothbrush, the mirror. The water scalded her skin a bright pink. Even after the ocean bath, the hosing in the yard, there was still blood trapped in her hair, in the nooks of her body. She took shallow breaths as thick chocolate rot ran from her hair down the drain, taking breaks to lean out of the shower and spit bile into the toilet. Soap mixed with whale blood created a mauve lather.

She heard JLL and Marty talking and laughing outside the bathroom. Marty's excited voice carried over the sound of water hitting porcelain. Around JLL, he seemed like a different person. A mesmerized child. Thrilled to be alive.

Julie filled her mouth with water then let it spill down her chest. When she'd lathered and rinsed a dozen times, she turned off the water. Throwing the shower curtain open, the whale smell was overpowering. Now clean herself, it attacked full force. She dropped her clothes in the bin and tied the bag shut.

There was a tap at the door. Marty whispered through the door crack. "Jules. Thanks for bringing her here."

"It honestly wasn't my choice, Marty." She grabbed a towel and put it to her nose. Rot had infiltrated the fiber. It was in the air too. Port Braid's breathing space overcome. "And don't get too attached. I don't think she can stay long."

"I haven't heard anyone puke like that since Midge," he said.

Julie closed her eyes. "What are you talking about, Marty?"

JLL called, "Marty! Who's Midge? Old girlfriend?"

Marty yelled back that it was his dog.

Julie sat on the edge of the tub, rubbed her face with the towel. "JLL doesn't want to hear about Midge."

Marty tapped on the door again. "Kiddo, why is there a raccoon in the backyard?"

She wrapped her housecoat around herself and opened the door. "That's my new friend," she said.

Marty stood before her, gave her a look. She gave him the finger.

"I know, I know. Your mysterious no-pets policy. It's temporary, but you can't kick him out because I've named him. He's Bert now."

"What are you going to feed it?"

Julie entered the kitchen, where JLL sat munching an apple and sipping the coffee Marty made for her.

"You have a pet raccoon," JLL said.

"Yep." She looked in the fridge and inspected the containers of leftovers, bags of moulding fruit. She grabbed a pack of bacon from the fridge, sandwiched a few slices between sheets of paper towel and put them on a plate.

"Bacon seems as good as anything." She stared into the microwave as they cooked.

"Don't do that, Jules," Marty said.

She reached for a loose piece of tinfoil on the counter and slapped it against her forehead. Light from the microwave reflected off the metal. "Better?"

Marty rolled his eyes.

"By the way," Julie said, "why did you take my lamp?"

"Need more lighting for the stage." He scratched under his bandana. "For tonight."

"You cleared out the living room, your bedroom, the kitchen. Where am I supposed to read?" The timer beeped and Julie opened the door. Steam poured out. "You bought the cheap watery stuff again." She reached in to grab the plate and recoiled.

Marty took the plate out with his Captain Hook. "You're feeding it to a raccoon, Jules."

Throughout their argument, JLL continued munching on her apple, not seeming interested in what either had to say, but when Julie carried the plate of bacon toward the backyard, JLL tossed her apple core in the sink and followed her. She told Marty he should come witness the spectacle.

One look at Bert, and Marty implored her to call the SPCA. The little animal made circles in the crate, cowered in the back corner as Julie opened the wire door. Marty and JLL took several steps back, both of them with arms crossed over their chests.

Raccoon nutrition was a mystery, but if they could survive off the contents of trash bins, whatever was in the fridge would do. Bacon, table scraps and the occasional fried piece of fish. Having a pet raccoon would be a dream. Wild ones were assholes, obviously, but what better way to beat a species than to mould them into tame citizens? It worked for dogs. She would train Bert to defecate in the toilet and shake paws and possibly ride on her shoulder to the envy of all.

JLL leaned in to look at Bert. "Why is this raccoon your prisoner?"

"I killed its mom." The animal didn't shriek when she scooped him under the belly. His body fit along the length of her hand.

JLL re-crossed her arms. "And now you're forcing it to live in a box."

"Screw off, I'm taking care of it." His soft fur brushed her hand. His body shook. Was there a flash of recognition in its beady eyes? She handed Bert a morsel of bacon, which it grasped between its paws and gnawed from the side of its mouth.

"You're coddling it," JLL said.

"Yeah, I'm pretty sure the options are coddling or death."

"So. Let it go." JLL reached toward the raccoon, but Julie shoved her hand away.

"To die?"

"Yeah, to die. Why not. Better than living in a little box in your backyard."

"It won't always be in a box." She touched Bert's head. He flinched but didn't try to escape. His cheeks puffed out as he ate. Julie held the raccoon in her lap and fed him another piece of training bacon. Released into the yard, Bert moseyed around the grass. Every time Bert bumbled over, she handed him another morsel of bacon. Positive reinforcement. He soon curled up beside her leg of his own volition. He became a mini mattress pump, little squeaks as he drew in air. The warmth reminded her of having Billy Poole fall asleep with his head on her lap, but without snoring or expectations of future encounters.

JLL lit up a cigarette and sat beside Julie on the grass. Marty set up a lawn chair. The sky glowed orange, a particular shade that the Port Braid dusk offered only for a short time in summer, when the path of the setting sun traced the slope of Mount Denburn, which rose from the Pacific a kilometre off the town's coast. The sun's rays were split and refracted through the lacy foliage of cedars on the mountain until finally the sun dipped into the ocean.

JLL puffed clouds of smoke into the air. In this pose, in this light, she seemed harmless. But it changed as soon as she spoke. "Marty. Your daughter and I were talking earlier. She had some doubts about what you told me. About when you nearly killed yourself."

Marty glanced at his daughter. He rubbed at the skin under his bandana. "She wasn't born yet."

JLL dragged on her cigarette. "That doesn't mean she oughtn't to know. Right?"

Marty leaned forward in his chair, rubbed his face. He turned to Julie. "Actually, I was going to tell you this."

Julie stared into the grass. She watched as the sides of the raccoon rose and fell, his breathing permitted only because of the delicate, toothpick-thin ribs just below his skin.

"Go on, then," Julie said. She stroked Bert's fur.

"I don't want to tell it now," Marty said.

JLL tapped off the ash from her cigarette. "You already told me. I'll go inside. If you want me to go inside." She rose to her feet, stubbed her smoke out against the bricks of the house. "But tell her."

Once JLL was inside, Marty sighed, rubbed his face. "Julie."

"Where is this all coming from?" Her throat was getting tight, threatening to cut off words. *Why is this happening now?*

"It's just a story about Midge. That's all."

"That's all?"

He put a hand on her back, rubbed it like he used to when she was sick, when they were falling asleep in front of the TV.

"I'd like to get it off my chest," he said. "I think it's important to me."

ten

1992

Marty sat in the back of his reclaimed van with the doors and windows closed, his eyes shut, letting the sauna heat soak his brain. His retreat from the house. The world, through closed lids, glowed red. He held Midge's collar, played with a tuft of fur caught in the plastic buckle. After that first Midge sighting, there had been no other reports. According to Nancy, it was a family of four who saw a long-legged hound with a lizard in her mouth somewhere outside the park. The dog was skinny. They whistled and she looked up and wagged her bony tail. One of their boys held a peanut butter sandwich in the air and the dog came over. The dog grabbed the sandwich, but when they took her by the collar, she slipped free. She had trotted away across the sand, PB&J in her jaws.

The interior of Marty's van looked rough. The upholstery on the seat backs was ripped from Midge's trademark scramble to the captain's chair. He would always put her in the back, but before he could even sit down, she would have clambered into the passenger seat. He would crack the window and off they would go.

Marty rolled onto his side to sleep. The hot air coated his lungs.

He heard a knock on the window. His mind swam. The van was sweltering. A thick blanket of sleep and heat confused his thoughts. Through the window, Nancy's face loomed over him. He shrunk in her gaze.

She mouthed, "Open the damn door." He did and a gust of cold air swept in. He knew it wasn't actually cold air. It was just a breeze. Any breeze.

"What's wrong with you?" she asked.

"Beats me."

She crawled into the van and flung open the remaining doors. "You're trying to cook yourself." A cross breeze carried through the interior. Her eyes had sunk in the last month. Her eyelashes interlocked over her eyes. "You can't even share a house with me anymore."

Marty shook his head. "It's just this place, Nancy." He used to like T or C, but day-by-day it was transforming into the other place. He had to avoid the beige. The beige set him off. Cots, beige, big rigs on the highway. The list grew.

"Well, you had this thing towed over here. Maybe it's time to use it." She glanced at him.

"Won't run yet."

Nancy scrambled out of the van and slammed the driver's side door. "If that's all that's stopping you, then get on a Greyhound. Oh right, you spent all your money. It's nice that you can't even buy us wine anymore, by the way."

He muttered. "The van's for Midge."

"What's that?" She leaned close to him.

He repeated himself.

Nancy covered her face. "Oh my God. Dog's worth more than me." She looked at the sky. Cirrus clouds etched fish bones across the blue.

"Nancy." He emerged from the van, slid on his shoes. He couldn't touch her. He watched her shoulders shake with distant awareness. "You're keeping me alive." The sauna sweat on Marty's face and neck dried and the wind felt hot again.

Nancy eyed him. "I know."

He forced a smile. "So when are you going to stop doing that?"

She laughed. "I guess I don't like the idea of you going before me." She dabbed her eyes. A droplet travelled down her finger and disappeared into her palm. A line of ants made their way across the driveway and Marty wondered how their legs didn't burn off. "You think you're the only one who needs to get out of here."

Marty considered this. "You could take off for a while. I'll look after the kid."

Nancy laughed again. "The way you are?"

"The way I am?"

Nancy eyed him. "You're half dead. I don't trust you with the toaster."

Her words should have stung. He stood and faced the road. A car full of teenagers rolled by, playing some boy band crap. A flash of panic stabbed his heart. Even teenagers riding in cars could set him off. He was so tired. The boy band voices dropped with the Doppler effect.

"You made up that story about Midge, didn't you? You want me to stay here."

"You think I want you around that bad?"

"Yes." Marty popped the hood of the van. He'd make this thing run.

"Marty," Nancy said. He turned around and Nancy shoved the collar in his face.

Marty stared under the hood. The engine, covered in fine white gypsum, relayed no relevant information. Each part was silent and still.

A shriek came from the backyard, and Marty nearly banged his head off the metal.

"You can just stay there." Nancy dropped the collar onto the engine. She ran behind the house to get her daughter. Marty followed.

Behind Nancy's house was a small pond lined with Painter's Plastic, refilled every few days with the garden hose. Scavenged bricks made up the circumference. Victoria crouched by the water, holding her hands away from her body. Marty stopped by the house, but Nancy ran on and picked her daughter up. She nearly dropped her.

"Oh, Victoria, what happened?" Nancy wiped something from her arm and dipped Victoria's hands in the water.

"I squeezed it by accident, and it splurged everywhere. It's dying." She sniffed.

Marty then spotted the lumpy brown toad struggling to surmount the bricks. Transparent silly string, dotted with black seeds, the distended innards of a kiwi, was strung around it.

Marty covered his mouth. "Oh no, she made it splurge." He started to laugh between his fingers.

Victoria ruptured into sobs, and Nancy shot him a look. But she was holding back laughter too. The corners of her mouth upturned.

Marty came over. "It didn't hurt it, kiddo." He scooped up the stunned toad and placed it near some sagebrush, out of sight from the kid. The spawn, he brushed into the water. "See, the tadpoles will be all right too."

Victoria wiped her eyes and inspected the floating spawn.

Nancy scooped her up again and carried her toward the house.

Just as she was opening the back door, a hawk landed by the sagebrush.

"Oh no." Before Marty could jog over, the hawk grabbed its prey and pumped its wings once, twice, landing on the telephone pole. The toad's back legs dangled and kicked. Its tiny arms splayed out from the hawk's beak.

Victoria's mouth stretched open and a fresh cohort of sobs burst forth. Nancy, on the verge of hysteric laughter, rushed Victoria inside.

That night, to make up for the trauma of the toad, Nancy promised Victoria her favourite meal—mac and cheese. Marty and Victoria sat on the plaid couch of the living room and the musty smell of the fabric embraced them. Some past owner of the furniture—or maybe Victoria's dad—had smoked. The smell mingled with the trapped dust. Marty stared through the living room window while Victoria tried to braid his sideburns. If he sat here for a few more years, his hair would grow, and her fine motor skills would develop enough to get the job done. She'd finished crying over the toad now, but red was rubbed deep into her eyes.

In the kitchen, Nancy pulled glassware from underneath the stove. A thin river of steam poured under the lintel from kitchen to living room. It carried with it the essence of cooked pasta. Marty closed his eyes and listened to the rhythmic chopping.

He felt a dull pain around his breastbone each time he exhaled. He tried to breathe differently—shallow breaths, deep meditative exhales, sighs, Lamaze exercises—they all ended with that ache between his ribs.

He craned his neck to watch Nancy. She stood at the stove. Her head pointed toward the window and her movements were slow. He knew she felt the same as him. The depression had unravelled its tentacles. You could no longer step around them.

She assembled the dish, slid it into the oven and joined them in the living room. She laid her head on Marty's lap, and Victoria transferred her efforts to Nancy's hair. Nancy sat up every once in a while to sip on something clear, and Marty wondered if it was water or if she was holding out on him. And what happened to the rule about drinking in front of the kid.

The timer on the oven went off, and Nancy fetched the mac and cheese. She placed the casserole dish on a towel. Nancy passed out forks, and they dug in together. The smacking of their mouths took over the silence. The air was tight. Every few minutes, Victoria and Nancy took turns sniffing.

The macaroni trudged down Marty's throat. The world outside was dark, and he wondered what was outside the front door. The apocalypse could be long over. This dinner could have started ten years ago. Maybe he was stuck to the couch and didn't realize it because he never tried to move. He shifted. The couch creaked. Victoria and Nancy looked up at him. He wondered if he should make a proclamation. He didn't.

The thought of death came to him like an epiphany. *If I die*, he realized, *then this dinner will be over. If I die, I won't need to look at macaroni ever again.* He stabbed a noodle with his fork.

"If I die," he said, "I won't eat macaroni and cheese anymore."

Victoria scrunched up her face, but Marty didn't care. Nancy rubbed his back. She misunderstood. She thought that he wanted to keep eating macaroni and cheese forever.

"Victoria," Nancy said. "I thought of something I wanted to tell you about the toad."

Victoria held a mouthful of macaroni in front of her lips. "What?"

"It's sad what happened, right?"

"Yeah."

"But sometimes sad things can make other things stronger."

Victoria put her fork back in the casserole dish. The noodles tumbled back into the pile. "Like how?"

"Well, think about that hawk. It needed to eat dinner. Maybe it even has babies to feed." Nancy swirled her drink, took a sip. "And there's another part to it too, but it's harder to understand. If the stronger toads survive, and the weaker ones are eaten by hawks, then all toads get stronger over time."

"Why?"

"Because stronger toads have stronger babies."

Victoria tilted her head. "But that toad had babies."

"True."

Victoria stabbed a noodle. "Then shouldn't we get rid of those babies?"

Marty interjected. "I don't think so, kiddo."

Nancy nodded. "What if there are some strong babies? We should give them a chance."

Victoria nodded and went back to her meal.

After the day with the toad, Marty told Julie, he and Nancy got worse. They started drinking more. Nancy quit her job. Or got fired. Marty wasn't sure. And it was around that time that his hair first started falling out. Clumps of it in the shower. Marty used the word *depression*, and this was the first time Julie heard her father say the word.

Marty and Nancy moved in each other's orbit but stopped touching. The fridge was empty. Nancy ended up calling Trent, Victoria's dad, to take the kid for the weekend. Marty knew that wasn't great, but he was too busy staring at baseball on TV. More socially acceptable than a blank screen, he learned. Before Victoria left, she told him he should take the bandage off his stump.

He followed her instructions. He stood in front of the bathroom mirror and unwrapped his stump. A scar ran down the middle with wrinkles puckering outward. It was smooth where the skin was pulled to cover the bone. It wasn't the worst stump he'd seen. It was less useful than one of those elephant trunk ones, with the small bit of muscle past the elbow, but he preferred it.

Inspecting his wound launched Marty into his first full-blown flashback. Burial detail, post Highway of Death. He is walking beside a soldier he hasn't met before. Together, they lift the bodies of Iraqis. Marty takes the feet, the unknown soldier takes the arms. The other soldier is American, involved in battles instead of engineering. He might be a rifleman. He wears khaki camo and a dark green vest.

The bodies they pick up, however, don't seem like soldiers at all. Something has gone wrong. They lie outside of cars filled with food, blankets, photos. Ordinary things. These aren't war vehicles. The war is meant to be over. Some of the U.S. soldiers pocket items of value—jewellery that could be family heirlooms of the people lying here, or stolen from Kurds. Either way it's stolen from the dead.

Dust mixes with smoke, fills their lungs.

The bodies aren't bodies. The bodies are black husks, and some of them implode as they're lifted. A bus lies on its side at the end of the line. Word around burial detail is that the bus carried hospital patients. Maybe they were bad guys before, but they didn't put up a fight last night. They were supposed to have safe passage. Something has gone wrong.

The American chatters about how he finally got his first fucking kill, and his second, and his third. They work side-by-side moving the bodies. The man is excited. The whites of his eyes flash above the bandana that covers his mouth. They approach a car that still burns. Marty sees a figure inside. It's someone alive shadowed against the flames. Hope. He sees the perfect profile of a face, with a roman nose and an open mouth, and he starts to run. He can save someone. There are two figures in the back of the car too, and one of them is small. His partner yells after him to chill the fuck out. There's no rush. But there are three people who don't have to end up in the unmarked trenches. The unmarked trenches are filling up fast.

Marty gets to the car. The mouth that a moment ago seemed to be crying for help now transforms into something else. Marty sees that open mouth is burnt into a permanent grin with coal for a tongue. Flames lick out of eyeholes, and then Marty is blown backward. The gas tank has finally gone off. He feels the black ashes of a family fly against his face and whip into his nose. The ashes entrench themselves in his diaphragm. He can feel them smouldering. They will stay there. The American runs to his side, tries to keep him from looking at his injury. His hand is ribbons of skin with white tendons snapped into toothpicks.

Marty woke from the flashback in Nancy's arms. He was yelling, but it sounded like someone else to him. She had a red mark on her arm and he understood that it was from him. He turned on his side, heaved. His skin slick with sweat. His heart aching.

Later, in the kitchen, Nancy prepared their drinks. Marty walked around the interior of the house, turning corners whenever the walls did. He started this journey in the bathroom, stepping into the bathtub to follow the tiles until he was out the door and walking through the hallway. He touched the front door and turned the two corners there and proceeded to tour the living room, making a slight detour at the television. He was having trouble remembering the layout of the place. In the kitchen, he found a dirty cutting board and took a break to clean it. Tomato seeds were suspended in their goop. The vegetable world's frog spawn. The hues of the rooms darkened with each rotation he made of the house.

Marty made it to the bedroom for the third time. A dark filter modified the furnishings. He heard the clink of ice as Nancy entered the room behind him. He was crawling across the bed-sheets, pulling his stump along the headboard. They got under the duvet. It was time. He felt so relieved.

"Do you want to fuck one more time?" she asked him.

"Do you?"

She shook her head.

"That's good," he said.

Nancy asked him how he wanted to do it. "Romantic or dramatic?"

"Which is which?"

"Let's call poison romantic. Let's call breaking the skin dramatic."

"So that's your slit wrists, throats, guns."

"Guns don't count as dramatic."

"What do they count as?"

"Messy." She smiled. "And easy."

"I like easy."

"I can't do guns. I can't pull a trigger. I can drink poison beer. I can't pull a trigger."

"I can."

She put a gin and tonic in his hand, dropped a mound of her prescription sleeping pills between them. "Will these do?"

"You've been saving them," he said.

With each sip of their gin and tonic, they popped another pill. He waited to start feeling nervous but it never came. Outside the bedroom window he noticed that the street lamp was missing. *That's funny*. No light at all came through the window. He stood up and walked over to the glass. The sky should have held a few stars, but it was as though someone had lined the window with black construction paper.

"I want to go outside a minute," he said.

Nancy patted the bed beside them. "Stay with me."

He looked at her and noticed that her hair was made of the same black construction paper. He sat down to look at it more closely, and Nancy held his stump.

"I can't see your scar," she said. Then she laughed. "Or your . . . mouth?"

Marty opened his mouth as wide as he could and she laughed harder.

"No, no." She nearly rolled off the bed. "I can see it. I can see it too much!"

"What's it like?"

"You're swallowing me!"

He knelt over her and motioned as if to ingest her.

"Stop! Stop! Monster!" She shoved him and rolled over laughing.

They polished off their gin. Marty climbed off the bed and got them two beers from the fridge. They'd have to down more pills if this was going to work. The liquid looked strange so he poured one into a glass. Thick ink oozed out. Marty sniffed it. It smelled like beer. So he tasted it and it tasted like beer. He carried them back to the bedroom and Nancy squealed in delight.

Her mouth became a gaping hole too. She transitioned from clown to undertaker, and it almost made Marty laugh. He caught himself.

Nancy sipped the beer. "I never should have had a kid."

"It's good you had her."

Marty could see down her throat and into the cavern of her ribcage, where her ribs glowed white and made waves through the darkness, and her lungs gulped up black blood and turned it to nothing. His belly started shaking and then his chest starting shaking. He was laughing. His guffaws bounced off the walls and swept Nancy to do the same.

"Isn't it funny," he said, "how I didn't believe this would happen?"

The two of them hung in the blackness between the ceiling

and the carpet. Water the same temperature as their bodies rose up beneath them. Marty felt it lap around his arms. Nancy paddled away. He heard the splash of her arms and then a bigger splash as she dove, and then she was back and placing more pills in his hand.

"We'll set her free," Nancy said. *Her* was Victoria.

"Her sad story." Marty took one and washed it down with hand-warmed beer. The sweetness sunk into the cracks of his teeth. He took another. He heard barking outside. Nancy took a pill and then another.

Marty's feet sank downward in the water, which turned to warm yogurt or honey. He rotated to a vertical position, and his feet met up with Nancy's. He pushed his arm through the substance and found her waist, pulled it close to his own. Where Nancy was, parallel to his own body, was even more black than the rest of the room. Their skin slid against each other and Nancy fed Marty another pill. The barking outside transformed into an electronic pulse. It vibrated the liquid and his skin. Marty shook his head and concentrated on Nancy.

He found that if he squinted his eyes, he could use his eyelashes to filter out the darkness, and that's when he noticed that Nancy's eyes were closed and mascara ran down her face. She grimaced.

"What are you doing?" His words slurred. He realized that his head had sunk under the liquid. The words tried to make a space for themselves, but Marty wasn't sure if their bubbles reached Nancy's ears. He took a long drag of beer.

The electronic pulse stopped and the liquid grew still. A thumping sound started from another room. The sound drummed on Marty's forehead. He couldn't drink more beer so long as it was happening. His skin melted away from his muscles. All he needed to do to reach the other room was glide, no paddling necessary.

"Wait for me." He squinted to see Nancy's head bobbing up and down. He moved through the house and rebounded off walls to make his way to the front door. The walls remained hard but furniture and knick-knacks formed black pudding. He felt the door with his hand, found the knob, opened it.

The liquid flowed out of the house and Marty saw a dog standing in front of him, its tail tucked between its legs.

The dog looked like Midge. He had to look at her through filtered eyelashes.

Midge turned on her haunches a few times and then sat down. She didn't greet him. Maybe it wasn't Midge. It didn't make any sense. Perhaps she had died and he had also died. The dog's ribs poked through her skin and her hips stuck up like a cow's.

The liquid in the house drained fully and Marty looked down to see that he once again had skin. Light seeped into the house, starting through the doorway and winding its way around corners.

"Nancy!" he called. "Nancy!"

Marty jogged back to the bedroom and saw Nancy with her eyes rolled back. She had four pills left in her hand. How many had she taken? How many had he taken? Marty removed the rest of the sleeping pills from Nancy's hand and tossed them in the bedside trash.

Midge walked into the house. Her claws tapped on the linoleum. The sound was real. He strode to the kitchen and downed cold coffee from the pot, picked a fruit fly from between his teeth. He took a pack of sandwich meat from the fridge and dumped it on the ground—Midge sniffed at it but didn't eat. Marty touched her ear.

"You saved me, kiddo," he told her.

Marty swept Nancy over his shoulder and dumped her in the car. He took Midge for the ride too. Marty cranked the air conditioning as high as it would go and sang along to David Bowie on the way to the hospital. He stayed conscious just long enough to check her in, and then he fell asleep in the car with Midge in the passenger seat. By the time he woke up late the next day, Midge had defecated twice in the back seat. They were small, sad shits that smelled like tar. It was early afternoon and the car interior was on fire. Midge still slept next to him.

Marty checked at the front desk to make sure that Nancy was alive. She was. He bought a plastic water bottle from the gift shop, filled it for himself and Midge and drove away from T or C in Nancy's car.

eleven

SOLE

*Chuck Berry is my fairy godfather. Because, prison
visits aside (illegal to cross state lines with a white girl,
especially a white girl still living with parents), he is
still the sanctified Pied Piper leading the kids through
the glistening halls of rock and roll as though behind
the marble aren't the beginnings of freer things.*

In the hours leading up to JLL's first show at The Halibut, Julie lay
on her bed, alternately thinking about Marty's story and flipping
through JLL's strange journal of rock legends and suicidal beasts.
The edges of the journal were dyed brown and swollen from
their journey in Julie's pocket during the whale explosion and her
ocean bath.

JLL and Marty had both left the house. Marty had taken his pile of lights into The Halibut to set up the stage. JLL, after leaving her belongings in the small attic space, had taken a small backpack and left to "prepare for the show." Julie hadn't questioned JLL on what *preparations* entailed.

Julie separated the pages of JLL's journal carefully and wiped away any debris. Only the edges were waterlogged. Miraculously, the centres of the pages were dry, and JLL's penmanship was unscathed by salt water.

The bungalow swam with heat, windows closed against the night breeze that carried with it the gaseous form of the decomposing whale.

Her father had tried to kill himself. This new knowledge disrupted her understanding of her own origins. Her father had attempted to end his life before hers had begun. Her existence was thanks to the timely, and implausible, arrival of a runaway dog. Every human on Earth, she knew, was the result of innumerable chances. Each one of us an impossible coincidence within the doughnut of the universe. And yet, this reverence for our unlikely existence only makes sense from our own perspective, wherein we are an important outcome that the universe had to conspire to create. If you take the view that we are no more important than a bacterium in the Arctic or a chunk of iron ore on Pluto, which required the same degree of happenstance to build, a skinny dog showing up on a doorstep means nothing. Her father could by now be nothing more than a skeleton, and that too meant nothing.

And yet the possibility remained vivid. A grave somewhere in New Mexico. Marty, underground, a collection of calcium twigs in a plywood box. It should make her feel grateful, she supposed, that she lived in a reality where her father existed, even though her mother no longer did.

After abandoning Nancy, Marty never tried to contact her. He had told Julie that. All these years, he never thought to look her up in a phone book.

When it was time for JLL's show, Julie shimmied into her tightest black jeans. She didn't know what to expect from the performance but hoped that it would be a failure—a group of bored Port Braidians around the piano, glancing at their watches and waiting for the strange girl to finish singing her songs.

Before Julie headed out, she walked to the living room, enjoying the cold feel of the tiles on her feet, to check the news on her laptop. There was an article about the fight between the coast guard and townspeople to see whose responsibility it was to haul the whale back into the ocean. It seemed like no one really knew how. Local residents should have a whale burying party—dig a really big hole and roll the carcass in there—so at least the stench of death was covered. They did it for the UBC blue whale when it first washed up in Nova Scotia. Julie had admired the UBC blue whale's skeleton suspended in the Museum of Biodiversity in Vancouver. The building was built to showcase the animal. It was all windows, so you could see the behemoth from the road. At night, it looked like a phantom blue had coasted down the sidewalk. Inside, you could descend the steps, gaze up into the whale's ribcage and imagine how many copies of yourself could fit in there. The lower jawbones were diverging canoes. The whale had decomposed underground for a decade before someone at the university had the idea to dig it up and bombard the Nova Scotian town a second time with a wave of half-rotted flesh. Probably much worse than the first time around. She pitied the people who were hired to clean the bones with toothbrushes.

The landscape architecture department had a small graduation celebration there. Parents were invited, and Marty drove from Port Braid in a single day to make it on time. She told him to refrain from a speech, regardless of what other parents were doing at the microphone, but when proud mom after proud dad started going up there, Julie saw Marty get restless.

She'd told Marty her stomach was hurting and that she wanted to call it a night. The blue whale hung above their heads, and Marty looked up at it. He put his beer by her feet and walked toward the mike before the previous person had finished. He waited for them, foot tapping. Then he was up there. Silent. He stared at Julie. She shrugged her shoulders, shook her head at him.

Finally—"I've known Julie for twenty-three years . . ."

The audience tittered, but Julie knew it wasn't meant as a joke. They were just the only words that came to mind. He froze again. The stage light caught the sheen of his forehead. Julie squeezed her wineglass. She considered dropping it. Cutting herself with glass to create a diversion. She and Marty could wrap themselves in capes, materialized at just the right moment, and escape into the night, the audience wowed at the mysterious duo. With her wineglass poised, she looked at her father.

"But it feels like a hell of a lot longer."

The audience tittered again.

Julie downed the rest of her wine in relief.

Walking to The Halibut, the smell of lindens intermingled with the whale. Street lights blinked to life one by one. On one of the lampposts, she spotted one of Marty's grotesque flyers, which he'd distributed around town. He chose puke yellow paper and clip art. *The Halibut presents* was written in Century Gothic. Below that was a cartoon image of a fish, as if to say that The Halibut was presenting a fish, but if you managed to keep reading, you would see *Jennie Lee Lewis, the most extraordinary Jerry Lee Lewis impersonator*

alive today. To accent the masterpiece, there was another clip art image of a man at a piano. The hair suggested Beethoven.

When she turned the corner for The Halibut, she saw a large group of humans loitering around the door.

All the people from town were there. Janice Erickson and her husband, Hal, chatted with their now-teenage son. Julie used to babysit him, back when static hair and sweatpants defined his personality. Now, he towered over his parents. He used the sleeve of his oversized T-shirt to block his nose from the whale smell. Ms. Halbert, probably the oldest person in Port Braid, sat on a camp-stool someone had brought. She too covered her nose.

Then there was Billy Poole, who flashed his canine grin when he saw her. He was with the two girls from the other night, Marjory and Lisa. Their hair was wrapped into topknots, and they smiled to say they knew she fucked Billy but weren't passing judgment. More like *Thanks, he needed that.*

She mumbled, "Hey guys," and squeezed through the door. The tables were stacked in one corner, making the place standing room only. Even Ian's table had been moved to the back room with the mop and cleaning products. Julie spotted him back there, still eating his fries and ketchup at his regular table in defiance.

Marty's obsession with the *stage* came into focus when Julie spotted the area surrounding the piano. Cheap religious candles from the dollar store lined the performance area. The lamp from Marty's garage workshop was now positioned over the piano keys. To the ceiling, Marty had tacked a line of silver streamers that blew in waves every time someone flushed the toilet. Too beautiful. Even Fran, the fish delivery woman, had contributed. She was tacking up a homemade banner across the ceiling that read, *Welcome, Performer,* the final couple of letters squashed against the border.

Her father flitted about, dunking things into the deep fryer and delivering plates of fried fish and potato wedges to customers, who tore pieces off and ate with their hands. Marty even used his Captain Hook to help customers, which he usually avoided, transporting bottles of beer. He called out to her. "Kiddo, a hand?"

Julie squeezed her way behind the bar, and Marty whispered to her that he had already brought in a thousand dollars, his best business ever. "I'm down to selling the sole, and she's not even here yet." The stage was the only clear space in the restaurant. Julie's bedside lamp was perched on top of the piano and shone its beam at her mother's ass groove. Leaning over the piano was the rented microphone from Alan's shop.

Julie worked the deep fryer while her father made rounds. Excited chatter filled the restaurant, people greeting those they hadn't bumped into for a while. Port Braid was a small town, and yet a lot of these people managed to live solitary existences, content on their acreage. They shuffled around until those outside were able to push their way in. The performance was meant to start in ten minutes and JLL was nowhere to be seen.

Julie felt a hand on her shoulder. Alan had managed to find a Jerry Lee Lewis T-shirt for the occasion, featuring the man himself perched on top of a piano bench, leaning over the keys of a grand piano. Forever the fashion innovator, Alan had paired his T-shirt with a pair of neon pink bicycle shorts.

Alan gestured at the deep fryer. "Career change?"

"You know I've always wanted to be a fry girl."

"Excited about the show?"

Julie shrugged.

"Well, I am. You should come by the shop soon. We'll debrief. Talk about the musical merits."

"Sure thing."

Alan disappeared into the crowd, and Julie turned her attention back to the fryer. She dunked in the last piece of sole and told her father that deep-fried Mars bars and French fries were all they could provide. Mars bars orders poured in and the cooking oil took on a healthy brown glow.

The murmur of the crowd dropped off. Julie looked up and saw JLL striding along the sidewalk smoking a cigarette. She wore a loose-fitting striped shirt—something like the Newcastle jersey—that hung over her black jeans. Her hair was slicked back, greased into a smooth wave that bounced with each step. Where in town had JLL transformed into this character? In the bathroom of The Lion's Den? Behind a gas station? Or a secret lair in the forest?

Julie glanced at her father. He wore the bewilderment of a child. "Do you even like Jerry Lee Lewis?" she asked.

He shushed her. JLL's cheekbones looked more cut than before, like she'd shaded them for effect. JLL stomped out her cigarette. She stood in the entrance and took in the scene. Julie suspected this was a better reception than she got in most towns. Half these people, herself included, wouldn't be here if there were a single stripper in Port Braid.

The crowd cleared a path for JLL, and she approached the piano. She sat in the centre of the worn groove, as though the groove were her own. JLL tapped a few keys with a single finger and ran the back of her hand across the length. She hit the keys three times each, starting from the high end and going to the low. Someone coughed at the back of the restaurant.

Marty leaned over the bar and whispered to her, "Do you want me to introduce you?"

JLL ran a hand through her hair. "Nope."

She started into a cantering chord progression. A steady, slow build. Here and there her fingers fell into a wild-west flutter of keys, the whole thing more country than rock and roll. The piano climbed and JLL's voice poured from her mouth, deep and accented with twang. *You win again.*

Julie looked around and saw the people from her town swaying to the music. They picked up flakes of fish or scooped up Mars bar goop in time with the music. Mesmerized.

Billy Poole was a person who listened to Tool twelve years after that was a thing people did. He proudly hung that Pink Floyd poster with their album covers painted on women's naked backsides. And here he was in a family-friendly fish and chip shop nodding his head to glorified country western, eyebrows lowered in consternation.

Jennie Lee Lewis's head wove side to side like a horse bored in its stall. Her voice dipped and hovered in unexpected places and when the song was over, the people clapped hard. Marty nodded ferociously.

Next, she sang "Great Balls of Fire," which was the one Jerry Lee Lewis song that Julie remembered. Kids at her elementary school used to giggle scream the lyrics whenever they wanted to reassert to their peers that they, in fact, knew what balls were. JLL gave no hint of the comedy, though, and no one in the audience had so much as a smirk. JLL stopped playing the piano each time she sang the main line, then leapt back with her key-pounding. She lifted her foot onto the keys, stepping down and releasing a crush of sound.

JLL was good. Julie wanted that to be untrue. With each song she played, the applause grew louder. JLL cut through their applause by starting a new song, and the audience sucked their screams back to listen fully. She sang "Breathless" and "I'm on Fire."

Before applause could subside, she started into a boogie-woogie lilt. Her voice came from somewhere deeper in her lungs, underscored by a sharp edge. She held her voice suspended over a straight razor, gave the impression this was a common occurrence. There was no need for panic—just a calm walk over a bed of nails.

Come along my baby, whole lotta shakin' goin' on
Yes, I said come along my baby, baby you can't go wrong

Janice Erickson, with moves revived from another era's school of dance, was the first to start really moving. Her hands began to clap, and then clap above her head. She began swinging her shoulders and hips. She held a hand to Hal. He kept his gaze on the floor but shuffled his feet and rotated his shoulders in what could have been a gym class stretch if not for the rhythmic knee bends. Their teenage son, instead of looking embarrassed, bobbed his head like a vulture in front of carrion.

The door to The Halibut hung open as more humans tried to press through. The whale smell swirled through the restaurant, kicked into motion by the flailing of dancers' arms. It was breathed in, exhaled, embraced as a necessary part of the scene.

Jennie Lee Lewis's face contorted with the lyrics. Her chin jutted to the side to allow enough room for the words to emerge. All the while, her hands flew across the face of the piano, giant claws swooping on the keys and clamping on the chords.

Well, I said come along my baby, we got chicken in the barn
Woo-huh, come along my baby, really got the bull by the horn

The next people to join in, to Julie's surprise, were Billy's crew. The dance that took Marjory and Lisa looked to be a precursor to headbanging. It was unintentional headbanging; they were overcome, controlled by their bodies' childish need to respond to stimulus. Their heads bobbed and tossed their hair forward over their faces. Billy's canines flashed in the stage lamplight.

Well, I said shake, baby, shake,
I said shake, baby, shake
I said shake it, baby, shake it
I said shake, baby, shake

JLL kept her face turned toward her fans. Her eyes roved and fixed on different people. When she locked onto Marty, he began to move. Julie's father had neglected to dance at Ian's wedding. Now, his chin angled skyward and his eyes closed. Just hours ago, he had spoken of dying, and now his body rolled and fell with the music. How could Julie deny him this? A seeming moment of happiness donated by the person who wished him harm. Marty's mouth opened. He sang along with JLL's voice.

Well, I said come along, my baby, we got chicken in the barn,
WHOSE BARN, WHAT BARN, MY BARN

JLL's legs spread wide and her entire upper body played the piano. Her knees bounced in unison as she balanced on the apex of her shoes. At line breaks she flung her head downward and loose curls broke away. A wall of hair fell before her face.

Ms. Halbert occupied the only remaining bar stool. Her eyes, like Marty's, stayed closed, and she hammered on her knees with her blue-veined hands. She was a baby demanding food from a high chair. The restaurant descended into childhood.

JLL halted the movement of her one hand. The audience paused with it. She kept only the bass line thrumming. It galloped onward and the bodies in the audience twitched, hypnotized. Only Julie stood stark still. JLL brought the microphone up to her lips and spoke to them.

"Easy now," she purred. The piano hand drummed on. She fixated on Julie and a smile crawled across her face. She then locked on to Marty. She half-sang. "Marty, shake it one time for me." Marty's eyes stayed closed and he rocked left and right. JLL focused on Billy's two friends. "Just move it around, a little bit." JLL twirled her finger and the girls rotated their hips. Julie looked around. They all had their eyes closed. The whale perfume seemed stronger now, a catalyst for leaving this world and entering another. Faces were no longer scrunched against the scent, but innocent, blank, open to whatever the world fed them.

JLL's hand hovered detached from her body—a floating appendage travelling the length of the piano. The drumming of the keys became an unnoticed background noise while JLL called out commands to the various attendees. She pointed to Billy. "You, let me see you move."

Billy pumped his fists as though at a malicious god.

JLL started a long hum. She let her eyes fall shut and she swayed along with the rest. The hum rose in pitch, starting in the bellows of her lungs and ascending to the attic. Her teeth flashed white. She exploded back into song.

SHAKE IT, BABY, SHAKE
SHAKE IT, BABY, SHAKE
SHAKE IT, BABY, SHAKE

The Port Braidians lost all semblance of control. Their bodies flung and rebounded. Julie watched as her father climbed on the bar and reached for his dusty bottle of Scotch. The uncapped bottle was passed from swinging arm to swinging arm, each mouth taking a drag. Marty twisted his body with the music and gave a pained yell.

SHAKE IT, BABY, SHAKE

The music lost its credibility as a song. JLL hammered the keys. She kicked the piano bench back. It slammed on the ground, shooting dust into breathing space. Julie jumped forward. It sat there unbroken.

Beside Julie, Janice and Hal's teen danced a Muppet dance, his limbs springing up in jubilation. One of his elbows came down and smacked Julie's nose. The pain shot through her sinuses and a drip of blood sunk out. She dabbed it with her finger and gave the teenager the finger. The air smelled of used deep fryer oil, sweat and rot. It constrained her breathing.

Julie pushed her way past the revellers. Marty tried to grab her hand from his perch atop the bar. She shook it off and escaped the restaurant.

The cool air enveloped her in the lamp-lit dark. Through the restaurant windows, shining like a television screen, she saw a man she couldn't believe was her father. Sweat poured down his forehead and dripped onto people below him. His face was red and his expression blissed. His skin was red and unwrinkled.

Julie sat on the window ledge and wiped her nose. The glass muffled the lower piano notes, but JLL's voice rang clear. Each syllable pushed out with muscle.

Waiting for the performance to end, Julie wandered the streets. Besides the glowing entity that was The Halibut, lights in the stores that lined the main street were off. It wasn't like the city, where business owners kept their window lights shining until morning, the tops of mannequins' bare scalps reflecting LED lights, in hopes of drumming up the future business of late-night passersby.

After a couple of blocks, the sound of music faded. The neighbourhood turned residential and in people's yards the moon glanced through black arms of Sitka spruce. Beyond someone's fence was a small pond, bulrushes growing from the water. Julie heard a frog trill. Or maybe it was a toad—the ghost toad from Marty's story, crushed torso, haunting her.

A mosquito whined by her ear. The insects comforted her—they were the other side of what was happening in The Halibut. Insects were all utility, completing their tasks in straight lines. Be born, get food, fuck, die. What was happening in The Halibut was none of that. Humans had scaled the hierarchy of needs and reached for what hung above it. By the morning, the Port Braiders may have fallen to the bottom of the pyramid and would need to start over with food and shelter.

In the small park at the end of Basser Street, Julie lay along the plastic slide with her feet hooked over the top ledge. When she felt like the performance must be over, she let her body slide down.

She watched from across the street. The first sight to meet her through the windows of The Halibut was her father grinding against JLL's thigh as she sang. His eyes were open but unfocused. The rest of the crowd closed in around them ready to lift them up. Marjory and Lisa spilled from the restaurant and grappled over a sewer grate. Marjory reached for a palmful of gutter water and flicked it on her companion. Lisa shrieked and charged at her friend. They toppled into the gutter and rolled over, laughing. Marjory hoisted Lisa up and they zigzagged back inside.

When the song ended, Marty stumbled back from his grind. JLL took a bow and righted the piano bench. Though people chanted for an encore, JLL shook her head. Her lips read "next time."

The singer edged her way out of the restaurant, removing hands as they took hold of her arms. She slipped away down the sidewalk. A few people, Billy included, milled around outside The Halibut, trying to see which direction she'd gone, but she'd slid into the darkness. Gone as seamlessly as she'd arrived.

Julie sidestepped into The Halibut as the last guests were wandering out. Sweat transferred from their doused arms to her own. Salt and unwashed hair assaulted her nose along with the toxic whale. Marty and Ian sat on the bar, their foreheads pressed together, locked into some giggling discussion.

When he saw her, Marty hopped off the bar and grabbed her shoulders. "Jules!" He kissed her forehead, even his lips slick with sweat. "Jules. Isn't everything so good?" The Halibut was coated in greasy tray liners. Glass crunched under Julie's feet as she shifted. The excited voices of the last guests faded into the night. Ian stumbled into the back room to be reunited with his beloved table. Marty used his shirt to dab his face. "I just feel so good."

"That's really great." She joined Ian in the back room. He slumped over his table, passed out between crossed arms. She extracted a broom and started gathering the discarded trash and trampled French fries. Someone cackled blocks away.

Marty collapsed onto a bar stool and rubbed his face. "There's something I want you to do for me," he said. "I want to get in touch with the guys from my unit."

"Your unit?"

"The twenty-first. You think you can find them online?"

Julie swept broken glass into a big pile in the centre of the room. "Anyone else? My grandparents? Or that Nancy woman?"

Marty looked down. His face still glowed red from the excitement of the show. "Nah. Don't worry about those just now."

"Just now?"

"That's right."

Julie rubbed her eyes. "Yeah, all right. I can help you with that."

Marty tapped his hand on the bar. "Good. Good."

They finished cleaning up The Halibut together, putting glasses through the dishwasher, stacking steaming plates. Snores emanated from the back room, where Ian slept beside his unfinished fries. They left a glass of water and the spare restaurant key by his head when they left.

twelve

SKUNK

According to the Illustrated London News, *in 1845, a Newfoundland dog jumped in the water and, after a long life of successful swimming, declined to paddle its paws. It was rescued, but tried the same tactic again and again, dipping its head under the water until finally no one bothered to scoop it out. It drowned. This breed, it should be noted, has webbed paws and was bred for the express purpose of rescuing people at sea. The Newfie dog Gander, recipient of the Dickin Medal, saved Canadian lives by retrieving a grenade and returning it to Japanese lines. But grenades in the mouth are bad for one's health.*

When Julie and Marty got home from the show, JLL was not yet there. While drinking tea, they watched another episode of *The Golden Girls*. Blanche was writing love letters to a man in jail.

Marty was still worked up. He tapped his prosthesis against his mug. He made trips to the kitchen for no reason. Julie went to bed around two, but Marty stayed up. Where did JLL go in these hours absent from the house, in this small town with nowhere to sit at night but outside?

In her room, under the harsh overhead lights, since her lamp still resided at The Halibut, Julie flipped through the whale-desecrated pages of JLL's journals, reading her tidbits about self-destruction. JLL arrived home around three, just as Julie switched off the bedroom light and tucked the journal away.

Later she was wakened by muffled voices coming from outside. She slid her bedroom window open and listened to Marty's and JLL's voices melting together in the night. Marty's voice slurred as he spoke. They spoke quietly, intimately. JLL's cigarette smoke drifted past the window and toward the moon.

"I do think about whether she'd come back here," Marty said.

"That's what you think about?"

"She's not too fond of anyone here." His voice was soft, reflective. A tone Julie was unused to.

"You'd prefer she, what, take up residence in your bungalow."

"Nah. Just. She'd never come back. She's got no reason. The place she grew up."

"And that's your main concern."

There was a pause.

"Don't know."

"You can't decree where home is."

Julie heard JLL crush her cigarette. The patio door opened and closed, and the only sound left was the raccoon in the crate below the window, making circles. She'd build him a bigger enclosure tomorrow, she thought, and closed the window to block the sickening breeze coming from the ocean.

The digital clock counted the minutes. She heard the sounds of JLL and Marty moving around in the kitchen. The fridge door. A bottle opening. Glasses taken down from the cupboards.

Her heart thumped in the dark room. JLL's and Marty's movements quieted, but Julie didn't sleep. She focused her anger on the woman in the other room.

In the morning, Julie lay in bed and listened to her father make his breakfast. His usual routine. Bread lowered into the toaster, the crinkle of the cheddar package, the microwave beeping to announce the arrival of his cheese toastie. Finally, his keys jangling, the door carefully shut, leaving silence behind. Another day at The Halibut.

When she emerged from the bedroom, she filled the kettle and placed it on the ring. Water sizzled and spit out. JLL's footsteps sounded overhead. Her place was in the crawl-space attic. A futon had sat up there for decades, waiting for guests. Other than the futon, the space was unfurnished and mostly unfinished. Marty brought up a set of pink sheets familiar from Julie's childhood and a lamp that he'd picked up at the thrift shop that day to replace the ones he'd thieved. More lighting for JLL. With the addition of a milk crate for her night stand, the bedchamber was complete.

Julie started making almond milk to go with her breakfast. A bowl of soaking almonds had been sitting in the fridge for a day. She squeezed them between her fingers so they popped from their skins. She blended the naked almonds with water, dates and a pinch of salt in the food processor. Squeezed through cheesecloth, the liquid came out thick into the glass jug, the remaining almond fiber a desiccated lump in the cloth. With a small poke it crumbled into the garbage bin. Julie took a swig of the fresh almond milk, swished it around her teeth.

She scooped a cup of steel-cut oats into a pot and threw in a handful of dried cherries, a tablespoon of cinnamon, a sliced banana and a douse of maple syrup. When it came to a boil, she turned off the heat and let it rest. Outside, she collected some blackberries from the edge of the yard. The whale smell was stronger than the day before.

Under the tangled branches of the blackberries, she spotted something. A crumpled heap of black and white. A skunk. One leg pitched outward. Julie froze. The skunk was chewing on something. Its teeth scraped along exposed white bone. It snapped at a piece of tendon. Julie traced the bone upward, attentive of any twitch of the tail, and saw that the bone was attached at the skunk's hip. She covered her mouth. A gust of whale rot sent her back into the house, her collection of blackberries held in the cradle of her T-shirt. She breathed into a musty tea towel until her heart slowed. A red pool from the crushed blackberries spread through the cotton of her shirt.

"Holy shit. Were you stabbed?"

She turned to see JLL standing naked in the hall. Her blond puff of pubes resembled the top of a Pomeranian's head. Julie dropped the blackberry remnants in the oatmeal pot and shielded her eyes.

"Come on. What is this?" Julie asked.

"You didn't give me any clothes."

"You don't have clothes? I'm pretty sure I've seen you wearing clothes."

"Christ." JLL shook her head. "They're dirty."

Julie gathered a pair of jean shorts and a ratty red tank from her own floor. Her clothes weren't clean either, but she wasn't convinced JLL would know the difference. She opened her under-wear drawer and debated whether she'd rather spare a pair or have JLL going commando in her shorts. She opted to surrender a twice-worn pair of boy-cuts.

JLL dressed in the kitchen. Julie thanked higher powers that her father was out of the house.

"There's a skunk eating its leg in the backyard," Julie said.

"Did it spray you?"

"No. You don't think that's odd?"

JLL shrugged in reply. "I'm not familiar with Canadian wildlife."

JLL's abdomen struck Julie as solid. You could poke it and it wouldn't give. Her breasts were little more than pecs, but they had a nice triangular point and for a second she thought about putting them in her mouth. She told her brain to shut up.

JLL served herself half of Julie's breakfast. They ate out-side. JLL picked up globs of oatmeal and let them fall back into the almond milk and crushed the blackberries with the back of her spoon.

"What do you want to do today?" JLL asked.

Julie felt like a kid during an awkward sleepover morning. *I'd like you to leave.*

"Who said we're spending the day together?"

"What else am I going to do?"

"OK. We could talk. How soon are you leaving?"

JLL scoffed. "Try harder. Ask me something else. And I can't leave now because I have shows coming up."

Julie took a spoonful of oatmeal and dipped it in a pool of syrup. She wondered if it was better to let JLL play the shows. If she yanked the parasite too fast from its host, she risked killing both.

"All right," Julie said. "Tell me how you can live with yourself, convincing someone it's fine to kill themselves."

"It helps that I believe it." JLL heaped oatmeal into her mouth, talked through the mush. "So, you're really convinced it's never fine to kill yourself?"

Julie crossed her arms. "It's not fine. It's cowardly. It's inflicting the worst kind of pain on people left behind."

JLL tapped her spoon against the bowl. "I happen to disagree."

"How?"

JLL shrugged, spooned more oatmeal into her mouth and swallowed. "Just to be clear, you can imagine no circumstances, ever, that it would be fine for a person to end their own life."

A hawk overhead made lazy circles. Julie watched its wings cut ever smaller circles in the sky. "None."

"Then I think you have a poor imagination." JLL pushed her bowl away. "If you think they're cowards, it's not worth talking to you about this. Self-destruction can be a lot of things. Sad. Devastating. Quiet. Glorious. Sweet relief. Comfort." JLL leaned toward Julie, flicked her temple. "And it's up to you, girlie, which one it'll be." She stood up. Turned back to Julie. "So, you would really never accept Marty's death?"

Julie's stomach clenched around the mound of ingested oatmeal. It burned. "Never."

While doing the dishes, Julie heard footsteps tracking from one end of the attic to the other. After cleaning up, she hid out in her room, laptop in bed, and looked for Marty's old regiment. The 21st Combat Engineer Squadron, it seemed, was no longer operational. Hadn't been for years.

Next, Julie typed *Jennie Lee Lewis* into Google. The first result was for a real estate agent in Phoenix. The second was an actress in the UK. The third, though, was JLL's website. Julie clicked the link and was brought to a Wordpress page. The background image was a black-and-white image of JLL standing, playing a grand piano, her back turned to the camera. Even in the static image, JLL's speed was apparent. Her hands hovered above the keys, about to bring down wrath. Across the top of the screen, bold letters read, *JENNIE LEE LEWIS (Jerry Lee Lewis impersonator)*. Down the left-hand side, in a curly font, were the headings *Past Performances*, *Reviews*, *Videos* and *Book JLL for your event*. Julie clicked on that and saw JLL's schedule. She had been booked solid, with only a few weeknights off. But, starting from nine weeks ago, the schedule was blank. Nothing at all.

The page for JLL's past performances contained a long list of cities and drinking establishments, shows played in Washington, Oregon, California, New Mexico, New York, New Hampshire, everywhere. She had played in Mexico but never in Canada.

The ladder in the hallway squeaked as JLL descended. Julie held her hands poised over the laptop, ready to close it if JLL came in.

JLL asked through the door, "So, really, never?"

"Fuck off."

Julie waited until the front door opened and closed so she could resume her research. A three-minute JLL rendition of "Great Balls of Fire" from a performance in Austin. Twenty-somethings crowded around JLL. A shaky video, probably shot with a cell phone held above the crowd. The stage lighting blurring JLL's likeness. Even with the poor quality, you could see the sweat pouring down JLL's face. The crowd gyrated as she belted out the lyrics, all of them singing along. In the last ten seconds of the video, a beer glass sailed over the crowd and smashed on top of the piano. JLL continued like it was nothing. A group of three guys tossed their beer steins at the camera-holder. The video stopped.

There were no remnants of Victoria Shipton online. Scattered people of the same name, but no one of the right age. A search of Nancy Shipton brought up a recent result.

Julie read the obituary. She'd died two months previous, aged sixty-one. Survived by her daughter and by her mother. The funeral was to take place at Kirikos Family Funeral Home in Truth or Consequences, New Mexico. Donations could be made to the National Geographic Society. For once, Julie felt glad her father was a Luddite, that he would never come across this information on his own. Marty dangled from an increasingly sparse array of threads, and this was one more cut. The obituary told her nothing, and it told her everything. Nothing about how Nancy may have died, whether JLL was there, if she attended the funeral, whether it explained her appearance in Port Braid. Everything about finality, Marty's dwindling connections to this world, that his story would not end with him reconciling his wrongs. The ending had been written in his absence. He was, as always, too slow, too withdrawn, too preoccupied with keeping himself safe from self-harm to tend to the people left drowning in his wake. And now it was clear that JLL and she shared something. Motherlessness was a coating over Julie's skin. Over the years it had latched on to every downy hair, only becoming apparent again when someone touched her, said, *I'm sorry, I didn't know.* But for JLL this must be a new feeling, to think about talking to her mother, realizing instead she'd be talking into a vacuum. Worse than talking to one's self. Talking into an absence, a soundless hole in space. That is, if the two were close. But given the story from Marty so far, Julie could imagine no less than a codependence forming.

In the afternoon, Julie built a new crate for Bert. With scrap fence boards from the back of the yard, she hammered together the four sides of a pen and attached with hinges a framed chicken wire top. In the corner was a sheltered area where Bert could nap during the day. She placed the structure under the shade of the cedar in the back corner of the yard. She lifted Bert from the dog crate and set him on her shoulder. He was learning to flex his paws around the curve of her collarbone, holding himself steady as she carted him across the yard. Sitting in front of the new crate, she allowed the animal to crawl across her body, tug at the buttons of her shirt in much the same way that Billy Poole did. He clambered up her shirt, grabbing onto the breast pocket, and felt Julie's face. His lengthening claws scratched her skin lightly, feeling along the creases by her mouth. One tiny finger slipped in.

"Oh, no, no, no, little buddy."

She placed Bert back on her knees. He sat there, hunch-backed, front feet splayed. If ever there was a nerd in the animal kingdom, it might be this raccoon. Each of his advances seemed like a fumbling sexual touch. Patting her belly, picking at the button on her jeans. The black mask around Bert's eyes made him look both concerned and evil. Eyebrows permanently raised. Where the windows to its soul should be, black holes. He used his nub of a striped tail as a counterbalance to his movements.

Under the pale sky, heat soaking the earth, seagulls calling from the ocean, it was easy for a moment to forget about Marty, about death. The raccoon was the near and now, tentatively exploring the life of the backyard, feeling the underside of leaves, experiencing the squish of grubs in his mouth.

Though the tightness of a sunburn crawled up her arms, Julie stayed in the backyard with the raccoon until the early evening when Marty arrived home. He came through the gate into the backyard. "Playing with your rabies baby?"

"Better than playing with myself."

"Christ." Marty shook his head. Set up a lawn chair next to her on the grass. Bert wobbled over to his shoe, worked on undoing the centuries-old knot that held on Marty's sneakers.

Together they watched as the tone of the sky began to change and the shadows between blades of grass began to lengthen, merge. Julie told Marty the news about his unit, that there were no new members being sucked into the role he'd once had. At least not under the same name. She asked him why he'd never kept in touch with the other men.

"*Ubique*, that was our motto. *Everywhere*." He scratched under his bandana. "We were supposed to be the first guys in. The last guys out. Dismantling mines, IEDs, on our hands and knees. And I get blown up because I couldn't figure the gas tank in a car was about to go." He gave Julie a weak smile.

"So you were the first guy out."

Marty shrugged, rubbed her back in reply.

"I don't think anyone would blame you for that," Julie said.

"Sure. But I didn't want them to know me after the war." Marty bent down, stroked the raccoon's back. Bert grasped his finger and Marty pulled away. "Sorry, Jules."

"Fucking military," Julie said. She yanked at blades of grass. "Fucking sends people out to fuck over other people, to get fucked up themselves."

Julie looked up to see her father massaging his chest.

"Don't," he said. "It's not your place."

She should stop talking. She picked Bert up and placed him back on her lap. He curled up in the crease between her legs. "But they gave you nothing. They deny you're sick. And what did you do over there? Achieve peace?"

"I'm proud of what I did." Marty's face was getting red.

"And now you have to fill out a form every year, saying you're still missing a hand. And did you know that new vets are getting lump sum payments for their blown-off limbs? No more ongoing care. Pay them off, get them out."

Marty tapped his prosthesis on the arm of the lawn chair. She waited for the fallout, for her father to stand, to lock her out, to lay on his bed and grind his teeth until the anger passed. But the red drained out of his face. The tendons around his jaw were strained, but he was breathing. After some time, he asked if she might look up a couple of names for him, just to see what became of the others. If they had turned into old men like him. He wrote the names on a receipt from his pocket, and she tucked it away.

She stood, lifted the top of Bert's new pen, placed him inside. The raccoon circled around the enclosure, tested the limits of the space. Before long, he found the sheltered area in the corner and curled up for a nap.

Her father's face was relaxed now, resigned to her callous comments. Julie sat back by his feet.

"Tell me about Midge," she said. "Tell me what happened to her."

He turned his face to her, raised his eyebrows. "You want to hear it?"

"You can even tell me the stuff in the middle."

thirteen

1992

In Nancy's car, he was driving along the California coastline. A tarp laid across the back seats so he didn't have to pull off the road. Midge was throwing up every thirty minutes. The car stank with her bile. The California coastline passed by the driver's side of the car. He wound through the hilly countryside of sagebrush and grass slopes, with the occasional conifer pushing through.

He should have gone that way sooner. The green hills induced fewer flashes than the dirt of New Mexico and Arizona. The ones he got now were mostly auditory—manageable faraway bangs.

The dividing line between desert states and green ones was Utah, and going through there, Marty understood why Mormons deemed it a godly place. Deep red earth was exhumed in the bursts of tabletop cliffs. These plains stood miles above other land for no discernible reason. In Utah, light travelled in reverent shafts and bounced off bloody stone.

California was quieter. He sometimes passed a farm, and Midge looked up at the cows. The road took him away from the water. It teased him by slipping away from the coast during the best views, but then it would swing back and the ocean would open in front of him. Far below, he could see rocks poke from the water, surrounded in white churning waves.

Marty wondered if Nancy was home from the hospital and if she would report her missing car. Or was it an acceptable sacrifice, if it meant he was gone. If she got the car back, she'd be upset to find the spare tire and tool kit gone, but he needed to pay for gasoline.

He wondered about Victoria, whether her mother would be allowed to care for her or if she'd have to live with her father, or with someone else entirely. Either way, best it wasn't him.

Midge coughed again in the back seat and left yet another pile of frothy mush on the tarp. Marty pulled off the road at the next gas station. He had to pull over anyway. Things on the horizon were starting to quiver.

The gas station was a little family-run place with outdated pumps. Marty went to use the bathroom. When he came back, an old man in an L.A. Angels cap was tapping the glass of the car and waving at Midge. Midge licked the glass on the other side.

"She's looking a little hungry," the man said. Wrinkles stretched out from his eyes like sunrays in a child's drawing. Marty knew he was being accused. He explained that Midge was a stray in the desert. The man told Marty that this was his place. There was a restaurant in the back where his wife cooked.

"Mind if we give her a little something? You can have something too, if ya like."

"She won't touch it. Or she'll throw it up. I can barely get her to eat more than a spoonful of wet food."

"Maybe she'd like to chew on a bone and have some water then?"

Marty looked around. The gas station overlooked the water and enjoyed a salt-tinged breeze.

"Sorry, I have to go," he said.

"Come on. I'm feeding you lunch." The man opened the van door, and Midge jumped out. She sat at his feet wagging her tail.

"Likes you," Marty said.

The man ruffled her ears. "You can bring her right in. Nobody else around." The man held the door open, and Marty was hit in the face by the smell of French fries. Red plastic seats and Formica tables filled the space. A small window led to the kitchen, where the man's wife manned the deep fryer. He watched as she scraped a plate full of chopped vegetables—a medley of carrots, broccoli and pepper, plus what looked to be mixed nuts—into the deep fryer.

"You just throw anything in there, huh?"

"Why not. Makes everything better." The woman wore a grease-covered apron. "Plus, the locals love it. We have a 'Bring Your Own' day."

The old man entered the kitchen and rooted around in the freezer until he found a decades-old T-bone. He dropped it into a pan with some oil. It began to sizzle.

Midge remained at the front door with her eyes closed, panting. Marty looked at his dog. Her collar had rubbed her neck bare in the short time they'd been reunited.

The man put the bone in a bowl and whistled for Midge. She got to her feet and wobbled head first into Marty. She stood with her head low and started to whine. She turned in a circle and bumped into him again. Maybe she was blind from the desert sun.

He stood to the side and Midge passed him by and wagged at the man. She lay down to eat, using her paws to manoeuver the bone. Her appetite seemed better, but Marty dreaded the meat throw-up.

The man put out a bowl of water, and Midge switched between the bone and bowl until she was finished both. She curled into a ball at the man's feet.

"Looks like she wants to stay here," he said. He scratched behind her ear.

Marty had been buying himself chips and hot dogs from 7-Eleven to save money. So when the gas station woman served him a piece of fried fish and hand-cut potatoes, it was the best thing he'd ever had. On the side were a few florets of broccoli and samples of the other vegetables. He squeezed lemon over the crisped batter. There was an extra taste in the batter, and Marty asked about it.

"Most people wouldn't think to put a Mexican spice in there, but there's nobody who doesn't like cumin." She'd grinned and folded her arms over her belly.

Midge remained asleep for the entirety of his meal. Her paws twitched through a dream. After Marty ate the last bite of soft fish, it was time to go. The woman paid no attention to him. She was occupied washing dishes and prepping for the night. The man left at some point to serve the few customers who drove into the gas station.

Instead of waking Midge, he scooped up her thin frame and carried her back to the van. Marty paid for his gas and tried to give extra for the food, but the man waved him off. "Just take care of that dog."

Midge threw up the steak half an hour later. Marty pulled over and wiped it off with paper towel. He stroked Midge's head and told her it was OK.

They stopped for the night in Redwood National Park. He

opened the van door and Midge jumped out, banging her head off his knee as she came down. She stumbled and righted herself. Marty checked her eyes for cataracts, but they looked clear.

The early evening light illuminated the dust particles in the air. Old-growth stumps, probably sawed off in the last century, dotted the forest along with clumps of fern and younger trees. There was room for a family-sized tent on each of the historic stumps. He rolled his thrift store blanket out on the biggest one he could find. He lifted Midge up so she could curl up by his side.

The two of them hung out on the stump and waited for night. After Midge fell asleep, Marty was left on his own to wait for morning. The thought occurred to him that the world couldn't be much prettier than this, and he pushed himself to enjoy it.

Over the next day, the throwing up became worse. Midge's declining health and increasing strangeness affected Marty in unexpected ways. Her heaving sides, instead of inspiring sympathy, made him feel hate. The rage always passed quickly, but it would return with the next bout of strained regurgitation. He felt anxiety, his chest strained, when she had been silent for a stretch. He could only think about how the sound would be back soon. His stump throbbed as he drove. IEDs exploded in his gut. The dog was making it worse. She was no longer the silent hound keeping him alive.

Early one morning, Marty pulled over when saw a sign for a vet off the highway. Midge sat stoic in the back seat. He slipped a collar over her head. Beside her haunches a dark stain sank into the upholstery where she lost control of her bowels. The car had an overall smell of bile and feces. The vet office wouldn't open for another fifteen minutes. While they waited, Marty spent some time stroking Midge's face. He pulled his thumb along the muscles of her cheek, and Midge closed her eyes and panted her sour breath in his face.

"Good girl."

The vet's office was in a strip mall—the last in a line of businesses that included a walk-in clinic, a pharmacy, a beer store and a plus-size clothing shop. The parking lot had room for a single line of cars, and only three of the spots—his own car included—were filled.

The clouds swirled above their heads in hues from dark grey to black, and the wind threatened cold rain. The northwest was an entirely different world than the southwest. Where moisture was sucked clean from everything in New Mexico, here was saturated. A drop of water could remain somewhere for weeks. The car seats were cold and damp.

Marty saw the *Open* sign flip on the vet's door, and he lifted Midge out of the car. The receptionist was a man in his fifties wearing a backwards baseball cap. He didn't look like he cared for animals. "Name."

"Marty Bird."

"Dog."

"Midge."

The man jotted the details down and passed a form for Marty to fill out. Midge stood beside him and gazed at his shoes.

The vet, unlike the man out front, made Midge wake up.

A lab coat hung off her shoulders. Midge wagged her tail. It twisted around like one of those wooden snakes. Midge's tongue darted out and wiped her nose.

"So, what happened here?"

Marty told the story yet again and the vet lifted Midge onto the examining table. She prodded at her, massaged her sides and looked at her ears.

"I think she's losing her eyesight. She bumps into me every time—" Marty stopped talking. He refused to embarrass himself here.

The vet shone a flashlight into Midge's eyes and waved a treat across her field of vision. Marty watched as Midge's eyes followed the cookie.

"I can't see anything wrong, to be honest. Seems like she's had some trauma. It could be psychological."

"Just like that?" Marty crossed his arms and the vet looked at him quizzically. "Just shine a flashlight in her eyes and that's it?"

"She can see fine. But you've got a very sick dog, Mr. Bird."

She prescribed an eating schedule, six meals a day. The throwing up, the vet said, was most likely a result of meals that were too large for Midge's stomach. Being fed too much at once can destroy the balance of acids, minerals, and make them sick. So long as she was up to date on her shots, her deworming, she would make it through this.

Throughout the check-up, Midge remained calm. A couple of younger people in lab coats—vets-in-training, Marty guessed—poked their heads in and each time Midge turned her head in their direction and thumped her tail.

"Is there anything—" Marty started. "I'm not sure how to put this. Is there anything that would make a dog forget who you are?"

"Sure. Senility, for one." The vet frowned and shook her head. "But she's on the young side. I think you just need to give her time. She'll come back to you. It sounds strange, but it might be worth treating her like a puppy again. Give her treats when she responds to you."

As Marty and Midge were about to leave, the vet added, "Bring her back next week. I really think she'll make it." Marty nodded and exited the vet's office. He lifted her body back into the car.

That night, they camped at Crater Lake. The drive took them past miles of lodgepole pine that must have been planted after logging the area clean, spaced an equal distance apart and with the same girth. The trees stood as soldiers in a salute to the sky.

Midge began whining as the trees whipped by the windows. It was a mosquito in his ear. A missile overhead. He told her to shut up. She got louder.

The road cut a straight line through the faux forest and ran flat for a long while before finally climbing upward. The road twisted and the air thinned as they got higher. Cold wind came through the windows in bursts. Marty rolled the windows up to keep him and Midge safe in the confines of the car. This amplified her whining. Marty reached back and grasped her snout. He looked at her eyes in the rearview. "Stop. Stop."

She whined through his fingers. Louder. He yanked the steering wheel to the side. The car screeched to a stop. Dust clouded around the windows. Marty got out and pulled Midge from the car by the scruff of her neck. He grabbed the skin under her ears. She cowered, whining.

"Stop!" She had to stop.

At the gate to the park, a woman who wore the same uniform as Nancy took his money.

"For one?"

"One plus a dog."

The woman looked in the back seat. "Well, if you have a dog, you gotta keep them on a leash." She waved him forward.

The road climbed further and wound around the rocky landscape. The trees thinned to make room for boulders and lichen. The car turned a sharp corner and Crater Lake came into sight far below the road. It mirrored the blue sky, but added a richness and depth that the sky lacked. The cliffs around the crater framed the mirror. Marty considered the size of explosion that had blasted the ground away.

He always thought it was a meteor, but, according to his

brochure: Mount Mazama erupted 7,700 years ago with such ferocity that a mountain was inverted to become a 592-metre-deep hole in the ground—a massive caldera. Only the perimeter of Mazama remains, leaving a rocky rim around a lake. There are no tributaries or distributaries for Crater Lake, meaning that the dark blue water filling it is all from rain or snow. It is the deepest lake in the United States, the tenth deepest in the world. It probably took 720 years for all of the water to be trapped. There are two islands— Wizard Island and Phantom Ship Island. These are cinder cones formed as Mount Mazama tries to resurrect itself from the water. There used to be no fish. But then, in 1888, a judge named William G. Steel thought, *Hey, what a great place for fish,* and tried to transport several hundred fingerling rainbow trout. Unfortunately, only thirty-seven survived the hike to be released into the clean water, but fortunately, they were wildly horny and their offspring now populate the water in the millions.

This part is a mystery: the algae layer in Crater Lake doesn't start until a hundred metres down. That means that you can dive in a vertical line, kick your legs, and churn up no plant life until the weight of the water starts to crush your head.

The water is clear. Glass. That helps with the dark blue.

Marty parked in a mostly empty campsite behind Crater Lake. It was housed in pines and had Steller's jays swarming the garbage bins. With no pigeons or rats, the worst pest this place got were the beautiful jays with their black-crested heads and indigo wings. Marty was happy to share scraps with them.

When nighttime came, a spread of stars emerged. It was like nothing Marty had witnessed before. There were stars between stars. He'd seen bright stars in the desert, of course. But here in the cool air, the light cut more cleanly and the Milky Way carved a distinct path. He was used to individual points of light in the evening sky, but from here he could see that it was a continuum.

Marty scooped a few spoonfuls of wet dog food into a plastic bowl. The campsite was silent. For himself, he emptied one can of tomatoes and one can of beans onto dry rice and boiled the lot of it together. When it was cooked, he opened tiny packets of salt and pepper from Wendy's and sprinkled them on top. With the addition of Tabasco sauce, his meal was ready. He ate at the picnic table and tilted his head up while he chewed. The sky seemed to come down around him. He breathed in as deeply as he could and enjoyed the sting of cold air.

Marty heard the muffled sound of whining coming from the dark, near the tent. He looked up again and saw that some of the stars had disappeared. One chunk of the Milky Way was swathed in oily blackness. His tent retreated from the campsite. Midge faced him with her tail tucked between her legs. As soon as their eyes locked, a low growl poured from her. Her head lowered and her shoulders formed two points along her hunched back. She erupted into snarls. The camping pot slipped out of Marty's hand and clattered to the ground. He looked behind him to see if a raccoon or bear or mountain lion stood behind him, but there was nothing but a few scattered family campfires. Midge bared her teeth and exposed her black gums. Droplets of saliva flew from her mouth and with each bark she took a step closer to Marty. A shadow extended behind her and into the trees.

A couple of laughing girls walked down the trail toward the restrooms. They would pass by Marty's campsite any second. Marty pictured Midge galloping for the girls and tearing out their throats before he could get to her. He grabbed a stick and lunged for his dog. She leapt at the same time but Marty managed to get the stick between her jaws and swing his leg over her back so he was riding her like a rocking horse. Midge threw her head side to side and backed up. Her sides contracted to nothing. Marty tried to grip Midge with his knees but she wriggled free. The girls passed in front of the campsite and Marty yelled at them to grab a stick and back away. If they ran, Midge would chase. Both of the girls—holding their family's dirty dishes—kept their feet planted. Midge flew toward the girls. The older sister yelled something. Midge spun around and headed back toward Marty, but he caught her by the underside of her neck and managed to slip his good hand between her front legs and belly, flipping her to the ground. Midge thrashed like a fish while Marty pressed all of his weight against her. Sweat dripped off his forehead. For a dog that nearly starved to death, she was strong. Teeth snapped by his eyes. It occurred to him that his strength might fail. He scrambled to return the stick between her teeth, yelling to the girls to go back to their campsite.

"Why are you doing that?" one of the girls yelled.

Instead of the expected rabies foam pouring from her mouth, Midge's gums looked grey and her mouth pasty. She twisted her body again and the stick snapped between her jaws. Quickly, her teeth sunk through his skin just above his severed elbow. He cried out.

And then he was back amongst the dunes in Iraq, red mist and an acrid smell filtering through the air, holding down a woman who struggled toward the strewn parts of her husband and son, who must have known it was Marty's job to clear mines and that he hadn't gotten to these ones soon enough to save her family. He pressed on her clavicles to keep her still, and she spit on his face. Her hot breath pounded against him. He held a cool stone, but knew he couldn't do that. There was a child watching, even if it was a dead child.

Returning from the trance, he felt hot tears streaming down, either from the stress or from the wound, and then, when he didn't expect it, Midge's body went limp. Under the rock, she licked her lips and started panting. Marty perched on top of her, waiting.

Pine needles and pebbles dug into his kneecaps. The adrenaline faded from his system. His heartbeats were audible. Midge's panting was hot against his hand and he felt her sides heave. Her ears perked up and her eyes rolled back to where Marty was sitting. Her tail thumped against the ground.

"Hey," the girl called out to him again.

Marty decided to keep quiet. He took a breath and dismounted his dog. He lessened the pressure on her face, and she stayed put. Carefully, he stepped over to the picnic table and grabbed her collar. He slipped it over her head and tightened the buckle. This was no longer his dog. This was some other dog walking around in her skin. It made it harder. Marty wished that Midge had died.

He turned toward the girl. As soon as they locked eyes, she sprinted off.

Marty built a fire using twigs that he found around the site. All the while, he checked Midge for movement. Her legs twitched in a running motion as she dreamt, but otherwise she was still. Spent.

The fire spit and cracked and shot shadows out to the trees around them. It replaced the star continuum with glow and sparks. Just as well. A really clear night sky becomes overwhelming after a while. It reminds you that even if you open your eyes, your mouth, your nostrils, your asshole, everything, as wide as you can, you can never take in enough. There will always be more stars in between the stars. You get full too easily. He wasn't religious, but his conception of godly people, the real godly people, were those that could remain vacuums a bit longer, who could suck in something a bit bigger than gas prices and love stories. Religious people, though, could be just the opposite. They closed things off early to keep God in their torsos, swirling around with the petty stuff. He knew the fire was blocking the good stuff out now. But he was tired.

Midge's head lifted from her spot on the dirt. Marty tensed and lifted the stick, but she just slunk over to the fire and lay down.

She panted. The light from the fire outlined her hips and ribs, and Marty tried to imagine her living a year from now. He couldn't.

Normally, Marty would have Midge in the tent with him, but not tonight. He brushed his teeth and spat the toothpaste into the embers. A sizzle of smoke rose into the air. He crawled into the tent and took one last look at the site. Midge stared in the direction of the tent and her eyes glowed with the dying flames. As he zipped the tent flap, he heard Midge whine.

He shivered through the night. The cold air seeped into the tent and brought moisture into his sleeping bag. The last remaining flickers from the fire lit the fabric and exposed the small moths that clung to the walls. Midge's whining continued for hours. It rose higher and then dropped to a low growl and then climbed back to high pitches. At times it could be mistaken for the whine of a mosquito, and at others the grunt of a bear or elk. Marty tossed as he tried to sleep and peered out a few times to see that Midge still sat in the same spot, eyes still focused on the tent.

He slept in spurts, while Midge infiltrated his circular dreams. She was in the tent. She was lost in the woods. She snapped at him, she bit his skin. The car exploded as the ashy tongue emerged from the mouth. He pushed her into the dirt. She sunk into the earth. She died. She attacked him. The body crumbled between his hand and hook and he scooped up the bits. He ran in the woods to find her. He found her, and she was a puppy at the pound. He pushed her head into the dirt and a little girl pounded her skull with a rock. She licked his face. She licked the wound on his arm. She died.

Each time Marty woke up, he sat up in his sleeping bag and tried to bring his thoughts back to reality. He poked at the moths, whose wings were stuck to the condensation from his breath.

Finally, Marty decided to get up and stay up. He slid his shoes on and walked over to Midge. It might have still been a dream.

She remained motionless. He reached his good hand out carefully, ready to pull back at any moment, but Midge only continued her singsong whine, unaware of his presence. Marty touched her fur and untied her from the tree.

Using the map from the parks woman, they drove to the easiest water access as the horizon coaxed the first hint of morning. The earliest rising birds sang from the pine trees.

The hike down to the water was beautiful. Marty led the way and Midge trailed behind, pulled by the long rope. At each switch-back, the lake came into view. Finally, they were by the water's edge.

A breeze rippled the surface. Marty shivered and looked back to see that Midge did the same.

"Come here, girl." Midge slunk over to him and lay down by his side. Marty ran a hand over her fur and felt her thin skin vibrate over her bones. She sneezed.

"*Gesundheit.*" Midge looked in his direction, but still her eyes wouldn't focus on him. Her left ear hung over his leg and he stroked it. It felt like silk. Once Midge was gone, he would be alone. As if on cue, following that thought from Marty, Midge rose to her feet. She walked away from him to the water's edge. She lapped up the cold water and then stuck her front paws in.

"Midge, come on." Midge never had any trouble coming when she was called. Lots of hounds could ignore their names once they had a goal in mind or as soon as they caught a scent they liked, but Midge always came when called. He could call her from the other end of a forest and she would come back to him. Now, Midge kept her head pointed forward.

"Midge," he said louder. She looked around, then back out at the water. "Midge!" She started her whining again and walked in a circle. Her whining was more frantic now. She was looking for him. "Midge!" Marty slapped his knees and whistled, but Midge leapt into the water and started to swim. She turned in a few circles and then set on a path toward the centre of the lake.

"Midge! For God's sake!" Marty stripped off his shirt, his pants, his shoes, and he stepped into the frigid water. It sent a shot of pain up his calves but he dove in. His lungs constricted and he couldn't breathe. His brain shrunk from his skull. He blinked his eyes hard and looked over the water's surface for Midge. She swam fast for a dog. Her legs paddled out in front of her with ease. Marty tried to yell after her again but his breath was caught. He front-crawled after her. This was his first time swimming since losing the forearm, and it slowed him down. The handless arm slid through the water too easily. His other arm worked harder to keep his path straight, but he ran out of breath quickly. Panic set in. Marty bobbed in the water to try to get sight of Midge again. Her head and shoulders skimmed along the top of the water about fifty metres in front.

Marty squeezed out a "Midge" and gulped some Crater Lake water. He sunk down. He coughed and spat and tried to float on his back until he could regain his airflow. He gazed up at the sky, which radiated purple-red. The cold stung his body and cramped his muscles. He couldn't catch up to her. He couldn't bring her back.

Marty swam back to shore and hugged himself as Midge got farther away. She slowed down and her head angled higher. Her nose acted as a periscope above the rippled surface. For a moment she floundered, and then she bayed and it echoed off the cliffsides. Marty imagined it waking the girls at the campsite. Her head disappeared and reappeared. Then, the top of Midge's head sank beneath the surface of the water, and stayed down.

The lake returned to silence. The lack of splashing, the lack of birds and even the lack of insects crawling along the stones grew unbearable. He slumped to his knees and watched the spot where Midge went down. Ripples moved outward and created a target, but soon that spot would be nothing. Marty waited for some miracle where she would appear, maybe at the shore, maybe dropping from a tree above his head. Maybe he would look over to Wizard Island and Midge would be there, wagging her tail and barking for him to join her. He waited for a long time. What else was there to do today? The waves dissipated and the only movement was the cold wind that picked up. It dried the moisture from his skin and pulled goosebumps up from his flesh. He kept his eyes on the water as he retrieved his clothes and dressed himself. When he pulled the sweater over his head, he felt the warmth of his own body.

Her heart may still be beating. She could still be under the water, still in the process of drowning. Marty pulled at his hair and stared through blurred eyes at the water. *Her heart could stop now, or now, or now.*

fourteen

COYOTE

*Female animals are more likely to commit suicide than
males, or so it says in Antonio Preti's "Animal Model and
Neurobiology of Suicide." Humans are an exception. Boys do
it more than girls, but girls attempt more often. Vertebrates
do it more than invertebrates. Although, the invertebrate
Globitermes sulphureus, a termite, will cling to predators
with its mandibles, then proceed to squeeze its own abdomen
until its head explodes, covering everyone with poison. In
2008, twenty-six dolphins filled their lungs and stomachs with
mud and beached themselves near Cornwall. One hundred
and fifty-two landed themselves in Iran the year before.*

Over the passing days, the whale's body was being released from
its ocean-dwelling form. Its fins, tail, baleen plates lost shape and

travelled outward as a gas that wound its way around the limbs and necks of Port Braid residents. It was becoming a part of the town, ordinary as road signs. It entered through doorways and infested upholstery.

From the back of Marty and Julie's backyard, the skunk had disappeared, likely dragged off by a coyote, only tufts of fur left behind, but around the town the remains of other wildlife became apparent, roadkill lining the edges of rural highways.

On the evenings of JLL shows, as the afternoon light gave in to dusk, Port Braiders meandered past the bungalow. Great clouds of smoke moved with groups of former environmentalists and anti-corporation activists as they sucked on cigarettes and blew pollution at street lamps. The Gregion Lake cottagers, whose orbits never intercepted the townspeople's, joined the tail end of the migrations, wearing headlamps and Gortex, ready for whatever weather phenomenon—eclipse or rainstorm—might interrupt their gentle roadside hike. They linked arms and shouted, every action out of character. Two young parents crouching on the curb to light a joint. A man with a white ponytail walking by, tapping white powder into toilet paper, twisting tight balls for any passersby who wanted to swallow his offering.

Julie avoided the shows, staring at the pages of a book until midnight, when faraway singing floated through the bungalow windows. She would open the front door and stand on the porch, take in the whale smell swimming in the evening dew. In the night air, the smell slid into the darkness between oxygen molecules. The singing rode over waves of ocean-cooled air.

Liquor laws dictated that The Halibut should be cleared before twelve, but the shows were never over by then. Julie wanted her father home, and the bottom of her lungs burned during these waits. She checked the time on her phone, stood on the stoop, watching for bodies to come around the corner. She would slide on a pair of flip-flops and walk to the end of the street, crossed arms, an angry parent waiting. As the singing grew louder, Julie's heart beat faster.

She had always been able to depend on Marty's whereabouts at different times of day. From nine to seven, he was at The Halibut, at night, home. Julie could call him during those hours whenever she'd had a bad day in Vancouver and never miss him. Three rings and he was there. *Hey, kiddo.* They had their prescribed conversation, Julie never even mentioning whatever personal crisis had made her call, but still Marty would make everything better. But now he was out, always out. Happy. He was *singing*, maybe. But JLL could spout her identity at any moment. She could grab the microphone, say, *Hey, slow it down a little bit, Port Braid,* turn to Marty, lock eyes. *You abandoned my mom in her time of need.* Then even if she kept singing, and the town kept dancing, Marty would be in the throes of something new.

On one of these nights, Julie walked to The Halibut to check on him from across the street. The night was cool, damp. Down the block, she passed two figures tangled together on a park bench. Clothes heaped on the ground. The bones of elbows and knees striking as if they fought to devour one another, emanating moans. Julie hurried by, hopeful they wouldn't drag her into their struggle.

One block from The Halibut, a shrieking contingent of tweens sprinted across the street, stripped down to briefs and training bras. They brushed by Julie and rounded the next bend, a flock of banshees. The singing from The Halibut lost shape. A dissonance of voices spilled from the restaurant. Julie stood across the street and looked into the restaurant to see a swarm of barely clothed bodies. A laugh escaped her. How nice it would be to join in. But somewhere her father was entwined with the mess. Torsos, hips, stomachs and breasts bounced and shook. The one fully clothed member of the scene stood at the front of the crowd, singing into a microphone, blond puff of hair bouncing. Julie searched the bodies for her father. Music pulsed the walls.

Liam Parks had his hands pressed against the front window, head bowed between his arms, his pale hips swinging. Marjory and Lisa tossed their hair around, strands whipping eyes, dipping in drinks. They pressed their foreheads together as they danced, and Marjory began braiding them together. Conjoined twins at last.

She spotted Marty, shirt wrapped around his forearm instead of his torso. He gyrated on the bar top. Julie covered her mouth. He picked his belly up and dropped it, his eyes squeezed shut. Julie kept her eyes trained on his face, but she could see the shadows of scars on his chest, scars he was so careful to keep hidden at home.

At the stage, hands clawed at JLL. She used her right hand to hold the mike and the left to caress the outstretched needy hands of her followers. When she turned back to the piano, they reached for her shoulders and neck. Her voice rode over the ambient yelling of the crowd, sharp-edged but full.

Julie turned back to Marty. His arms rose into the air as he shook. His hook and hand clasped over his head as though in desperate prayer. A woman used Marty's leg as a support beam. Her hands crept up the length of him. She scrambled onto the bar, finding her footing amongst bottles of forgotten beer until she was upright and able to lock her mouth onto Marty's neck.

Julie walked toward the restaurant. Marty opened his eyes but kept his rhythm. He leaned over the woman and took a handful of her hair to stay upright. He didn't know where he was. He didn't know what was happening. He couldn't. Neither could this woman.

Julie flung the door open and twisted her way through sweat and skin. The floor was blanketed with shed garments. Next to Marty's legs, Julie reached up to guide the woman away from her father. "Marty, come on. Marty, come outside."

His eyes opened but a haze of bliss kept him in a separate place.

Julie pulled harder. "Marty!" Nothing. She tried a different tactic. She danced. She wove her fingers between Marty's and coaxed him down. He turned and hopped off the bar, rocking with some faraway rhythm. This close, she could see how Marty's skin had deteriorated, the psoriasis claiming his arms, swathes of his abdomen. His fingers, entwined with hers, had yellowed tips, something she'd never noticed. She encouraged him forward, forward, until they exited the restaurant.

Marty smiled and blinked. "Let's go back inside. It stinks out here." He turned.

"I'm Julie. 'Let's go back inside, *Julie*.'"

Marty faced her. "Yeah. Julie. I know."

The smell of alcohol poured out of him.

"God, Marty. Did you bathe in it, or are you drinking hard liquor?"

"I had a drink. I had a drink." Marty watched the spinning bodies in the restaurant.

Julie took his chin. "Marty, I came home to Port Braid to help you."

He removed her fingers. "That's a bad reason to come home." The haze dissipated. His pupils shrank. He focused on her face.

"Please just come home with me this time."

"It's a bad reason to come home, though." Marty looked inside at his bar. Liam Park's back was now pressed against the glass. A stretched and freckled canvas. A great mass of bodies behind him had linked arms and swayed with the lilting piano.

He came with her, though. Julie walked her shirtless father home. That night, she heard animal noises coming from Marty's bedroom, and only realized once she pressed her ear against his door that it was the sound of crying. She wished for a moment that she'd let him stay at The Halibut, a stranger caressing his chest scars, no awareness of time or place.

When Marty emerged from his room just before noon the next day, he was red-faced, bags under his eyes. And yet his expression was serene. He told her, as she tried to force him to drink water, that The Halibut would have to remain closed for the day. His stump throbbed, he said, an old memory of ruined mornings, phantom fingers pulsing with each heartbeat. But at the same time, he'd slept. No 3 a.m. pacing. More than eight hours without getting up to pee. He'd had that old dream about Midge, where they were walking through some field together. For once, he didn't think it'd ended badly.

He made no mention of the sobbing, and Julie didn't bring it up. She instead took a loaf of bread from above the fridge and put two slices in the toaster for him.

He went to the bathroom to piss, so hard it echoed in the bowl. When he came out he sat at the table, head on his hands. *He must not remember much*, Julie thought. He looked so unaffected. Even though it made her unhappy to think about the scene, it was a worse thought that he couldn't remember breaking through his asexuality in that free gone state. He made no mention of the woman. Julie waited for him to bring it up.

"Drink the water," she told him.

"Give me a minute."

Julie nodded. She looked him up and down. "Are you ready for coffee or will that make you yack?"

"Yack."

Julie plonked the dry toast in front of him. She handed him a cool washcloth. He laid it across his scabbed scalp. He told her to stop playing nurse as though that were an option.

Despite the descending madness of her performances, life with Jennie Lee Lewis in the bungalow developed its own type of normalcy. When Julie and Marty watched their episodes of *The Golden Girls* from their seats, JLL set a pillow between them, placing a bowl of popcorn on her lap and sticking in her tongue like a lizard to select individual pieces. She asked questions about the show. *Why is that one older? Why does no one slap Blanche?*

They ate dinner when Marty got home from The Halibut. Julie cooked. JLL paced the attic or smoked cigarettes in the backyard until it was time to eat. Sometimes she passed through the kitchen, snacking on raw ingredients and making comments on Julie's creations.

Usually they ate in silence, but on the Saturday following Marty's drunken escapade at JLL's show, as they sat together at the small table, eating a meal of pork chops, rice, and green beans from the garden, Julie broke the standoff. JLL was putting whole green beans into her mouth, folding them so they fit around her teeth like a retainer, chewing with all her teeth.

"Why did you choose Jerry Lee Lewis?" Julie asked.

JLL, hunched over her meal, folded another bean into her mouth before attempting to speak. "What?"

"I want to know, out of all the performers in the world, you decided to impersonate Jerry Lee Lewis."

Marty held his fork steady with his prosthesis, sawed into the pork chop. "Her name is Jenny Lee Lewis, Jules, who else would she choose?"

"He likes piano; I like piano." JLL stabbed her pork chop, moved it around her plate.

"That's not it, though," Julie said.

"Jules . . ."

Julie looked at her father. "No, Marty, that's not it. There's Billy Joel. Ray Charles. Elton John. Aretha."

"Oh God, come on. I couldn't be Aretha. Only Aretha is Aretha."

"Tell me why Jerry Lee Lewis," Julie said.

"No," JLL said.

Marty put his fork down. "Drop it, Julie."

"I'm also curious about this impersonator thing. You can't write your own songs? And then, when you choose to suckle off someone else's fame, you choose some cousin-marrier?"

The air grew tight. Julie felt her father's eyes on her. JLL chewed her next mouthful. She swallowed, licked her lips clean. She spoke slowly.

"Here's my take," JLL said. "Jerry Lee Lewis was a southern church boy who knew that the devil flowed from his hands when he played, right? And that it was dirty sin, but he couldn't help himself. Hated himself for it. But then he goes further with it than anyone in rock and roll. He doesn't ruin himself with drugs, booze. Nope. He stamps on people's safe morality by marrying his baby cousin. No one could stomach it, right? He's dragged through slime and hated by everyone, and then in the depth of the slime, he plays and records this show and releases *Live at the Star Club, Hamburg*. Amazing. They're devil spawn, the audience." JLL took a forkful of rice, gestured with it as she spoke. "They don't know where they are. Jerry Lee Lewis, this awesome monster, hates himself, hated by everyone, starts playing piano and takes their limbs up and tosses them to the wind. He murders the piano. They're decimated. They bang their heads, and no one had even thought up headbanging before. They fling their bodies. They're gone. Jerry Lee Lewis got decimated, self-destructed in the most beautiful, ugly way, and then he returned the favour to those kids. Halle-fucking-lujah!" JLL shoved the rice into her mouth, took a small bow.

Marty nodded, impressed. "See, Jules?"

"Bullshit. He's the only one of your idols that gave up on legend."

"I'm tired," JLL said.

"He's even still alive." Julie's voice rose. "There's nothing less sexy than marrying your too-young cousin. Right? There's nothing that makes you less of a rock and roll legend than that. He gave up on it because he loved a girl. That's it."

JLL pointed a green bean. "You're talking from your asshole."

"You know it, though. You must have chosen him for some other reason. Jerry Lee first got married as a teenager, so to him, marrying a thirteen-year-old probably didn't seem like such a sin. He wasn't being self-destructive. He wasn't doing it to break taboo, and he wasn't being rock and roll."

"Actually, Marty was right," JLL said. "I just chose him because our names were so similar."

Julie talked through her mouthful of food. "I just see this falseness. You're selling this wild freedom, but your idol didn't give a shit about this stuff. You're promoting this manicured self-destruction. Totally fake. You're not this bright, burning star. You're an impersonator."

Julie felt something bounce off her cheek. A piece of pork fell to the hardwood. JLL grinned at her, her fork a covert catapult by the edge of the table.

Marty stood, said he'd had enough and was going to sit in front of the TV with the rest of his meal. Julie turned to JLL. "Your mom died recently, didn't she?"

JLL and Marty stared at her. She hadn't meant to spit this out, use it as a comeback to some minor slight. She pushed food around on her plate. The pork chop seemed somehow grey under the dining room lights, rice creeping over its side like maggots. Instead of walking to the television, Marty went to the kitchen, set his plate on the counter.

"That true?" he asked. "I'm sorry to hear that."

JLL confirmed she had. She spun her plate so it rattled on the table. "Went peaceful as a lamb. Really very unremarkable. Don't worry about it."

"But it's why you came here," Julie said.

"You got weird ideas, lady," JLL said. "I came to the little town of Port Nothing because my mother passed away?"

Marty came back to the table, reached his hand toward JLL, who declined to accept the gesture.

Julie rubbed her forehead. "So why did you come here so soon afterwards?"

Julie's father told her to shut up, but JLL waved him off to say it was all right.

"OK," she said. "My mother died a really long death. It was shit. Both of us had a shit time of it. I don't want to see anyone else go through that." She winked. "You get me?"

Marty looked perplexed. "Sorry, why did you come here?"

JLL stood, gave Marty a smile. "Looked pretty on the internet."

Julie saw something else hiding behind her expression. JLL left her plate, retreated from the table, and climbed to the attic.

That evening, Marty and Julie watched their episodes without the questioning figure seated between them. The programs were the same, as were the missing pixels in the bottom left corner of the screen, the single dusty cobweb hanging above the television, the squeaking La-Z-Boys, but, for the first time, they felt the weight of the gap between their seats.

fifteen

PALLID BAT

David Bowie is my magnetic north because of all
the young dudes in tow. The sudden freedom of
the strange bestowed on the rock and roll suicides.
Mick Jagger is the south for the way he pouts.

Mist floated down from the slate sky and coated the backyard surfaces. Julie sat cross-legged behind the patio door, a damp raccoon
in her lap, and watched the trees try to wave the precipitation away.
The house was quiet. Marty again at the restaurant and JLL losing
herself in the streets of Port Braid, perhaps accepting handshakes,
pats on the back, a love that this town never showed anyone.

The red journal lay on the ground beside her. Since it came
into Julie's life, it had been leafed through, soaked in the ocean,
involved in the explosion of a whale. It had its pages ripped apart

where congealed blood held them fast. It was beaten, abused, but now it gave up the information in its pages easily. Despite the hardened paper, Julie could flip from one page to the next, use scraps of text to assemble a fuller picture of JLL, but whether these words told Julie about her fears or loves was impossible to say. She only knew that these things were important enough to write down.

Outside it was silent. The mist stopped the vibrations of the natural world and caused all creatures to hunker and wait. The mist glommed onto the airborne particles of whale, pulled them to the ground, gave the town a reprieve.

There was a tap on the glass. JLL stood on the other side of the door. Her tank top was soaked through, clinging to her body like a used rag. Her hair, slicked to one side, dripped from its curly tips. She swayed where she stood. Julie closed the journal and set it on the ground. She unlocked the patio door and let her inside. There was no use concealing the journal. It was in plain sight between them. JLL snatched it up.

"Good reading?" Her breath stank of alcohol. The undersides of her eyes were like pillows. Red rays struck out across the whites of her eyes.

"I don't really get most of it," Julie said.

JLL smirked. "Guess you're not the intended audience." JLL wobbled past Julie, seated herself in one of the La-Z-Boys.

"Where were you drinking?" Julie asked. If there was a moment for an apology, for her prodding questions about JLL's deceased mother, this was it.

"Not The Halibut. The Lion's Den." She looked at the ceiling. "Giving Marty the day off."

Bert yawned in Julie's lap. He stretched his claws out, caught threads of Julie's jeans. Julie watched JLL flip through the pages of her own journal.

"It means a lot to you, this rock star stuff, doesn't it?" Julie asked.

"*This rock star stuff*. You practise being patronizing?"

Julie stroked Bert's fur. "We all have our talents."

JLL snorted. She pulled the chair lever and leaned back. Outside, the wind shifted and mist speckled the glass. The bushes at the end of the yard leaned side to side, moving together like a drunken cohort coming home from the bar.

"It does mean a lot," JLL said. "You couldn't understand how much." She ran a hand through her hair as though to negate the words. "I have a show tonight."

"So skip it."

JLL shook her head. "They'd eat me alive."

Later, Julie packed a spinach salad for Marty. She loaded a Tupperware container with greens, a boiled egg, bacon bits, orange slices and ranch dressing. When she left the house, the mist was still floating down. She wore only her tank top and shorts. Before long the rain coated every angle of her skin.

On the way, Julie thought about a concept her roommate once described to her. Lucy described certain people in the world as *feelers*, people who felt everything more strongly. Art stabbed them in the belly. They could reach transcendence through music. There was the good side of being a feeler, but they felt the pain of others more acutely than their own.

Lucy thought of feelers as hungry ghosts gorging themselves on sorrow, and in the last decades, sorrow has become available in infinite supply. As they gorge, they grow bigger and darker. Feelers clump all the pain of the world together, and they forget where each morsel came from. They forget that the pain can be divided amongst many. They think the pain is all theirs, and it can be absolute.

But we shouldn't ask the feelers to stop feeling, Lucy said. They're our civilization's redeemers. The ones able to see and understand beauty so the rest of us have lived for something.

Maybe JLL was one of these. Maybe that's why it was easier to be an impersonator. And she'd chosen Jerry Lee Lewis, a person who'd been through a shitstorm, in order to ingest and broadcast that seed of pain.

Rain dripped down Julie's shoulders, covered the underside of her chin, plastered her hair to her neck. She walked with her head bent down and watched the worms coil onto the sidewalk, where they'd later be baked. An old Cadillac slid up beside her and splashed a puddle across the sidewalk.

Alan Cheung rolled down the window. "Hey, maniac! Get in the car!"

Despite the summer temperatures, Alan had the heat blasting inside the Cadillac. It began to dry the rain from her skin. Alan wore his favourite Hawaiian shirt, with the blue flowers and palm fronds.

"Here, put this under your ass," Alan said. He reached into the back seat and grabbed a beach towel. Julie tucked the fabric under her body. Alan shook a finger at the towel.

"You know, actually, I got that thing for you, when you were a toddler."

"No shit?" Julie dabbed water from her hair.

"Yes shit. One time I was going to take you to the beach, and so Marty got you all packed up, had you waiting by the door when I came by. Sunscreen, little hat, frilly bathing suit, bottle of juice."

Alan braked at a stop sign, put on his indicator. He leaned his head forward to see both directions like a caricature of an elderly driver. "But then we get to the beach and the towel he sent along was this hand towel. Pretty fancy one, with embroidery. And you and me, we're sitting on the sand, watching the seagulls. And I don't have a towel either. I'm sitting on my shirt."

Alan turned onto the next road, hand over hand. "So you keep waddling over to the next group over. And the couple there, tourists, think you're in love with them. They're cooing and peek-a-booing. But you wanted their towel, Julie Bird. You tried to pull it out from under them."

Julie smiled. "And did I cry like a baby when they took it back?"

Alan shook his head. "You think I'd let you cry? No, no. I bought that towel off them." He laughed. "They thought I was strange in the head, but they sold it."

The windshield wipers squeaked as they scraped water away. The grey sky hung heavy over them, but Julie felt protected in Alan's car. For the rest of the drive, he told her about Marjory and Lisa, Billy's friends, who had taken up residence near Tallicurn Beach. Alan had hiked down there one day with a scarf across his nose. Just to see what the place looked like now. Marjory and Lisa had their own little camp going on the unscathed side of the beach. He didn't know how they could stand it. They had laundry lines strung up between tree branches. Around the smoking remnants of a fire, Marjory was playing the guitar and Lisa sang along. As far as Alan knew, Marjory made appointments for a dental office. Lisa was a substitute teacher. But it didn't look like either had left the beach in some time. Cans had been stacked like a house of cards.

Alan pulled up in front of The Halibut, and Julie thanked him for the ride.

"When are you coming by to see me?" he asked.

"Soon. I promise."

The door to The Halibut was closed and the lights dimmed. Julie knocked on the door and heard a crash. She pushed it open and peered around the corner to see Marty holding his chest. A box of knick-knacks was spilled onto the floor. He wore his ratty California T-shirt over a pair of jean shorts. "Startled me," he said.

She put the Tupperware on the nearest table and bent down

to help him gather the things. They smelled of dust. On top of the pile sat his hula doll, the one with the real grass skirt that Ian brought back from Hawaii. Marty said that he had too much junk lying around. He was collecting things to donate. Leaning close to her father to collect the knick-knacks, she caught a slight chemical trace on his breath. Like something was going sour in his mouth. She wondered when he'd last brushed.

He hadn't made much progress boxing the things. Only one wall had been stripped bare, particleboard exposed behind the shelves. He asked her if she'd looked up his military friends.

She told him she'd found five of the seven online. Two had passed away. One was cancer, but the other, Julie suspected from the obit write-up, was a suicide. She told Marty all of this, gave him the names.

He nodded slowly. "But James, Reg and Walter are around?"

She told him they were. Reg, it turned out, owned a B&B in nearby Livelton. She asked if he wanted to plan a visit.

He rubbed his head. "Just wait on it, Jules." He turned to the shelf on his left and started removing the tacks holding up a Union Jack. "Good you could contact them if need be, though."

Julie picked up a small alarm clock. She wiped dust from its face. Its hands had stopped turning long ago, stuck at the ten and two. She put it in the box with the rest. She mentioned the JLL show happening that night, said he must be excited.

"Tell you the truth, Jules, I'm getting tired."

Her heart jumped. "We can ask her to leave," she said. She worked with Marty, removing tacks from the flag.

"Not tired of her. Just of everything going on. The shows," he said. He picked at a stubborn tack in the corner. "By the way, you could stop being nasty to her."

"You don't know who she is."

"She's my employee, and she needs a place to stay."

Julie scoffed. She stopped herself from saying more. Marty ripped the flag from the wall. The last few tacks flew out and bounced across the ground. He sat at a table and opened the container of salad.

"You gotta stop making food for me." He took the napkin off a fork and knife on the table and started to eat.

"I like making food for you."

"I know. But you're my crutch." He smirked down at the spinach. "I remember when I had to eat your meals all the time. There was the time, when you were twelve, that you learned from some cookbook how to cook rice. I got home and you made me sit down at the table, lit a candle and served me soupy mush with a black crust. Still don't know how the hell you managed it." He stuffed one half of the hardboiled egg in his mouth.

"You ate it, though."

"Oh, I always ate it." He gestured at the salad. "I'd always eat it."

The mist outside still came down hard. Businesses were beginning to switch on their lights, which reflected off the lustre of the road. Marty and Julie sat together over salad and coffee until people began to arrive for JLL's show. Marty kept the door locked for a little while, and the townspeople peered in the windows, tapped on the glass as though the two of them were zoo animals. But it was safe and warm in The Halibut, cold and lonely out there. Finally, when Marty unlocked the door, Julie got up to leave.

"Stay for the show," Marty said.

She shook her head. Before she left, he pulled her into a hug. One of his encompassing Marty hugs. It'd been years, she realized. She breathed in the smell of his laundry detergent and that faint chemical twinge.

sixteen

THE MOOSE

In Val d'Or, to celebrate a year of slaughtered moose, the
whites strap moose heads to their automobiles and drive to
the dump to watch them tumble down, antlers over noses,
but Willy Mitchell, he rescues one in town for the soup pot,
not where it belongs, but a lot closer. In the '30s, Robert
Johnson traded the Devil his soul for a guitar at the cross-
roads. In '69, a police officer shot fifteen-year-old Willy in
the head for being Algonquin and holding stolen Christmas
lights, and he lived to trade his $500 settlement for a
Fender Telecaster Thinline that sang Fuck you, po po.

A knock on her bedroom door woke Julie that night. She squinted
at her alarm clock. It read 4:17 a.m. The door creaked open. Billy
Poole's face poked in.

Julie sat up and covered herself with the bedsheets. Billy came in and closed the door behind him. The green light from the alarm clock bounced off his eyes.

"So this is what the bedchamber looks like, huh?" he said. "Not as much gilded shit as I imagined."

Maybe he was some sort of weird teenage vampire after all. Maybe he floated right through the wall. Or she left the front door open again. He seated himself beside her on the bed. "You gotta come now." He held out his hand.

Marty. Julie listened for her father's snoring or his nighttime pacing. Silence. She swung her feet out of bed and threw on the first clothes she found. Billy reached for her thigh as she dressed.

She slapped his hand away and pushed him out of the room. "What happened?"

"Just, come on."

He led her in the direction of The Halibut. A car outside the restaurant had its mirrors and back windshield smashed. Pebbles of glass covered the ground. A few people kicked the pieces under the orange street lamp. Liam Parks leaned against the wall, holding his elbow. Dark streaks ran down to his fingers. Julie's chest seized. She ran toward him, but Billy grabbed her.

"No, no. He's good. This way." They ran. Two blocks down, Billy turned right.

There, a massive form lay draped over the pharmacy's spiked metal fence. Julie stopped. Antlers the size of snowshoes dangled above the ground. Billy started laughing. "Fuck, it's huge!"

As Julie got closer, she saw the moose with its entrails hanging out like spaghetti. Its front legs and back legs were on opposite sides of the fence. Its eyes rolled around in its head. As it grunted, waves travelled through the dangling intestines.

Moose impaled on fences was something that happened every few years. Two years ago, a mother moose failed to hop a fence for fresh grass and incited a campaign to ban picket fences, but the love of the Moose Meat Lottery outweighed the concern for Moose Lives Lost. But moose don't hop fences in the summertime. It only happens when they're desperate.

A puff of smoke rose up from beside the creature. Julie looked down to see JLL smoking a cigarette. Marty lay with his head in her lap. His eyes half open.

"Look who turned up." JLL shifted her weight, and Marty rolled over.

"She had to see the moose!" Billy said.

"Yes, thank you," JLL said.

Billy ran his hand through the bristles at the moose's fetlocks.

Julie knelt by Marty. "Marty." She shook his shoulder. "Marty."

One eye opened and fell shut. "Hey, kiddo."

JLL ashed her cigarette. Bits fell onto Marty's forehead. His bandana was missing and his scalp was covered in continents of chipped skin.

"He's drunk," JLL told her.

"Yeah," Julie said. "I can tell. What the fuck."

JLL shrugged. "He's all grown up." Beside them, Billy wrapped a length of intestines around his wrist like a bracelet. The moose kicked its back legs out and sent up a flurry of dead leaves. Julie jumped up and punched Billy in the arm.

She listened to the moose's laboured breathing. "We gotta kill it."

JLL laughed and blew out more smoke. "That's a change of heart, isn't it? Don't you want to take it home, keep it in a crate?"

Julie looked at the viscous blood moving down the fence posts. "Bert didn't have his insides in the dirt."

"No, not exactly." She ashed again. "Go on, then, kill it."

Julie ran her hands along the moose's two velvet antlers. She grasped the brow tines and attempted to twist the moose's head. The head wobbled, in no danger of harming a vertebra.

Julie's voice squeaked as she talked. "What did you do to this thing?"

JLL's eyes widened. "Me?" The moose grunted. Drops of blood fell from its lips. "I think it's funny that you don't think they could do it themselves." She ran a finger along the moose's hanging lip. "You don't think things could get bad enough for them to want to die." She shrugged. "Maybe we've made the world shitty enough that they're opting out."

"Bollocks."

A light breeze picked up around them, carrying with it the distant scattered howls of Port Braiders. JLL measured her palm against the underside of the moose's hoof. "You think we own these fellas? That they're here just because we enjoy their style?"

"I think animals lack the ability to make those decisions. They lack the sense of self."

"God, humans love to think they're unique."

Billy howled and slapped his knee as though this were a verbal smack down.

"Anyway," JLL said, "I doubt a sense of self is necessary to feel like shit, or to stop doing the things needed to stay alive. Like a dog whose best friend dies. Stops eating, follows suit." She stood. Marty's head fell in the dirt. He tried to prop himself on an elbow but collapsed. He reached for JLL. Leaves stuck to his face.

"So they're just responding to conditions," Julie said.

"Isn't that what humans are doing when they kill themselves? Responding to conditions?"

"We know what we're doing."

JLL faced Julie. "But you do believe humans can make those decisions?"

"Actually, I'm in the *free will is an illusion* camp. Our decisions are made before we're conscious of them." Billy tried to caress

Julie's arm. She pushed him back into the moose's head. "Our brains only justify choices we've already made."

"God." JLL placed her smoldering cigarette butt on the moose's tongue, which lolled halfway to the ground. "So what are you so worried about, then?" She gestured at Marty squirming in the dirt at her feet. "Just sit back and see how it all plays out. He will or he won't. You'll stop him or you won't. According to you, the decisions have already been made. We'll just have to justify it later."

Julie prodded JLL's shoulder. "You fucking disgust me."

"That makes me genuinely sad. I like you," JLL said. She shooed Julie with her hand. Julie grabbed onto her fingers. She squeezed until she felt one of the joints pop. The moose's breath came in sharp bursts.

JLL pulled her hand away, pointed down at Marty. "Good luck with that, then."

Billy was having a staring contest with the moose. JLL gestured for them to leave. They disappeared into the dark.

Julie tried to make Marty sit up. His body was a rag doll. Finally, she turned him on his side and let him sleep. As the night wore on, dew set in. The moose went silent. Its blood began to congeal on the fence posts, layering over itself like dripping wax. Julie spent her time counting pine needles in the dirt in the hours until Marty was conscious enough to be led home. On the way, they passed street trees strewn with discarded clothing, decorated for some parallel universe's Christmas.

The Halibut, of course, would be closed for another day. The curtains in the bungalow were drawn against the morning sun. JLL was still tucked up in the attic. Julie left a glass of water and a cheese sandwich on the counter should Marty emerge from his bedroom. She put Bert and his crate into Marty's Buick and began the drive to Livelton to find Reg.

With the sun returned the whale smell—once again strangling the air. As she drove along the coastal highway, the tainted wind from the ocean whipped through the window. It was many kilometres before the briny smell of the Pacific returned. The highway curved away from the water and led through the coastal mountains, still capped with snow this many months into the summer. The mountains' bald heads poked above the treeline, a playground for mountain goats. On the four-hour drive she stopped only once at a ski chalet reimagined as a mountain biking destination in the summer and ate a bowl of thick chowder. She collected pieces of sand-riddled clam in a napkin and later fed them to Bert.

Livelton sat in a valley between three peaks. The town was much smaller than Port Braid, so finding Reg's address was easy. The road to his B&B ran along a ridge, the houses set high above the valley, overlooking the vein of water that separated the three peaks. She left the car in the guest parking spot and placed Bert in a shady place under a cedar.

It was a two-storey cottage with a balcony running around the entire second floor. Impatiens tumbled out of flower boxes around the railing. The house's white doors and window frames stood out against dark wood. A man in a bathrobe answered the door when she knocked. A pipe hung from his lips.

He had the raspy voice of a perpetual smoker. "Help you?"

Julie explained her relation to Reg's old unit mate.

"Marty Bird. Marty Bird. I remember that gentleman well. First one up in the morning, first one to pass out. He's not passed, is he?"

Julie shook her head. Reg invited her in. They crossed the living room, where Reg introduced his wife, who sat reading on a loveseat. They proceeded to the dining area, where there was an oak table large enough to seat twelve, draped with a lace tablecloth.

The room was encased in bookshelves. Large provincial things with bevelled edges. Reg bought a tray with a fine China teapot and cups.

Julie didn't know exactly what she wanted from this man. Beside the smoker's voice, he seemed so far to be Marty's opposite in health and wellbeing, his hair full and silver, his tawny skin firm from years of sun exposure, his muscles on his calves and forearms taut. Reg hadn't heard from Marty since the Gulf.

He shook his head. "I go a couple decades not hearing nothing from these guys, and the first thing I get to hear about them is they're sick or dying. Sorry, darling."

He poured tea into their mugs and dropped in a lump of sugar each. "So maybe you can fill me in on the details. Let's not jump the gun to the nasty stuff. He got married, he had kids, right?"

Julie sipped the syrupy tea. "Just the one kid. My mom died right after."

Reg stopped stirring. "Jesus H. Christ. How much tragedy is a person supposed to sustain?"

His wife said something from the other room.

"We're fine in here!" he yelled.

Julie didn't know what to say to him, so she asked about his time spent in the military. Reg paced around the table and told Julie that he'd been a lifer. He'd had to move units in '97 when things were reorganized, but he was a combat engineer a long while. Afghanistan was the last place he'd worked in the field. Sixteen combat engineers from Canada had been killed. After that, Reg had moved up the ranks, spent more time in an office.

"So you never had any trouble? Um, readjusting?" JLL asked.

"PTSD? You can say it, darling. I was one of the lucky ones, I guess. Never know who it's gonna hit. Marty?"

Julie nodded.

"Not still?" he asked.

She nodded again.

Reg turned a chair around and straddled it to face her. "Now, listen. They got new things now. There's this program out of UBC, supposed to be one of the best in the world. And that's including the States where they got a lot higher stakes in fixing this. Dr. Marvin Westwood, Veterans Transition Program. If you can talk him into it, well. Here." Reg fetched a scrap of paper from the living room and jotted down the information. "You women, you're good at getting help. Men, not so good."

After their tea, Reg gave Julie a tour of the B&B. There were three rooms upstairs.

"If this wasn't midweek, they'd all be full up," he said.

Outside, his wife had constructed a small pond. A painted turtle swam circles around the lily pads. From the end of the backyard, the mountain slope rose steeply. Douglas firs stood proud up the incline. Julie felt sorry when it was time to drive back to Port Braid. She thanked Reg for accepting a stranger into his home.

"Just take care of your pops. Tell him he has to call."

The drive back to Port Braid took longer than the trip up. She drove slower. By the time she reached the outer limits of town, it was nearly 6 p.m., but hot whale-infused air still pounded through the windows. Bert was getting restless in the back of the car.

On the way back to the bungalow, she spotted the dark stain at Marker 34 where she had hit Bert's mother. She pulled over, turned in her seat and faced the raccoon.

"JLL thinks I should have left you here." Bert turned a circle in his crate. "Fucked up, right?" Julie turned off the car and stepped out to stretch her legs. She wanted to think about how to approach Marty about Reg's suggestion. Just admitting she'd gone there without telling him would be difficult enough.

She pulled out the crate and opened the door so Bert could wander out. He sniffed the gravel and touched the stones. Julie wanted to see if he'd sniff the raccoon-shaped stain where his mother had been squashed. He sidled in that direction and sat on his back legs. He looked over his shoulder before turning toward Marker 34 and taking off into the Cold Forest.

Julie sprinted after him. Blackberry thorns caught against her legs as she ran. Under the canopy of trees, the temperature dropped by several degrees. Bert ran ahead of her, parting the underbrush as he went. Sticks cracked under Julie's weight. She stumbled, lost sight of Bert, but heard his progress ahead.

"Fuck." She bent over and tried to catch her breath. A glint of something by a patch of salal caught her eye. A pane of glass lay in stark contrast to the rest of the forest. Julie stomped over to it, and found the decaying body of a car in the forest. Its white body was badly rusted, and by the way it was grown over, Julie guessed that it had been here for a long time. Maybe it belonged to the farm, if the farm ever really existed. By its box shape, Julie guessed it was from the '80s or early '90s. She ripped away the plants that gripped the front grill and looked at the license plate: New Mexico.

094 MMR
Land of Enchantment

She could look it up when she got home, but she already knew this was Nancy's car. She imagined her father arriving in this town behind this steering wheel. Maybe it was where he finally ran out of gas. He would have driven it off the road and sat there, dumb to what his life would be next. A stranger walking into a town without means or connections. It was impressive, Julie thought, how much he was a part of Port Braid. She'd never thought of it.

But this discovery also reshaped precious childhood memories. While Marty was teaching her to swim in the Cold Forest pond, only a short walk away, he would have known that this beater was staring at them through the trees. For all of their swimming lessons, he must have had split concentration, one eye minding Julie's breaststroke and the other tracking the progression of rust across the vehicle's hood. While she paddled, it could see her, but she could never see it.

Julie cleared the underbrush away from the driver's side door and unlocked it through the open window. It creaked as it opened, and she slid inside. Specks of burgundy upholstery showed through the mould, but the inside of the car was mostly green. The interior smelled of damp moss and the seat soaked her jeans. She gripped the steering wheel and imagined driving through the bush—slaloming around tree trunks and flattening blackberry bushes. Julie inspected the buttons and dials inside the car. The gas gauge claimed that there was still a quarter tank, and the key was in the ignition. She turned it, but the engine was silent. Out the passenger-side window, she could just make out a truck passing by. The road lay less than twenty metres away.

She pushed a few buttons. The radio. The windshield washer fluid. She pulled the lever for the trunk. She heard a pop and looked behind to see the lid open. The last working mechanism.

Julie put her foot on the gas and resumed her fantasy of forging a highway through the forest, perhaps leading all the way back to Vancouver, where she would call home and Marty would pick up and everything would be normal. She would decline to visit Port Braid for another five years. When the novelty wore off, she tilted her head back and closed her eyes. Light from the roadside danced across her eyelids, and Julie marvelled at the number of times she had walked or driven by this wreck.

Her stomach rumbled and she decided it was time to go. She shoved the rusty door open and went to shut the trunk. It seemed right to leave the wreck as she found it.

Her breath stopped. When she looked inside, she saw a flat pile of bones in the shape of a hunched creature. She stared at the shape. Not human. No, not human, she reassured herself. Its spine curved into a perfect arc—a protractor of a spine with degrees marked by vertebrae. The skull was small and long. From her last visit to the Biodiversity Museum at UBC, where skulls of myriad creatures sat in glass cases, sometimes accompanied by stuffed versions of the same species, she knew that skulls always looked too small. Without cheeks and skin and hair, we disappear. The skeleton had a tail, which curved on the same trajectory as the rest of the spine, and there was the ribcage, no longer a cage, but just a two-dimensional criss-cross of bones. Julie then noticed the fur that outlined the skeleton. It stuck to the upholstery all around it. The silkier stuff had blown to the back of the trunk when she pulled open the hatch. At the end of the tucked-in legs were black claws. There were four at the hind end, and five with the dewclaw at the front. It was a dog. She prayed that it was dead when it got shut in there. There was no sign of a struggle. A dog in distress wouldn't die in a perfect semi-circle.

Julie sat on the edge of the trunk and buried her head in her hands. It'd be so great if there was just one not messed up thing in Port Braid right now. Then she could leave in peace. One *not* messed up thing.

When her breathing calmed, Julie rooted through the car to see what she could find. There was nothing there, nothing even in the glove compartment, except an empty jug of washer fluid. She was hoping for an ice scraper so she could bury the bones. Later, she thought. I'll come back later. She left the trunk door open and fought her way back to the road. Before she broke through the last layer of trees, she heard scuffling in the gravel. Bert picked his way across the shoulder and sat back on his haunches to look into the car.

"You fucker. Couldn't make it on your own, huh?" Julie scooped him into his crate.

Julie sat in the front seat of the Buick and put her head on her hands. The occasional car whipped by. Then, a tap at the window. JLL's face was inches from her own, her curls pressed against the glass. What looked like a child's bike lay beside her on the shoulder. Julie swore to herself, rolled down the window. "You following me?"

"I like keeping tabs," JLL said. "What you doing way out here?"

"Come on. Throw the bike in. I'll give you a lift."

JLL looked over her shoulder, down the road. "Actually, no thanks. I'll stick here. I need the exercise getting back."

When Julie arrived home, Marty was chopping carrots for dinner. While they cooked and ate together, she revelled in the time spent without JLL, and she couldn't bring herself to talk about the program at UBC. It seemed wrong to waste the calm minutes. So they sat in front of the television together, as though everything were the same.

seventeen

OPOSSUM

Starting in the 1950s, in Minamata, Japan, cats began dancing around town. They whipped their tails and did barrel rolls, flung their limbs in rhythms, threw themselves off cliffs. Dancing cat fever affected more than cats. Crows fell from the sky. Fish trembled on the water surface. People lost their ability to dress themselves and open mussels. Their voices rose to cartoon pitch. Following the dancing cats they started their own wild convulsions: arms beating, praising higher things, heads and eyes rolling back, cigarettes dipping in and out of mouths. They sunk into comas, continued dying for decades, while Chisso, their employer on the water, continued making mad hatters of them all.

It was later that night, after having dinner with his daughter and watching their favourite reruns, that Marty sat up in soaked sheets. The night sky lay tranquil through his window. His duvet stuck to his stomach. He patted the mattress and sniffed the salted cotton. The house was quiet. JLL had come home and gone straight to bed. Julie was long asleep too.

Two weeks had passed since he last had a nightmare. But now, when he closed his eyes, he saw those flames licking. Human-shaped until his touch disintegrated it to carbon dust. And Midge in her curled *c* beyond a roiling field of mice. He tapped his temple to keep his thoughts here. *I am in a bed. This is an alarm clock in British Columbia. The smell of death through the windows is not human.*

He put his feet on the floor and threw open his blackout curtains. The street lamp cast a square of light across the laminate. As he walked to the door, grainy particles clung to the sweat on the soles of his feet.

At times like this, he recreated in his mind the last time he felt calm. The exact scene he imagined may never have occurred. Just as likely, it was an amalgam of memories selected by his brain as anesthesia. He lay on a towel in his parents' backyard. It was summertime, and he had not made up his mind about joining the army. It was only a dangling life choice, exciting as any other turn he may take. The pool's filtration system gurgled. Somewhere nearby there must have been roadwork because the air smelled of tar. Midge lay with her paws hanging over the pool's edge and snapped at waterlogged crickets as they drifted in the slow whirl-pool. His parents were in Phoenix and he was house-sitting. No one was coming home. Midge plodded over and lay parallel to his body. Her fur was hot from the sun. Sparrows hopped around in the bird feeder and scattered seed shells across the deck. The image stopped and looped from this point. His memory did not include going for a swim or having a drink. Just the sparrows, Midge's hot fur, the gurgle of the pool.

When he woke in a panic like this, as he had on thousands of nights before, he would walk laps of the house, touching objects as he passed to confirm their ordinary existences. The rotary phone, the humpback whale fridge magnet, the cedar breadbox, the oriole decal on the porch window. The flashbacks would draw him into a battle or he would make them submit.

Tonight, instead of his rounds, he stood halfway between the attic ladder and the door to Julie's bedroom. A flash pierced his sternum, stabbed the backs of his eyes. Desert and rot. Burning oil wells and flesh. So tedious, so tiring.

Speaking with JLL about death these last weeks had made him hopeful. Like some people desired sports cars or country villas, he desired to die. For his heart to stop seizing. For his blood to settle in his veins. For his synapses to stop shrieking. To be still and permanent, trustworthy and even. Death was shiny and smooth. A warm and still lake.

He passed Julie's door and walked outside for clean air, but out there the tide of rot flowed thicker into his lungs. Black smoke billowed from the gutted car and into the shadow of a fir. Marty got down close to the ground, crept along the grass, staying under the rancid flow. He waited for the pop of gunfire. He scanned the sky for blinks from choppers and instead caught sight of a yellow square of light. He blinked. A fresh yawn of metallic rot blew by his face. Whale, now.

What kind of a child was he that these imaginations could still carry him away?

Marty chose a stone from the driveway and tossed it at the attic window. Another flash gripped his chest. He selected another stone, larger and heavier in his hand, and threw it. The stone clanged off the glass. A moment later, JLL filled the frame. She threw the window open and raised her arms in disbelief. "What's this, Marty?"

"You're up."

"Now."

JLL wore a long T-shirt of Julie's—the stupid one with the multicoloured bear. Her pompadour was more of a tam, flattened against her scalp. A strong audio hallucination peppered Marty's eardrum.

"Come down," he said.

"I'm fucking tired."

"I'll pay you." Marty felt his pyjama pockets. "In the morning, I'll give you money, or, you can keep all the sales from the shows, or . . ."

JLL stood there a moment. Then she turned and mooned him. Her white butt cheeks hung over the sill, and she walked away. He heard laughter.

Hulking shadows moved along the sides of the house, hid in bushes.

"What can I do?" he called. "Name it." Marty stood staring at the window. He didn't allow his eyes to drift down to where the shadows might materialize into humans, dead or vengeful. *Just screw off.* He tried to lighten his tone. "I'll make waffles in the morning. Whiskey maple syrup."

JLL's face reappeared. "I thought of something."

"What?"

"Tell me about that dream you always have. The one that has you thrashing in the room below me. Not tonight. But a rain check."

"You can hear that?"

JLL shook her head, incredulous. "Yeah. I can hear you."

"It's a deal." Anything would have been a deal.

Five minutes later and JLL was outside, panted, barefooted and dangling his car keys on her middle finger.

"Where are we going?" she asked.

Marty took the keys and got in the driver's side. He leaned over to open the door for JLL. She slid in and crossed her legs. The black crusted sole of her foot grazed his driving knee.

Marty backed out of the driveway. He rolled down the windows and swung the car onto Sequoia Street. The back bumper clipped the garbage bin as he shifted from reverse to drive. Marty pushed on the accelerator and the Buick groaned to high speed.

With no JLL show that night, most Port Braiders were in their homes. For the people still awake, shadow shows of their existences played through living room curtains. Silhouettes of couples watching TV.

Wet, whale-ridden wind blew through the car windows, hitting their faces. The car skidded past a stop sign and righted itself on Lilac. JLL's hair whipped against her forehead. She held it back with two hands. She had to speak up to be heard. "Marty, I know you see me as Wild Thing incarnate, but I don't mind if you slow down." She dropped a hand from her hair and braced herself against the dash.

But the shadows from the bushes trailed in the exhaust stream of the car, and at this speed, they stayed behind. They billowed up and dropped away and never reached as far as the tailgate. Marty focused on the horizon.

The humans were in their homes tonight, but the wildlife was active. Along Highway 3, the street lights disappeared and iridescent eyes reflected the high beams from between the dark trees.

Marty stepped harder on the accelerator and saw a white flash in JLL's eyes. He flipped on the radio, and Nina Simone's gripped voice trailed out. Some late jazz show on the CBC. As he drove faster, the wind flapped a beat through the windows, and their clothes fluttered in time. The rise and fall in pressure equated to IEDs along the Highway of Death. Marty watched the sideview mirror for the stream of panic behind the vehicle.

JLL gripped the dash. Marty turned his head and saw her mouth moving, aggressive and wild. When he turned back he saw the white triangular face of an opossum in the centre of the road. He spun the steering wheel and the back tires slid out. The smell of burnt rubber wafted through the interior and the opossum passed between the wheels. The car fishtailed toward a pickup parked on the shoulder. Marty cranked the wheel the other direction, fighting to gain traction. It slid too easily in his sweaty palm. The right headlight smashed against the truck's bumper and the Buick rolled to a stop.

Hot blood pounded through his heart. Simone sang her last notes. Marty switched it off and the car went silent except for the scream of crickets outside. The glove box had opened and a thousand years of gas receipts spilled onto JLL's lap. A small contusion on JLL's forehead leaked blood onto the paper. Marty rested his head on the steering wheel.

He heard JLL tap the dashboard. "Hey, well, look at that. That was almost, almost, super fucking convenient. Ass." The door opened and closed. Marty looked up. They were parked by Woodlawn Cemetery.

JLL passed through the angel-arched gate. She shook out her shoulders and head and swore at the sky.

Marty felt along his body. His fingers and toes could move. He dabbed his hairline to check for blood. Everything was fine. The exhaust shadows must have launched past the crash and were somewhere far beyond.

On shaking legs, Marty emerged from the car. Electric pulses shot through his phantom hand. The passenger side was dented and headlight glass was scattered across the pavement. The engine hissed and popped from the effort, and insect carapaces exploded on the grill. The pickup was fine.

Marty followed JLL into the cemetery. A pair of granite tombstones stood sentinel past the gates, his and hers. He put his hand on the man's stone as he passed. A minivan screamed by on the highway and the headlights made sundials of the headstones. JLL was lit for a brief moment, sitting on a box marked for discarded flowers.

Marty knew only one person buried in the cemetery—Ms. Lemieux, Julie's kindergarten teacher. She was killed by her husband before Julie was done with third grade, and the parents made an unspoken pact to keep the details from her former students. Julie still didn't know. He felt sorry for that now, but it was most of the kids' first experience with death, besides their goldfish, so it had seemed like enough to sit them down on bedsides and confront tears, confusion and questions about the nature of mortality without having to get into the question of how people can be abusers. Julie was mostly stoic, but she asked question after question. All the typical ones. *Can anyone die? Why did she die now? Can I die? Can you?* Marty had crumbled and talked about heaven. He'd felt so tired, meeting with the other parents, going to Julie's regularly scheduled karate and French lessons. Ms. Lemieux was Catholic and unprepared to die at thirty-seven. And her husband hadn't paid for a plot. So the parents, school administrators and people from town donated to buy her a stone and a place to lie. The grave was tucked into the east corner of the cemetery. Marty could just make out the white spire under the willow.

There were veterans in the cemetery too, but none from the Gulf. Most Gulf vets he knew, the ones that went early, chose cremation anyway, returned to the ash and dirt that infected them in the east. The vets here were World War II vets. Marty walked past the ankle-high picket fence that kept their corpses separate from the civilians. They were celebrated vets. Wreaths and ceremonies. Modern vets were different. In thirty years, Marty figured the odds were nil that they'd ask him to stand wrinkled, shaking and proud at a Remembrance Day ceremony. No one saw his as a world-saving sacrifice. They didn't even think of him when they filled up their gas tanks. Instead, he had to prove by lengthy questionnaire every year to Veteran Affairs that he hadn't grown back his hand. He always drew a hook hand in the corner. Still a pirate. Every damn year.

Marty caught up to JLL at a newer grave and lowered himself to the ground next to her. The discarded flowers lent a funerary scent to the whale rot. He wondered when his olfactory senses would kick in and block the death smell.

"I'm sorry about that," Marty said.

JLL pulled a lighter and two cigarettes from her pocket. She offered him one and he shook his head. She shrugged and slipped it back in her pocket. The orange tip of her cigarette glowed in the dark.

"Well, you know how to let go," she said. "You can have that."

Marty sniffed. "That's not letting go. That's losing it."

JLL dragged on her cigarette. She stared up. A cool breeze came from the ocean and moved between the graves. "Must be exhausting, though."

Marty felt a sting in his sinuses. He blinked it away. "Sure."

"Reminds me of my mom."

"Yeah?"

JLL looked at him from the corner of her eye. "You'd have liked her. Nice." She blew smoke sideways. "But fucking exhausted as fuck. Daytime sleeper. She wasn't supposed to last so long."

"She sick?"

"Yeah."

Marty nodded. "Me too." He rubbed his head, smiled at JLL. "Made my hair fall out."

JLL nodded, sucked on the cigarette, shook her arms out. "God. I can't fucking believe you crashed the car."

The moon illuminated a stand of poplars. A breeze blew and shook their upright branches. The leaves shushed their conversation.

Another car glided past the angel gates, high beams drawing roadside trees out of the blackness. The lights caught the engraving on the war epitaph. He'd memorized Laurence Binyon's words years ago. *They shall grow not old, as we that are left grow old: Age shall not weary them, nor the years condemn.*

JLL rubbed the cigarette butt under her foot. "You gonna quit soon?"

"Quit? Drinking? I have before."

"No, idiot. End it."

That sting shot through his nostrils again. He breathed in, out. "I haven't told Julie." His heart beat faster.

"Why?"

Marty shook his head at the sky. He couldn't imagine the conversation with his daughter. It was a terrible thing to ask someone to accept.

"Shame. It's fucking shame." JLL pulled out the second cigarette. It dangled between her fingers. "Drives me insane. I mean, people shouldn't feel so bad."

"It's cowardice. Ending it." He smiled. "I oughta be a man about it. Hang on."

JLL shook her head. "That's bullshit, though. And in fact, you're being a woman about it."

"What's that supposed to mean?"

"Statistically speaking, 'hanging on,' you're being a woman about it. 'Being a man about it' would mean going ahead. If you're going to make it a sexist dichotomy."

"So men are cowards, then."

"It has nothing to do with cowardice." She lit the cigarette and moved closer beside him. "It might have to do with which gender has more family obligations, more or fewer people to talk to, ability to seek help without having your balls chopped off. It's hard to stick around, but deciding to end it, that's hard too. It's not a wimpy way out. Where's the cowardice in holding a gun to your head? With no idea what it's going to be like?"

"I think I know what it's going to be like."

"You a heaven guy?"

He shook his head. "I still don't think it's the brave thing to do."

"Jesus, Marty. It's nothing to do with bravery. All right, so say you have a guy who, like, lost the family fortune gambling. And the shit's coming down, the gangsters are coming to the house to break his fingers, and the guy's like, *Ooh, owie, I don't want my fingers broken, ooh, owie, I don't want my wife to know I gamble*, then he slips into the Niagara River, then changes his mind and screams all the way down the falls." JLL flicked the second cigarette, mostly unsmoked, onto the cemetery path. "That guy's a fermented piece of chicken shit. But that's like one guy, ever, in a world of suicide. Most people do it because they're suffering and can't see past it. And they can't ask for help. Teenagers kill themselves. All the time. You think they're weak? You think they should 'man up'?"

"No."

"No. It's the saddest fucking thing in the world. No teenager should kill themselves. But people should be able to say *I really want to kill myself* without being called a pussy. That's why your shit about 'being a man' is vile, Marty. Don't spout that shit. People need to be able to say it out loud. Stating a fact, not admitting a weakness."

Marty felt a spider making its way over his hand. He brushed it away. "So we can help them."

A breeze rolled by and pushed JLL's second cigarette butt back in their direction. It still glowed orange on the path. "Yeah," she said. "Or, in some cases, we can finally let them go."

"No one could do that."

"I disagree. How could you disrespect someone who went through decades of consideration and made a rational choice because it's not getting better, and told the world, *Hey dude, I'm outtie?* Fuck. They deserve a farewell party."

"I don't know."

"I'm just saying I couldn't do it. Sticking around, I can do."

"I don't know."

"Christ, Marty. Don't swallow a fistful of pills tonight. Just lay off the self-persecution."

Marty took the lighter from JLL and turned it over in his hand.

"But what do I know?" JLL asked. "You got shit to live for. Your dick still works, right?"

Marty laughed. "No."

JLL covered her mouth. Her teeth shone in the moonlight. "Shit." A coyote howled somewhere in the forest. "I can't believe we're talking about this shit in a graveyard."

Another car drove past the cemetery. This one slowed down at the crash. Marty held his breath. The car paused for a moment, then continued on the highway.

The night had grown cooler in the time they sat by the flower box. The stars shifted by degrees each time Marty looked up. The moon advanced past the poplars, heading to the ocean.

JLL leaned back on her elbows and shifted her weight. "My fucking ass is asleep. I'm bored." She stood and stretched. Jumped up and down. "Let's do something fun."

Marty's knees cracked in two places as he stood. By the time he was up, JLL was most of the way to the groundskeeper's shed. Marty felt the soaked seat of his pants as he followed her.

The shed was constructed with roughly hewn pine. Marty leaned a hand on the wood and felt myriad splinters poke into his calluses. Dark knots covered the shed like Dalmatian spots.

JLL backed up a few steps, then flew at the door. She slammed her shoulder into it and the small latch burst. The door swung open and she went in. Metal objects clattered inside until JLL emerged with a hammer. She pushed the hammer at Marty. "Take this. Too heavy for a girl. Ha."

Marty took the hammer. It was a ball peen, rounded ends on both sides of the head. He ran his hand over the cool metal. "What's this for, then?"

"Smash a grave."

"I don't think so."

"Smash a fucking grave. Just do it. Come on." She grabbed his arm and dragged him to the nearest line of stones. The row was marked by identical heights and shapes. Classic rounded tombstone, RIP, perfect for a cobweb or skeletal hand reaching from the earth. JLL ran her hand over each as they passed them by.

"What's this supposed to do?" Marty asked. "Secure my immortality?"

JLL scoffed. "Sure, big guy."

Marty read the names. *Monique Jennings. Klaus Peters.*

"I feel strange walking across graves," he said.

The dark figure of an animal darted between the headstones.

"You know what's weirder?" JLL peered between the stones to see where it went. "There's a skeleton *inside* of you right now." She gave a fake shudder.

"Never thought of it that way."

"Of course you didn't. You know those old cartoons with the dancing skeletons? Check it out." JLL started to dance. She raised her elbows and let her forearms dangle down in rhythm as she danced a jig. "Dance, skeleton! Dance!" She howled with laughter. "Dance, other skeleton!" She shook his shoulders.

Marty bobbed his knees, stuck out his butt, churning butter with his arms.

"Yes, skeleton!" JLL yelled.

They stopped when they were out of breath. JLL leaned over, panting. "Here, all right. Choose a grave."

Marty scanned the options. "I choose Vera Olive Loveless."

"No. No, no, no. Sorry. That's the worst choice."

"Why?"

"Too awesome of a name. Vera Olive Loveless is amazing in her own right, obviously. She doesn't need a smashed headstone. And you can't deprive the world of a headstone that reads Vera Fucking Olive Loveless."

"Mary Garlick."

"No. No 1800s superheroes and no children's book characters. Here. John Short, who died in 1983, the most boring sounding year in history, except for being my birth year."

Marty looked at John Short's gravestone. The stone was single toned, no lustre, and John's name was written in blocky caps. Marty tapped it with the hammer. "Don't feel good about this."

"No shit. It's an immoral act." JLL ran a hand through her hair.

"What if it was your mother's?"

JLL turned away from him. The back of her head struck Marty as a smaller, distorted face. Two curls formed eyes, and the divot at the base of her skull was a gaping mouth. Another animal emerged from between the graves. Moonlight reflected off its eyes, tiny beads, and its white face. Marty wondered if it was the same opossum that made him crash the car. It raised its lips, exposing arrowhead teeth, but continued to waddle past.

"Watch your feet, kiddo. Those things are mean."

"Give me the hammer."

Marty held it out of her reach.

"Come on, Marty," she said. "This was fun a minute ago." She jumped up but couldn't reach it. "You dragged me out here."

Marty watched the opossum move toward an open grave at the end of the row. He couldn't think who in town would have died. Maybe it was earmarked for later.

While he was distracted by the animal, JLL yanked his arm down and ripped the hammer from his grip. She took a couple of steps back, hammer held high. She swung and hit John Short's stone. A small chip flew from the upper edge, but it was otherwise unharmed. She swung again, and a fragment came off above the *S*.

The opossum made a lap around the open hole in the ground and dropped in. JLL handed the hammer to Marty. "Here. Just do it. I want to go home now."

"Maybe it's better if I do it soon."

"What?"

Prickles ran up the length of his spine. Marty swung the hammer as hard as he could. New flakes came off with each attempt. The stone gained a backward lean until finally JLL ran at it and kicked it over. It thudded to the grass.

JLL smiled at the ground, gave Marty a nod of approval. She let a gob of spit drop onto John Short's resting place.

Marty's heart thumped against his ribs. He said a quick mental apology to John Short, but he felt good. Waking up JLL was the right choice. Sharp outlines framed the objects in the cemetery. Virgin Marys stood white against dark grass, their features set at high contrast. The row of poplars threw their branches up in silent disbelief.

JLL hooked a finger through his prosthesis. "Celebrate it, you know? No shame attached. John feels no shame. No righteous victimhood."

Marty nodded, slung his arm around her shoulders. "Home?"

"Nah. I'm hungry. Make me some fish and chips."

eighteen

ROCKFISH

*Bessie Smith is my illustrious leader. She opens and
closes behind her a stream of gates in picket fences and
sings things that cannot be said in an era. Hot dog in
my roll, sugar in my bowl. She wants it hot, not cold.
Mother, brother, father gone by nine. A husband, then
platonic life partner, all coupled with bisexual affairs, to
break 1920s rules. Ten thousand mourners and an unjust
death and a voice that leapfrogs the Great Depression.*

Previously, in Julie's entire life, Marty had never failed to return
home. There was never a date, a guys' fishing weekend, an out-of-
town reunion.

She didn't notice his absence until she woke at 4:30 a.m. and felt
the house too quiet. His car was missing from the driveway. The

ladder to the attic was down, meaning that JLL must be out with him. She'd give it two hours, she told herself, before calling the police. To fill the time, she played a zombie shoot-'em-up game, challenging enough to keep her preoccupied, mindless enough to calm her nerves.

The door creaked open at five. Muffled voices. JLL's steps going up to the attic. The ladder being pulled up.

She listened carefully. After a moment, Marty's steps continued down the hall. She expected him to go to the kitchen or his bedroom, but he paused in front of her door, tapped on the frame.

She closed her laptop, told him to come in. His face was flushed. He stank of cigarettes. And he offered no explanation for where he'd been.

"Ian's taking the boat out this morning," he said. "I want you to come."

"JLL staying here?"

"Yes, kiddo. JLL is staying here."

Julie pulled on clothes from the floor and followed Marty outside. She inspected the smashed headlight and new dent on the Buick. Marty got into the driver's seat, without any explanation of the accident, so she decided to let it lie. They drove together to the marina, where Ian's troller was docked. It was a windy morning. Tops of coniferous trees bent and snapped back with the gusts. In contrast to the rapid movements of branches and signposts, purple light crept slowly from the east, across the dimming stars.

Theirs was the only car in the parking lot. Ian usually walked to the pier if he hadn't spent the night sleeping on his boat. Julie hauled the sloshing cooler as they walked along the raised boardwalk that connected the parking lot to the docks, the smell of oil and wood mixing with the wafting whale rot off the water. There was another smell too, something fresher and fishy. The planks creaked under their steps. At low tide, as it was now, the boardwalk ran several metres over the muddy sand.

Her father was turned inward, concentrating on thoughts foreign to her. His face was up to the horizon, but he didn't seem to focus on any particular sight.

The dawn light was just beginning to illuminate the sand below. It looked strange. Normally the beach was scattered with the bony bodies of oysters, but now it was rippled and lustrous. She caught a flash of movement. And another. A tremor on the tidal flat. She put a hand on Marty's arm, told him to wait. She put down the cooler and leaned over the edge. Gradually it came into focus. A field of twitching rockfish, their orange scales grey in the early light. Their spiny dorsal fins cut into one another's sides. Their mouths gaped and closed, their startled marble eyes rolling. Hundreds of them, from the size of a minnow to the size of a dog, covered the ground below them.

Marty told her to hurry up. He didn't want to look at them anymore. Ian was waiting.

"Aren't they endangered? Shouldn't we throw them back?"

Marty looked at his watch. "The tide's coming up soon. It'll be faster than we could be."

When they arrived at Ian's boat, he was asleep in the captain's chair. They hopped on board and prodded him awake. He rubbed his eyes. "More notice next time you want to go out this early, 'kay Marty?"

They chugged out to the open water. Even though she'd grown up on the Pacific, it was Julie's first time seeing a sunrise from the ocean. Colour seemed to seep from the west, though the sun was behind them. Orange stole up the clouds, unfurling like tentacles across the sky.

The plan was to travel to the back of the Khutzeymateen Inlet, where there was a grizzly bear sanctuary. It was somewhere Marty had always wanted to go.

On either side of the inlet were grass flats. Behind them were snowcapped peaks. The wind-disturbed water chopped their reflection into small pieces. Ian stayed behind the wheel, the path too narrow to take his eyes off the monitor. Marty and Julie took their place in the lawn chairs on the bow, sharing a Thermos of coffee that Ian had brought.

"I need to tell you something," Marty said.

She heard the tension in his voice. No good news ever follows the phrase *I need to tell you something*. It never did soften the hard truth. It preceded bad news with nervous stress and anger, coming from the knowledge that an unpleasantness was about to be thrust upon you, and that you had no say in its content and timing. But curiosity prevents a person from saying, *wait, let's just finish our coffee first. Let's see if that brownish lump ahead is a grizzly. Let's, in fact, never get around to what you have to say.*

Marty picked at the moons of his fingernails.

"Do it," Julie said.

He wanted her to know that when he dies, the house will go to her, everything goes to her, but he doesn't expect her to hang on to it. He looked at her face.

Julie sipped the coffee. There was sourness from built-up milk under the rim. The boat chugged past the brown lump in the field of grass—not a bear but a turned over tree stump.

"I don't want to hear about the house," she said.

"Tell me what you want to hear about."

"I don't want to hear any of this."

Marty nodded, squinted at the horizon.

"Aren't you afraid of it?" she asked. Her windpipe felt as though it were closing.

Marty answered fast. "No."

The boat chugged around a bend and a new set of mountains appeared in the distance.

"There's this program at UBC," Julie said. "It's new. They get you to relive traumas with this group of other vets, act it out and then . . ."

Marty stood, walked to the railing.

"Why not?" she asked.

"I'm not joining some drama class to learn what I know."

"It helps people, Marty."

"I'm sure it does. It's been too long. Mine are buried deep."

"Stop holding your flashbacks sacred."

His face was getting red. He turned back to the water. "No drama classes."

"If you get cured, it means you wasted twenty years, right?" she said. Marty looked at her. She went silent.

The inlet closed in around them. Julie spotted a bald eagle perched on the top of a fir. It leapt from the tree and flew over the pass. The sun had risen higher in the sky, and the wind began to die down.

Marty scratched his head, gave her a sorry expression. "Shit."

Julie shifted in the chair. "Let's got to Mexico or some shit. Chile. Japan. I don't know."

A snorting sound came from the water as a seal poked its head above the waves, looked curiously up at them. Julie got up to stand beside her father.

"Dogs of the sea," Marty said.

"Thailand. France, anywhere."

He put an arm on her back. "You know travel sounds like hell to me, kiddo."

The seal turned circles in the water, dipped below the surface and reappeared behind the boat. It kept a safe distance behind them but stayed in sight. Julie's eyes stung with tears. She kept a hand shielding her face. "I'm not going to let you do anything."

Marty sighed. The smell of gasoline flooded the air as a gust of wind came up behind them. The boat went around another bend in the inlet. The grassy flats shrank back so the mountain slopes dove straight into the water. The seal was joined by a companion, the two of them tracking their progress further inland.

"This is just our reality, kiddo."

"No." She choked on the word. Tears flowed faster, infected her nasal cavities. She sniffed. "Fucking hell."

He pulled her into a hug, kissed her forehead. "All right."

He kept his arm around her as they undertook the coming kilometres. Soon the grassy plains around the inlet widened again, and more bald eagles dotted the sky. Eventually they reached the bay at the end of Khutzeymateen. There, lumbering through the shallow water were three grizzlies. A mother and two cubs. The cubs loped after their mother as she searched the water for fish.

Ian lowered the anchor and joined them on deck. He cracked open a beer and lay back on a lawn chair. "You two spatting over something again?"

Marty shook his head. "Appreciate you taking us out today."

"My pleasure." He pointed at the bears. "I spot three rides. Who wants to saddle up?"

The seals continued to make appearances around the boat, their heads seeming to glide above the water, then disappearing under. Whatever was disturbing the wildlife in Port Braid hadn't yet come this far. Here the wildlife was slow-moving, self-assured. There seemed to be no rush to track down dinner. There were spare hours to examine the curiosities in their lives. The bear cubs splashed in the water, jumped on one another, played tag around fallen stumps. The mother grizzly, the muscles under her cinnamon coat rolling in waves as she swiped, wandered around for almost an hour before catching a flapping fish. She ripped its skin off in a fluid motion and bit into its flesh. Once she and the cubs were done eating, the three disappeared back into the bush.

Marty, Ian and Julie drank beer and enjoyed the slow breeze. The day was surreal to Julie, and it soon felt as though the conversation with her father had never happened. He acted exactly like himself. Like the Marty she'd always known. Never smiling but always joking.

Ian drove them back to Port Braid in the late afternoon. They smelled the town before they saw the familiar docks and bays. On Tallicurn Beach the police tape still surrounded the whale, and there was the campsite Alan had talked about, that belonged to Marjory and Lisa, though the two were absent from the scene. The whale appeared darker now, almost black. Where Julie had split the thing, the dark intestines spilled onto the sand. Scavenging birds hopped around the beach. The seagulls seemed to have lost interest and now flew farther out to sea.

Marty had been right about the tide and the rockfish. As the ocean water had come in, it had lifted the rockfish off the sand. Many of them, though, must have been too far gone. The orange bodies of the fish floated on the surface.

The boat drifted through the bobbing bodies of the fish. When they got close enough to the dock, Marty stepped out and helped Ian tie off the boat. Julie waited until all the knots were secured and then passed the cooler off the boat. Marty offered a fish-and-chips meal to Ian for the day out. "You coming too, Jules?"

She shook her head. "I'm just gonna walk around for a bit."

She ate dinner alone at The Lion's Den. A server chewing gum and wearing a button-up dress slapped her all-day breakfast onto the table. Julie wondered if maybe they went to high school together, and if she'd made a bad impression.

The conversation with Marty played in her mind. Perhaps the damage that JLL inflicted could be undone just as fast. But there was also the chance that this was the new normal, and like some sick people needed IV drips, Marty would need regular supervision. She pictured a future with secret cameras installed around the house. A nurse paid to drop in at random hours. A compulsory treatment program. Her moving back to Port Braid permanently. She wondered how far she'd go.

She chewed her slices of bacon, and when that was done, she asked the server for a pitcher of beer. This elicited a raised eyebrow, but soon afterward the pitcher was slammed down on the table. Foam piled over the sides.

She drank pint after pint as the other dinner customers came and went. High school troupes, young families, older couples. The Lion's Den served every living generation of Port Braidians, where The Halibut tended to cater to outsiders. This was where Julie and her friends came when she was young. She remembered Billy Poole stealing salt shakers, and her friend Helena hiding rubber spiders from the dollar store amongst the packets of sugar. She finished off the pitcher, licked the last bubbles of foam from the spout. When the server came over, she ordered one more. A moment later she was back, but with only a pint glass and the bill.

"This is all you get," the server said. "Don't need you filling up the toilet bowl."

The numbers on the bill blurred, and she became anxious about how drunk she'd be once she stood up. Sitting still felt like the only safety. She sipped her pint as slowly as she could. The familiar paintings on the wall—the grizzlies fishing in front of a strangely stunted mountain, the little girl on the tricycle with the black eyes—brought uncomfortable familiarity. How many times she had seen these pictures. Loved them as a child, pointed out their details to her father or Alan as she ate chips. Made fun of them as a teenager for their inaccuracies and the ineptitude of the painter. And now, hated them for their lazy nostalgia. For being inadequate. Nothing was ever enough.

By the time she finished the pint, the last few people sitting at the bar had wandered out. The server came over and took Julie's bag from the back of the chair, fished for her wallet, took enough cash to cover the tab. She held up the bills.

"You want change?" she asked.

Julie shook her head, pushed herself up from the table. Out on the street the sidewalk waved in front of her. Particles of whale swam in the air, but otherwise it was dry, warm. The stars above pulsed on, off. The sharp stab of Marty's words was fading into an ache that rested on her sternum. A couple of street lights flicked on and off as she walked down the main street. Most shops' lights were off, so in their windows Julie could watch her hunched reflection stumble toward home.

The lights in Alan's store were on. From across the street, she saw him moving around in his shop. He was dusting the stereos at the back. He moved in rhythm to some song, flicking the duster like he was playing drums. Julie tapped on the glass. He squinted, trying to make out her features, then his face was overcome with enthusiasm. He jogged over, opened the door. David Bowie's "Kooks" played inside the store.

"Julie Bird." He looked her up and down. "You kind of look like shit."

He pulled her inside and swung her into a waltz. He spun and dipped her as Bowie sung about throwing homework on the fire. She laughed as Alan lip-synched, over-enunciated the lyrics. He danced them over to the glass counter and hoisted her up. The room continued to spin. He opened a couple of beers for them. It seemed to be the same pack as the previous time. Julie took a sip.

"Why'd it take you so long?" Alan asked.

"Been preoccupied."

"Well, I've been bored out of my mind."

"You went to some shows," Julie said.

"Yeah. You never came!"

Julie shrugged. "Kooks" came to a close and "Quicksand" came on next.

"*Hunky Dory?*" Julie asked.

"Always thought it was the best one. Hey, actually, with you here I can try my experiment." Alan switched off the music and went to the back. He returned with five copies of the album—a tape, CD and the LP that had been playing. There were two other albums—a greatest hits CD and a live concert DVD recording. All of them had the song "Life on Mars?" and Alan wanted to play them all at the same time.

Julie held the dusty CD case in her hand. "This is stupid, Alan."

"Yeah, I know."

Julie drank her beer and watched him work. He rolled out five TV stands, set them up in a circle in the middle of the store and dragged an extension cord to each one. He then fetched the boom box, two CD players, the record player and a small TV with a built-in DVD player. When he was done, he gestured for her to come over with the albums.

They loaded them into the five machines and queued the DVD up to the right chapter. The colour on the television was several shades too vibrant, the honeyed tones of the '70s concert coming through as primary colours.

"Now," Alan said, "the intro on the DVD version's a bit longer. I think there might be some talking. So we gotta wait until the first chord to press play on the other ones. You're in charge of the CDs. I'll do the vinyl because I'll have a hand free after I get the DVD rolling. Julie, hon, we're going to get this first try."

"OK."

"I mean it. We have to."

"OK, Alan."

"There are no second chances."

She gave him a shove.

"Ready?" He pressed play on the DVD. Audience cheering from the last track faded away. The band moved around the stage. Bowie looked at his feet, out at the audience. Then the first chord struck. Alan dropped the needle on the vinyl track, pressed play on the boom box, Julie started up the CD players. And there they were, the five Bowies, their voices only milliseconds apart, a dissonant fullness to the sound, the stilted need in his voice magnified, reassured by a choir of selves.

Alan cranked the volume on the devices and leapt from the circle of electronics. He grabbed a microphone from the stand and began to sing. Julie used her beer bottle to sing into. They cried out with the chorus—sailors, fighting—dropped to their knees at peaks, begged with their arms at lows.

The DVD version crept further from the other tracks until the song descended into chaos. When it ended, Julie and Alan leaned panting over the glass counter. Alan turned off the machines. Julie thought she might throw up on the glass. The cameras under the display spun. They sat in silence for a while, sipping on their drinks.

"Alan. Do you see Marty as being suicidal?" Julie asked.

Alan stared at her with his mouth turned down. With the music off in the shop, the hum of the air conditioning took over.

Finally, he said, "I've always thought of myself as a sort of emergency surrogate. But. He's doing good."

"How's that?"

Alan straightened his back. "Your mother used to come in here, you know. So we could chat. I guess Marty was, uh, well, you called it suicidal. He was like that back then." Alan spun his bottle. "He was talking about it a lot, I guess. But he's good now, don't you think?"

"But he was talking about it a lot?" she asked. The ache in her sternum deepened.

"Then you came along. And he talked about it less. And then, you know."

"She died."

"He stopped talking about it, though."

"Because of me."

Alan gave a sad smile. "You're worth it, you know. But I was always here for backup."

They had another beer together and talked about the town, and then Julie had to hear Alan's critical comparison of the JLL concerts. They discussed Julie's life in Vancouver. Whether a green thumb could be learned or whether she was doomed as a landscaper. It was two in the morning when she felt ready to go.

She felt like she was both hungover from her first drinks of the day on Ian's boat and still on the trajectory to getting drunker. She wanted to fall asleep in the back of the beater in the woods, by Marker 34. She wanted to connect with the version of Marty that existed in the era of that car.

In the morning everything would be clearer. They would talk about it, at least. What he wanted to do. She could be open.

She asked Alan to give her a ride to Marker 34, saying that her friend lived there and she was spending the night. She grabbed a flashlight and a pack of batteries from the shop while Alan was searching for his car keys. She hugged him goodnight as she got out by the highway marker.

"It's just up the drive?" he asked.

It was, she told him. She watched his taillights disappear in the distance.

Even at nighttime, when the cooler air flowed over the road, the Cold Forest still felt chilled. The cold air and the hike sobered her. She traipsed through the bush, shining the beam of the flashlight on tree trunks and brambles, looking for the glowing eyes of wildlife, until she came to the old car with the New Mexico plates. The trunk was open. She shone the flashlight into its cavern.

The bones were gone. Only the outline of fur remained. Even the dislodged claws had been collected. Julie looked around as though the culprit might be right there. She ran a finger through the loose hair and searched the ground. Ferns coated the forest floor. She swept them aside to look underneath. A glint of white poked through. A single dog rib, the lone survivor of the theft.

"What happened to the rest of you?"

She tossed the bone back in the trunk, where it belonged, and shut the lid. In the driver's seat, she found a note. It read only *I O U Midge bones.*

nineteen

MICE

Marianne Faithfull is my spirit, sacrificial lamb wrapped
in a sheepskin. Living heroine in London's alleys then
causing the defenestrated suicide of a man who loves
her more than a rehab centre's walls can contain. Left
with a voice that sings it all without the details.

Marty woke from a dream. The clock read 2:39.

The dream had been a bad one. His heart rate was raised and his stump throbbed. He sat up and looked at the sheet of black in front of the wall. His blackout curtains let nothing in.

Midge was in the dream. That's all he could remember of it.

The darkness around Marty pulsed with some outside noise. As he slid into consciousness he identified it as tapping. Tapping from somewhere inside the house. A dripping pipe or a faulty wire or a dog's toenails on hardwood.

In the dream, he and Midge walked through an Ontario forest. The path was wide and scattered with gravel. Somewhere near civilization. Sumacs lined the way with their red thumbs pointing the direction to go. Looking forward, the path had no end and no curves.

Marty rubbed his eyes and cracked his neck—crunching one way then the next. He lay back down and the darkness wrapped around the back of his eyes. He could go back to sleep with lids open, the darkness was so complete.

Midge had plodded by his side and her ribcage and legs were filled out—there had been nothing skeletal about them. The air flowed warm around the two of them and jangled the leaves of silver white willows. Poplar fluff came down like late winter snow, fat and soft. Whip marks from Toronto planes streaked the sky. In his dream, he could hear a plane and so could Midge, because they looked up at the sky together—both at the wrong spot—focusing on where the plane had been instead of where it was, closer now to its destination and farther from the invisible dog and man on the ground. Marty had two hands. But then, he always did in dreams, except in ones where he was losing one.

He placed his feet on the floor and the cold penetrated his skin. His eyes were caked with sleep. He let them stay closed until he was standing.

The tapping had a hollow quality. It could have been originating from wood or metal depending on how far away it was. It could be the sink or it could be a peg-legged man walking on rail ties a half-mile away. It could be the subject of that childhood campfire story about a hook-handed murderer knocking on the door—metal hook on wood frame—come to get him fifty years too late. It could be Midge walking in circles in the living room, doing her rounds to make sure the space was safe so that Marty could sleep soundly on his last night before going to the Gulf.

He loved when he dreamt about Midge, even though the dreams usually thinned to panic. Last year, he dreamt that he was a child and that there was a war in his house, and Midge was there though she hadn't been born yet. Young Marty hid under the dining room table and Midge sat there, and she moved her mouth and said, "Marty, this is all a dream. You can wake up if you like," and he was so thankful to that talking dog. That one wasn't a frightening dream, but stressful still. But this last dream seemed peaceful. There were birds, he believed. Planes and birds. So many things to look up at. A hawk followed behind them. As they walked, they kicked up mice, and the mice tumbled out of the ground and the hawk came down to get them. Yes, that's right. Mice churned from the ground. Midge and Marty were like giant ships dredging up rodents instead of fish, in a field instead of the Great Lakes.

Marty laughed, both at finally remembering the dream and at the ridiculousness of it. He stood and looked through the black toward the ceiling, trying to pinpoint the source of the noise. It seemed to come from everywhere. Outside the bedroom, each time he turned his head, the source seemed to change. First, the living room resonated with the sound, then the shower, then the cupboards.

He flipped on the kitchen light and watched the second hand of the wall clock tick in conjunction with the sound. There were two taps for every three seconds. Marty looked toward Julie's door.

There was something else.

The dream didn't end on the Ontario path or in a field of churned mice. They moved on. There was maybe a deer that Midge ripped apart, or maybe Midge found a ripped-apart deer. She had a sticky face at one point, with bits like candy-apple shell plastered in her fur. The hawk came down and grabbed mice and their tails kept falling in his path. There was a dark small place at the end of the dream. He shook his head to push it out.

Dark small places often entered his dreams. For part of the dream he wasn't himself. He was panting, and thirsty, and the small space moved up and down in jolts.

Marty visited Julie's dirty raccoon in the backyard to escape the untraceable tapping. The night air blew cool on his face. The animal walked circles in its pen and chattered a message to him in its truncated language. But at least the sound came from a definite source. The raccoon grasped the wires of its pen. Marty never liked raccoon paws. To him it looked as though someone had taken a human hand, smoked it and dried it, somehow turning it both stronger and more sensitive, able to locate and pluck fish in ice water.

Marty leaned over the cage and the raccoon gazed up at him. It'd grown a lot since Julie first dragged it home.

It chattered louder. It held the cage tight and the wire dug into its fur.

"Easy, little man." Marty put the tip of his prosthesis through the wire. The raccoon recoiled and bared its teeth. Fear pouring from its incisors. Then the animal spun on itself and grabbed hold of its tail. It clamped down.

When she turned eight, Julie became determined to get a pet. There were baby sparrows, voles that fell in the gap by the basement window. And every time Marty took them out at night, told Julie they healed or died or whatever it took. And on birthdays, for five years, she expected a puppy. He told her about imaginary allergies, financial troubles. He accused her of being incapable of walking the damn dog every night. But despite all that, despite fighting to keep non-humans out of their home for her entire childhood, it was still closing in. He had always been the black hole. He drew destruction toward himself, crushed to death everyone that got too close. The way that blue whale beelined for shore. Midge.

Marty backed away from the raccoon. When he closed the patio door behind himself, the *tap-tap* resumed.

The items in the kitchen glowed too brightly, like he'd eaten mushrooms sometime during the night. The microwave clock emanated abduction green, and its exterior hummed as though it was running. The tiles under his feet hummed too. And the fridge. The oven was trustworthy. It was silent and steady, and Marty focused on it to bring everything else to a level plane. Still, the tapping continued, but now from the other end of the house.

Marty stopped at Julie's door. Passing that was passing a threshold, and then he might need to keep going. He listened at the door for the sound of her breathing, but all he could hear were the taps. If there was life inside that room, it was drowned out. He placed a hand on the door and pushed. She wasn't there. The bed was empty. Julie asleep on that mattress, breathing, was an ageless image in his mind. Constant and outside the flow of time. In his first years of single fatherhood, he would stand in this threshold and listen to the rhythm of her breathing, proud the little thing was still alive. In the day, he had fed her, taken her to school, answered her questions. He felt himself the ventilator machine that pumped oxygen into her lungs. If he slowed down, if he allowed himself to stay in bed, the little creature would fade.

Marty slipped into the room and stood above the tangled empty sheets. A couple of times since she'd been back, he'd looked in to check on her. Since she'd come home, Julie's breathing had changed, that was the only difference from when she was a kid. It was more self-assured. But other than that, the smell of her room, the shape in the blankets, the mess of hair, she could have been four years old. Every night she slept in flamingo position, always had, one leg crooked up, the other straight shot down. There she'd be, fully formed. Able to inhale on her own, out of sight from him, far away from Port Braid. He wished she were there now.

The tapping sound pulsed against his eardrums, its origin still elusive. He thought about flipping on the television to block the sound, hoping for more reruns. He always preferred the reruns because the truth was, when he watched something new and good, it made him feel depressed. Every time he watched an episode it was closer to being over. It was the same watching his kid grow up. Seeing Julie learn to read, the first few times she sounded out words, it made him happy. But not happy enough. Hiding behind the pride he felt, it always hurt to see one more thing done.

The strange tapping sounded like raindrops falling around him, bouncing off the stove and tiles. He didn't want to drown it out. He wanted to track it.

He checked the radiators, the mess of cords behind the television. Or—what if—it could be Jennie Lee Lewis who pinpointed the attic floor spot that lined up with his position in the house, and who tapped it with a knuckle. *Hi, hi, hi. I'm above your head. Right here. Hi.* But then, would it be so regular? Wouldn't she just knock? Wouldn't she just come down to his door?

Except that would mean she had to walk past Julie's door. Just like, if he were to go and see if the tapping was coming from the attic, he too would first have to walk past Julie's door. He couldn't stop in to watch her breathe.

When Julie was a child, she insisted her door stay open, because if it was closed, it would lock the ghosts in. No monsters under the bed or witches in the closet for this one. And ghosts were fine, young Julie explained, so long as they could pass through the room easily. It was when they got stuck that they got mad. He always wondered if the obsession with ghost etiquette started with Brenda's death.

The other advantage of keeping the door open was that the sound of the television emanating from the living room always put Julie to sleep. That's how he put her to bed instead of good night stories. Sometimes he sat in front of the TV, put a pillow on his lap, and she fell asleep there. Then he would carry her to bed. If she woke up and the door to her room was closed, there was screaming. He was always amazed at the things that could make kids weep. It all has to do with how much tragedy you've experienced. His kid had come across none. Something like a closed door could set her off.

Midge had been in that small space in his dream. That was her panting. Or they were both there. It was hot and the air had been breathed in too many times. All they wanted was to be back in the field with a hawk diving behind them. Be in that field and stretch their legs out full length. Just once more. There was hunger in the small space and there was recycled air. Their lungs shrunk to prunes.

Marty tapped on the side of his skull. *Out, dreams.* He passed the threshold.

Past Julie's room, getting to the attic entranceway was easy. That's where the sound was coming from. It could only be above his head. Otherwise, as he walked through the downstairs, the pitch of the sound should have changed. It was a constant drum, a life-swallowing pacemaker. Marty put his two fingers on his stump wrist and found the same rhythm.

The ladder to the attic had been retracted and a string hung down from the closed hatch.

JLL might be out. She could be running wild.

He took the attic ladder string between his fingers. He pulled down slowly to prevent any creaking. The wood ladder slid down to the floor.

The tapping got louder. It didn't hesitate or accelerate. The light up there was off.

Marty noticed something new in the sound. What was hollow before started to fill out. It was more than a tap. There was more to it. He shut his eyes and listened. It pretended at first to be a double tap. Each drip followed by a back-up.

Tap-ap

Tap-ap

Tap-ap

But it wasn't that either. The second part was softer. Someone whispered after each hard consonant of sound.

Tap-shh

Tap-shh

It comforted him, the second part of the sound. Each tap grated on him, and each follow-up sound brought him calm. He was punched and pet, punched and pet. Marty rose up on the first step of the ladder and the sound sunk deeper.

Tap-shh-sh

He wanted so much to hear what it was saying to him, and so he climbed another rung and stuck his head into the attic. He was a groundhog rising into an unknown field. He was the mouse being churned from the earth.

Its voice became clearer and Marty thought that he could make out words, but the hum of appliances downstairs stepped in the way. Marty slid onto the attic floor and turned onto his back, like he was stargazing, except that he was looking for points of sound instead of points of light.

It told him about the small space from his dream. He could be in that small space now. He couldn't get his knees to straighten. This was a small space and there wasn't enough air to breathe.

Tap-shhhshhhh

He reached his hand to where the hole should lead back downstairs but it was flat and soft. Not carpet exactly, but something like it. He felt along his own body. His hand went up and over the contour of his stretched ribs.

The sound kept him pinned to the ground. It pinpointed his wrists and ankles and he was tied to the spot. He didn't want to listen to it anymore. The things that it had to say were wrong and they were unfair. The sound had lured him into a place he'd just escaped in his dream.

It was also familiar. He'd had this same nightmare again and again but this was the first time that he remembered its entirety.

The small space moved up and down, responding to bumps and jostles from outside it. He was a passenger inside of a cramped cavern. He was at the whim of someone else's journey.

He tossed around the hard surface and the voices pounded into his head.

He did this.

"No," he said.

Then, all movement stopped. He heard a sound, but it wasn't tapping. It was a voice. Marty moaned. The voice came again.

"What in shit's name are you doing? Marty. Marty, what in *shit*'s name. Are. You. Doing."

He sat up. A lamp with a pink shade illuminated the far end of the attic. It was perched on a milk crate, and under its grandmotherly light was Jennie Lee Lewis, who sat upright and naked in a pile of sheets on the futon.

Marty looked around. Across the ground, socks and music sheets formed a unified layer.

"I must have been sleepwalking."

"Do you usually sleepwalk into women's rooms at two in the morning?"

"Yes. All the time." He hoped his smile was convincing.

"Come here."

"What?"

She made no effort to cover herself up.

"Come the fuck here."

He did what he was told and sat on the end of the futon. He faced the wall so he could better control his line of vision.

JLL reached over and touched his back. He realized he wasn't wearing a shirt. He was wearing the ratty Molson Canadian boxers that he got free from a pack of beer twenty-odd years ago. There might be a hole in the back, he couldn't remember, but just in case he resolved to remain seated.

Here he was in his underwear, in his attic, with another human being, who he was staring at.

Last night's dream stabbed him again.

JLL looked different in the attic. The air around her body felt warm, whereas in The Halibut, even downstairs in this house, the air around her was cold. Her presence invited him.

She grinned. "You're a fucked-up guy."

"Yeah?" He tried to determine if "fucked up" was a compliment from Jennie Lee Lewis.

"You climb up to my room and writhe around on the floor in the black and then you sit on my bed and tell me that you can't feel the sheets. Yeah, you're a pretty fucked-up guy."

Marty took a pinch of his skin between his fingers. *Can't feel the sheets?* It was true. His nerve endings, in his ass and in his thighs, they registered nothing. It was such an astute observation, that the sheets and his skin must be one and the same. The particles of one travelled along with the particles of the other. They did figure eights around his legs and down through the cotton. The threads were woven together just as his skin cells were, everything the same temperature. He hunched forward and concentrated on the feeling of the molecules moving along their paths. His skin and the sheets shared a consistency with the thick darkness that he swam through a few moments before. If the air downstairs was like this, he never noticed it before.

"You all right there, champ?" JLL raised an eyebrow. Marty got on his knees on the bed. He kissed her. JLL positioned herself underneath him and wrapped her hands behind the small of his back. He could feel her hands even if he couldn't feel the sheets.

The two spots just above the waistband of his Molson Canadian boxers glowed with heat. His liver and his kidneys burned. His penis pressed against the boxers. Like a little miracle. Resuscitated after all these years.

She asked him if he was drunk, and he shook his head. She asked him if he was sure and he paused. Shook his head again. "No. No, I didn't drink anything tonight."

She shrugged and climbed on top of him. "This just doesn't seem like something you'd do."

"Really?"

If Julie came home, he knew, she would hear the unmistakable creaks of the futon and the scuffle of the metal frame on the floor-boards. But he couldn't stop himself.

He tried to stay quiet, his lips pressed like they were sewn together. He was a corpse, arms stiff by his sides, avoiding touching the woman rowing on top of him. Pressure built up on his bladder.

Her triangle chin hovered above him, a bird beak pecking into the dim room. He wished he was gone.

When they were finished, Marty lay back and felt his face. JLL laughed.

She turned to him and hugged her pillow. "So, what alternate reality were you in when you crawled up here?"

"I don't know." He looked at the black holes of her eyes. "It started with that nightmare I always get."

"The one you owe me."

"I can't remember it clearly." Marty listened for the tapping noise, but the room sat silent except for his thumping heart.

"You always turn it off."

"It's a nightmare."

"Walk me through it."

The room sunk and swayed. As he told JLL about the dream, his voice reached out to the items in the attic, swept across the floorboards, knocked dust off the window ledge, dipped into JLL's belly button. It dipped into the crevices of the dream too and pulled out invisible details.

JLL listened while he talked about the small space, the dwindling air. She leaned over and rummaged for something under the bed, pulled out a plastic grocery bag and placed it on the bed.

"What's this?" he asked.

The plastic crinkled as she opened it further. Inside was a skull and a pile of bones. He looked at JLL, shook his head, confused.

"Come on, Marty."

His heart seized. Something was off. He scratched his eyebrow. "I don't want to do this."

JLL rested her arm on his stomach. "Tell me what happened to Midge."

Marty reached into the bag and pulled out a vertebra. He turned it over in his hand. Its surface felt fibrous, soft.

"Time to face the truth, huh?"

JLL smiled and rubbed his chest. Marty choked on it. The words broken and far away. "She wouldn't be quiet. That whining. I lost it."

"Keep going," JLL said.

"I put her in the trunk. I forgot about her, didn't I? Her whines were something else to me."

"And what?"

"She was already in there when I drove into Crater Lake."

JLL shrugged.

"At the border I go in to buy some beer, open up the trunk. She's so far gone I can smell her."

Something lay suspended in the shadows, just out of view, but beginning to emerge. "And you're Victoria."

She nodded and shrugged. "I knew you'd get there."

"So Nancy's gone too."

She nodded. A wash of shame filtered through him, the smell of sex hanging in the air. She sat on the edge of the bed with her back turned to him. Her warmth radiated against his skin. Her vertebrae were reminiscent of Midge's curved spine. He ran his finger along them and she recoiled.

She shook her head. Marty focused on a dust bunny in the corner.

"I want you and Julie to look out for each other," he said.

"So you're going."

Marty watched a small spasm below her shoulder blade. It moved a freckle up and down. "Julie hasn't let me go."

She nodded again, still hiding her face. "Don't believe she will, Marty. Not until after."

He fished his boxers from the sheets and slid them back on. He stood. His knees shook under him. "Thanks for the send-off."

She turned toward him. The rose-tinted lamplight warmed her face. "You're welcome."

He returned to his bedroom and packed a small bag. Two pairs of underwear and one spare shirt. No toothbrush, but a vial of mouthwash. He picked up his car keys and inspected the key chain he got from New Orleans with his parents as a teenager. It was a Mardi Gras mask with *Louisiana* printed underneath. Or, rather, *Looisiana*, the *o*'s boobs with perky nipples. He smiled. Couldn't believe he still had the thing.

He got out of the house and into the car. His prosthesis stayed on the stand by the front door.

PART III

Three Days Missing

twenty

HYENA, JACKAL

In the 1800s a stag was chased by hunting dogs and came
to a cliff. It observed the gnashing teeth behind, the pointed
rocks below. It held its antlers high and jumped. This is
not suicide. Mice with Toxoplasma gondii will walk up to
a cat, beg to be eaten. This is not suicide. When it comes
down with an infectious disease the naked mole rat leaves the
safety of the colony. Not suicide. We, we know the results
we aim for. How might our actions differ if we didn't?

The plan today, day three, was to search the logging roads. Marty's
vanishing act was only just becoming reality. Day one, she expected
the door to open, Marty holding a bag of takeaway for them to
share. Day two, she expected a phone call, inquired around town.
Day three, it felt as though he were gone.

She stood by the open door of the shed and looked at the mass of floor mats from long-dead cars, unstrung tennis rackets, tools, and finally found her father's rusted mountain bike. Rust plumed as she yanked the bike out. The chain was a solid oval. She worked the joints one by one with oil to get them to move.

When Julie had found those bones gone from the trunk that night, she had run home, doing everything to keep the sloshing beer in her stomach from escaping her lips. But he had already left. She didn't know that then. She only knew he wasn't home. The car was gone. He was only out. The attic light was on, and Julie found JLL sitting on the bed, looking innocent.

The next morning JLL's bags and tent were gone. The sheets from the futon were balled up on the floor. With JLL gone, the fear deepened. There was no one left in the house to harass. Simple acts like buttering toast or showering felt selfish. Watching television would make her a monster. And so she spent as much time as she could out of the house. Day two, The Halibut was closed, of course. Fran was lingering around the door, looking in the windows, but the place was empty.

On Marty's second day gone, she visited the police station and filed a report. The officer sat across the desk from her, tapping his pen on the paper. He asked, *Hasn't this happened before?* Then she tracked down Ian at the pier. The wind made the masts swing like metronomes. She told him what the police had asked. Julie asked where Marty had been that time.

Ian had looked out at the ocean. "He was just home, kiddo. Avoiding human contact. Locked up in the attic. It all turned out."

Now, day three, she prepared the bike for her search. She changed the tubes, pumped them with air and wheeled the bike into the backyard. When she got around the corner, she saw Bert's head sticking through the corner of the crate. He had managed to pull the chicken wire away from the wood and had pressed his little skull through the opening. He tried to move back as she approached. His ears kept him stuck in the pillory. When she moved his fur to the side, she saw that the wire had dug into the skin. He could have been there all night. She ripped the chicken wire back and scooped Bert up. He squirmed in her arms and his claws dug into her forearm. There wasn't a good spot outside to leave him. She tossed Bert into her bedroom and shut the door.

She hopped on the bike and wobbled down the shoulder of the highway that led out of Port Braid. She hoped to see Marty, but mostly she prepared to come across JLL's orange tent on one of the forgotten back roads. She'd like to burn the tent down.

Julie pedalled down Route 50. The logging roads spread like veins from this main artery, and each of them had to be searched to its tip. The road glowed with heat. Sweat beaded on her face. Light reflected off the pavement, and Julie cursed herself for forgetting sunglasses. The first logging road separated from the highway at Marker 22, and she turned right. The first hundred metres weren't so bad. The packed-down gravel and dirt was sturdy enough for cycling.

She passed by a cleared area where groups of Port Braid teens held bush parties. She remembered coming here a decade ago. Like eagles building a nest, each new generation added on to the site. Beer bottles from different eras collected in the dirt and became a part of the foliage, and campfire and cigarette ash from thousands of drunken nights permeated the air. A faint whiff of puke and teenage lust on the breeze. Past that, the road was less developed. Potholes became the norm and her bike tires kicked up dust as she went deeper into the bush. The bike seat jabbed her crotch. Her tires made sticky contact with the ground.

The path narrowed. The farther she got, the more nature took back the path, until invasive blackberries blocked her from going farther. She picked a few berries and waited for her breathing to quiet. She licked the blood red juice from her fingers.

She tried the next logging road, and the next. Wondered what she was doing. The rutted road rose up steeply in front of her. She pushed on one pedal and the other, straining her back. The chances were nil she would find Marty standing in the middle of some unused road, but there was nothing at home either.

And then the pedals spun with no resistance and the bike stopped. The chain hung off the rear hub. She swore, flipped the bike upside down. Using an alder leaf she tried to ease the chain back onto the gears. She looked around. She was nowhere. This logging road looked exactly like every other one. Patches of deciduous trees, but mostly coniferous. Ferns. Dust. Sun.

After a while the rumble of a vehicle approached. She shielded the sun from her eyes. A pickup truck with a green body and blue doors came around the bend. Billy Poole sat in the driver's seat. He pulled over.

"Hey, Upward Mobility." He winked at her. She threw her bike in the back with the hunting rifles and gear, got in the passenger side and slammed the door.

"Home, driver," she said.

"Mine or yours?"

Julie thought about this for a moment. "Yours."

Billy looked at her from the corner of his eye, no doubt assessing whether she was sassing him. They turned onto the main highway. She watched the yellow lines pass under the centre of the car. He kept glancing at her. She corrected the steering wheel for him. He drove her to his mother's place.

They entered his suite from the separate entrance in the backyard. The unwashed boy smell in the suite was a comfort. For a while she could pretend to be an irresponsible teenager.

Billy plopped himself down on his futon and lay on his side. He made no indication of where she could make herself comfortable so she shoved him over and sat, with slow purpose, right in front of his cock. The first time they had slept together, Billy was relentless, picking at her buttons, sliding his hand down her side. Now she took that role. He looked disinterested. Probably stoned after not shooting any deer. But she set herself single-mindedly to the task. She played with his belt, undid his top three shirt buttons.

He stopped her. "Hey, uh. Isn't your dad missing, or something?"

She retracted her hand. "Yes."

"Do you want to kind of talk to someone about it?"

Julie focused on his Pink Floyd poster. The women's asses were such perfect *w*'s. "Yeah, let's talk about it, Billy." He nodded, too enthusiastic. She raised her eyebrows at him. "You start."

"Well, when did he go missing?"

"Two and a half days ago."

"Has he . . . called?"

She raised her eyebrows further. "No."

"Oh."

"That's not really how 'missing' works."

"Well, where do you think he went?"

"I could ask you the same thing."

"Well." Billy looked up at the Pink Floyd ladies. "You really have no idea? I mean, he's your dad, right?"

"Yes. He's my father."

"Maybe if retraced your . . ."

Julie looked up at his apologetic eyes. She headed for the door.

"Hey, Mensa." Billy sat up on the futon. "I thought we were going to hang out."

"We were."

It was late afternoon when Julie arrived at the bungalow. The sun stung the back of her neck. A wasted day. A useless bike and empty logging roads and a quick fuck gone off the rails. It would have been better to search the province's hotels or legion halls. The shade of the house invited her in, and she felt ready to collapse her head onto her pillow. Her head ached.

The first thing she saw when she opened the bedroom door was a hole in the drywall. Bert's beady eyes peered out. He disappeared into the walls. Pillow fluff was spread across her bedsheets. Her desk leg was chewed halfway through.

"I thought we were friends, Bert."

She could hear his fur rubbing against the plaster as he proceeded behind the wall into the next room. She sat in her office chair and leapt up again. Bert had peed there. In fact, he had peed in a lot of places. Her office chair, her side of the bed, on her day planner and, of course, on her laptop keyboard, which had stinking beads of yellow between the keys.

The raccoon moved deftly around the inner house. His claws clicked along the studs. The clambering sound travelled up to mid-wall. Bert was somewhere along the crown moulding over the living room entranceway. She closed her eyes and covered her ears, but the scratching sound of destruction crept through.

"I am the superior being," she whispered to herself. She'd fed him, housed him, saved him from starvation in the forest. But there was no sense blaming a raccoon for a lack of gratitude. And though the raccoon may inhabit the gap between the interior rooms and the outdoors, the space within was hers. She could own this place. Like an untrained dog she could mark the furniture and houseplants. Where Bert had to scurry and hide, she could move with confidence to any corner of the house, stretch out in the middle of the floor, create a ten-course meal and set it along the dining room table, live like a queen or live in filth. She might already own this place.

All Bert could do was breathe in insulation and snack on dust mites. Eventually, inhaling fiberglass shards would kill him. Then she'd just have to deal with the smell for a while. And the whale had made her a pro at that.

After a while Bert was silent. She suspected that he'd fallen asleep nestled between dead bugs and dust bunnies.

twenty-one

HALIBUT

Freddie Mercury is my saviour, soft-spoken behind
a stage persona that weeps strength. The man with
four octaves, in a power singlet, stirring something
deep in his crowds, is going back to the hotel, sure to
phone home to the cats before his night is done.

It seemed impossible that JLL would have another show. The owner of the bar was missing. The townspeople knew he was gone. JLL was either camping in the forest or back in New Mexico. But the day of the last scheduled performance, the sound of excited voices filled the air.

JLL might be the last connection to Marty's whereabouts, so Julie set herself up in a lawn chair across the street from the restaurant. A group of about fifty revellers milled around the windows. Some of them peered through the glass. Some talked, some shouted. The faces were unfamiliar. New fans from surrounding villages swarmed together with the Port Braiders. More of them rolled down the street from the elementary school, where the yard had turned into a parking lot. Julie couldn't hear what the fans were saying or catch their mood; their voices were agitated and jubilant.

As the crowd condensed and diluted, open passageways appeared so she could see inside The Halibut. The restaurant was dark and still. Chairs sat by tables, waiting to seat invisible diners. Napkins were squared between condiment containers. Clean glasses hung over the bar. It was a frozen scene that stood stoic in front of this frothing crowd.

A disturbance began at the far end of the throng. It resembled an early atom model, some central force, the nucleus, and the electron cloud. There were no discernible orbitals, just a confused swirl of humans. The mass grew and moved toward the front of the restaurant. One form with many parts. One body kept it together.

A gap formed in the crowd, and she saw the central point. Jennie Lee Lewis stood with her arms stretched to the side in a gesture part religious beckoning and part shrug. Julie's skin tightened. She searched the crowd for Marty. Maybe he'd been drawn by her as well.

There were familiar faces in the tumult. The people from the first and second concerts were there—Billy, Marjory and Lisa, plus Ms. Halbert, and even her first-grade teacher. They rattled around the street and bounced off one another's energy. Billy broke free from the rest and took an ornamental rock from the street garden. He felt the weight of it in his hand, then lifted it over his head and whipped it at the window. A star spread across the glass.

Julie stood. Marjory was the next to pick up a rock. She used it like a hammer against the glass. Once, twice. The window shattered down. Bits of glass bounced off the sidewalk, and the crowd cheered.

Julie searched the humans for a distressed man. Someone not celebrating the restaurant's destruction. A ghost of a person, a sunken face, standing still while the others celebrated.

The crowd pushed forward to enter the restaurant through the window. No doubt, JLL led the tickertape parade. From here, Julie could inspect individual faces. No bandanas. No checkered red skin. No Marty. The possibility that he had met up with JLL somewhere in the woods was quashed. She was here and he was gone. His restaurant was alive and he was gone.

The voices of the crowd softened as they put their energy into finding spots to stand. Their bodies rebounded off one another in the small space and they started passing chairs over their heads to be tossed out, to crash on the street in splinters. Those who couldn't fit into the restaurant strained to see the action from the sidewalk. Smaller fans were lifted on the shoulders of muscular ones. They wobbled and surged forward, the lucky few spilling through the broken window and fitting like keys into available gaps.

Julie spotted Ian in the mass. His head bobbed into view now and again as he jumped to see the front of the room, his eyes locked forward. Then, piano began to pour from the restaurant. Julie saw bottles of liquor taken from Marty's stocked bar and passed from person to person.

Marty had created this restaurant for all of them, and already they were celebrating in his absence. And maybe that was the right way to act. If they decided to lock their heads between their knees and weep Marty's name, he would still be missing. Here were people dancing and raising their arms in the air.

Ian, the person who should be most affected, headbanged and

pumped his fist in the air. His facial expression hovered between a grimace and a smile.

Julie sat on the chair and let the music wash over her. She scanned the streets to see if the Jerry Lee Lewis songs would summon her father, a stumbling figure in the dark, saved from self-destruction by a Pied Piper.

She tried to put herself in that place—the place where a missing person still exists in the world. To be the one who disappeared.

She disappeared for a night when she was twelve. Marty had messed up her birthday, so she had an unplanned sleepover at a friend's. While she was missing, she existed. Marty, a missing man, currently saw things, felt things. To glimpse through his eyes once—to know the things his eyes focused on, whether he was indoors or outdoors, whether there were buildings or trees—she would give everything.

The music inside the restaurant hit a crescendo. The heads of the crowd tilted up at the ceiling as JLL's hands thudded against the keys and sent a gruesome mash-up of sounds barrelling down the streets. The streets sounded like Halloween. Julie closed her eyes.

The music stopped. JLL's body was hoisted above her audience. Just like the chairs and the booze, they passed her from person to person. The crowd was sardined enough that her voyage around the room was smooth; she travelled on a conveyor belt of hands. Her arms stuck out stiff and her head cranked to the side, looking for a place to land. Then her arms flopped downward, the muscles in her legs relaxed. From her convex posture, she began to sing again in a low voice, something slower that Julie couldn't make out from her post outside.

There was a smash from the corner of the restaurant. One of the few remaining family photos had been knocked to the ground by the grinding crowd. She saw Billy Poole, his head bobbing, fling his arm and slam another photo into the ground. Cynthia Renalds, one of Marty's regulars, clambered up onto the bar and began dropping glasses onto the floor. People ducked out of the way.

Julie strode toward the bar. If Ian couldn't be bothered to stop this, she would. She would demand that JLL tell her where Marty was. She looked around for something with which she could demand attention and found a crowbar lying in the back of Billy's pickup. She entered The Halibut just as the crowd started singing in a drunk-freshman-style singalong of "High School Confidential."

Julie held the crowbar in the air and yelled, but the voices drowned her out. Only one person looked in her direction, and that was Jennie Lee Lewis. Her mouth gaped and her hair bounced as the crowd passed her around. She had stopped singing but the audience kept going. The song should have been over, but they looped the chorus again and again.

JLL mouthed something, but Julie couldn't make it out. Julie put her hand to her ear. JLL tried again, still meaningless.

"Hey!" Julie yelled again. She waved the crowbar around in the air, but the only response she got was a man reaching over the cash register and nabbing the last framed photo—Ian and the whale—and smashing it to the ground.

Even the people immediately around Julie ignored her existence. Half of them closed their eyes as they sang. Julie got knocked around by hips and swinging shoulders. Finally, the words JLL had mouthed appeared clear in Julie's mind. She saw JLL saying the words without the distraction of dancers, of music, of hysteria in a small town, alone in a bar with her, maybe sipping a martini and looking just over Julie's shoulder to demonstrate her superior knowledge on the subject, explaining that life from now on would march without false legends of her father's strength in the face of anguish, his duty to life, his permanence defined by the things he preserved.

"Piano's a goner," she'd mouthed. Just a moment ago, that's what she mouthed.

Julie looked over to see a woman tearing up the washroom postcards and rolling strips into tiny balls, feeding them into her mouth one by one. Billy's approach was more violent. He tore panels from the bar and split them in two with his boot, proclaiming his success with a wolf howl each time. The music became less like a song and more like a sound experiment of howls and barks and caws. The crowbar was pried from Julie's hand.

It was passed over the heads of three men. Julie jumped to reach for it, felt like a child as she did. It was passed forward and placed in the hand of JLL, who now stood back at the mike. Everyone, even those most dedicated to closed-eye dancing, stared at her with comic anticipation, but JLL simply passed the crowbar on to Billy, who held it up and flexed his bicep. He brought it down on the keys of the piano.

A mashed sound rang out, and Julie sank to her knees. The crotches of audience members crowded in and she could smell the stench of sweat and sex. She heard another crack and the splintering of wood, and she covered her ears. Someone stepped on her thigh and another dancer thumped a knee against the back of her neck. They howled in a unified voice every time the crowbar came down. They were taking turns at its destruction, she knew. They were passing around the pleasure.

Her eyes were pressed shut, but hot tears flowed out. She grabbed someone's pant leg to stop their knee from banging her shoulder. A hand reached down and hooked under her armpit, dragged her to her feet.

JLL's face met hers. She yelled over the noise. "You OK?"

Julie shook her head. JLL slipped an arm around Julie's shoulders and escorted her outside. The audience was so wrapped in their singalong that the two slipped out without a break in the gaiety.

Outside, cool air and whale scent flowed around them. JLL led her around the corner, and they sat in the alley. Sobs shook Julie's shoulders. An intense feeling of loneliness descended on her as JLL stroked her hair. There was no one to argue with, no wrongs to be corrected.

Julie looked up at the clouds blowing under the stars. "I just want to tell him Godspeed."

JLL pulled a piece of Julie's hair behind her ear. "Truly?"

Julie nodded, crossed her heart.

"I had an idea of where he might've went," JLL said.

"Where do we go?" Julie asked.

"It's out of town. Can we take the raccoon?"

"The raccoon is living in the walls now."

JLL squinted at her. "In the walls?"

"Yeah. Lost him to the walls."

"That can't be good."

"It's not great."

twenty-two

DOG BONES

When the west coast was run by areas of monopoly—that is, regions carefully managed by the Heiltsuk, Kwakwaka'wakw, Tlingit, Haida, Nuu-chah-nulth, and Tsimshian people— species' numbers were maintained. And then, with competition between the North West and Hudson Bay companies, the free market sent individual trappers—European, First Nations, Russian, no matter—into the bush to do their damage. That's where the million otter deaths come from. Extirpated. But as those Nations have reasserted territorial rights, the sea otters have reemerged from the waves.

They slept that night in the bungalow. Within his short residency, Bert had destroyed the place. The bedsheets were a mess of raccoon piss and tubes of feces. Bert had emptied the trashcan and spilled apple cores and discarded Post-its across the carpet. They didn't try to clean any of it before going to sleep.

Instead of climbing up to the attic, JLL fell asleep curled into one of the La-Z-Boys.

When Julie came out in the morning, JLL was already in hunter mode, her posture lowered. She had looped fishing line through the handle of a broom. She padded between rooms, listening to the drywall. At a large hole over Julie's bed, she stopped.

JLL handed the broom contraption to Julie and had her position the loop over the circumference of the hole.

JLL signalled for Julie to stay there. Then she turned off the lights.

By the second drywall hole in the bedroom, JLL's determined gaze was illuminated by her lighter. She lit up a piece of paper and blew smoke into the hole. When the flames licked too close to her hand, she dropped the paper into a tray full of water. She repeated this several times, dousing the flames once they got too large. Julie's heart pounded with the thought of twisting the little beast's neck.

On the fourth burning piece of paper, Bert flew from the hole. The fishing line noose tightened around Bert's belly, caught in his rolls of fat. Bert flung his body around and tried to bite Julie, but she held him at length with the broom handle.

Ungrateful little fucker.

While JLL worked on subduing the raccoon, Julie paid another visit to Alan at his store to ask whether she could use his car for the Marty hunt. Before she finished explaining her reasons, Alan was fishing in his pocket for the keys. He didn't hesitate handing them over. "I was waiting for the day you'd ask to borrow my car."

Alan's Cadillac was parked down the street. Its headlights were like grasshopper eyes, and the front seats were one long leather couch. The steering wheel reminded her of the one on Ian's boat.

JLL was standing in front of the bungalow, hugging Bert, when Julie pulled up. She stopped in the middle of the street.

"Nice ride," JLL said.

They blocked the passage from the back seat to the front with chicken wire they taped to the leather. They packed water, camping gear, un-raccoon-tarnished food from the fridge. They also brought the bag of Midge's bones, to be deposited where they'd been found.

"Why do you want the raccoon to come?" Julie asked.

"I think he's cool."

Julie looked again at her pet raccoon, who tried to pull at loose threads on the seats. She tried to think of him as cool, perhaps with sunglasses and a leather vest.

They drove east. As they passed through town, Julie noticed that the people in Port Braid were no longer walking around covering their faces. The town no longer used oxygen. It breathed whale. The rot had settled fully into the pores of the town, a steam that softened the residents' skin and replaced their oils with its own. An invisible temper, altering behaviour. Instead of chatting on street corners, people dipped into shops, got what they needed and went home. They walked with glazed expressions. Their focus was single-minded. She couldn't wait to get out of here, and she hoped JLL was right that Marty was already gone from this place.

JLL rested her feet on the dash and smoked a cigarette out the window. Bert fell asleep in the back seat, or at least he stopped tearing the shit out of it.

JLL's cigarette ashes tumbled down the side of the car. Marker 34 approached on the right. Julie pulled the car onto the shoulder, and the cedars slowed their procession to a crawl.

Julie put on the parking brake, grabbed the bag of bones. "Come with me."

"You need me to hold your hand?" JLL scratched her eyebrow, looked at Julie. "Fine." She blew smoke toward the cedar tops. The glowing tip of her smoke already kissed the filter. She tossed her butt out the window.

Before they entered the woods, Julie took a rib from the bag and placed it on the front seat.

"For good luck," she said. Perhaps she wanted another companion in the Cadillac to take some of the pressure off her dealings with JLL. Another party to break the silence now and again. The bone could say, *Hey, does anyone want to hear a joke?* And JLL and Julie would give each other a knowing look and indulge the bone.

What did the monkey say when he caught his tail in a revolving door?

Here, Julie would chime in.

I don't know, Bones. What did he say?

It won't be long now.

And JLL would take care of most of the laughing, but of course Julie would help out too.

And then maybe all of their muscles would relax and they would sit back in the car seats, blare the music, and maybe Bones would stick her head out the window to smell the northern air, and say, *This is so nice. I thought I was going to be in that trunk forever.* If Bones could hang her tongue out, she would do that, and slobber would dot the outside of the car.

Or, more likely, Bones would get locked in the back with Bert, because having a bone in your back seat beside your luggage might be frowned upon by police when she was pulled over for speeding. And who's to say that Bones's life with Julie would be any better than her life in the forest? Julie would have to put in an effort to make sure it was.

Entering the forest felt like sinking into a pillow. The air softened and sounds were muffled between the branches of oaks and broadleaf maple. The sound of insects could easily be mistaken for cotton brushing against your ears, broken by the sound of JLL's and Julie's plodding. They traipsed through the underbrush, following the path from Julie's last couple of trips.

At the beater, she pressed the trunk release. As she lifted the lid, the small pile of dog hair rearranged itself. Using the bones in the bag, Julie reassembled the skeleton as best she could. She no longer wanted the dog buried in the ground. Or at least not yet. JLL stood by the car with her hand on the hood. She circled around the vehicle, tracing the lines of scratches and dents. Vines held the back door shut, but JLL tore them away the yanked the door open. She sat in the back seat.

"So this was your mom's," Julie said.

"Yeah, no shit." She ran a hand along the upholstery and searched the pockets on the back of the seats. "The three of us used to drive around, you know."

An icy current travelled up Julie's shirt. She got in the back seat with JLL, who traced something with her finger.

"I used to carve things into the leather on the back of the driver's seat. I'd stop whenever I saw eyes in the rearview mirror. Check it out."

Julie inspected the seat. There were some scratches, but mostly the material had disintegrated. The leather peeled around a name.

"Victor," Julie said.

"Yeah, 'Victor,' dumb shit." JLL smiled, punched Julie's arm. "Maybe that's who I should have been. Can we go now?"

"You don't want to say goodbye to your mother's car?"

"You know. She met Ralph Edwards when she was driving this thing once. This gameshow host. Just before he died. She was driving away from the annual festival, and she passed him walking along the shoulder. They chatted through the window. She used to tell that story at drive-through windows, say, *I talked to Ralph Edwards just like me and you are talking*. It was so dumb. But your dad stole that story." JLL looked through the windshield. "You know she asked about him when she was dying?"

"Him?"

"Your dad. Not Ralph Edwards. Some idiot she knew twenty-six years before. I guess because he was supposed to accompany her to the other side. Fucking Midge."

The ground held Julie's gaze. Moss enveloped small rocks and spread as a lush carpet halfway up the trees. Should she stay there long enough, it would crawl up her legs too. She spoke softly. "But you got to be with her when she died."

"I'm helping you get to him, aren't I?" JLL asked. She scratched her eyebrow. "Curious. You say you're letting him do it. Have you started grieving?"

Julie thought about it for a moment. "No. I don't even know what it'll be like. And there's still this big thing that has to be done."

"Finding him."

Julie nodded.

"You never grieved for your mom," JLL said.

"Too young."

"Well, it's shit," JLL said. "You keep thinking it's going to be over. Then you find something of theirs." She tapped the headrest in front of her. "And it sucker-punches you."

The air in this part of the forest hung cold and the boughs overhead blocked out all light. It was a world covered by prescription sunglasses, a layer of dark separating eyes from the objects they tried to focus on.

Julie wanted to check one more place before she and JLL left. She told JLL she'd be back. As she walked away, from the corner of her eye, she saw JLL take a rock from the ground and hold it high above her head. She slammed it down on the rear window and the window shattered across the back seat. The sound rang through the forest. JLL's shoulders rose and fell. The pieces rained down into the ferns. Looked like it felt good.

A wash of cold ran over Julie's legs. After a while she came to a thin dirt path. Here the cold current ran close to the ground. As she penetrated deeper into the forest, the sun's rays lost their angle, the current overtook her body and she shivered. Figures of trees blended together. Julie's eyes adjusted, and she was able to see the dirt path splitting the forest in two. The path ran in two strips with a grass mound in the middle. Julie chose the one on the left and went forward.

The pond was somewhere around here, the place where Marty had taught her to swim away from the town's judging eyes. She was never exactly sure where to turn. Four years had passed since she'd last checked on it, and that was just to see if childhood sights were still the same. Most things shrank sometime between the past and present, and the pond had been the same.

She rubbed her arms as she walked. It was amazing that a short distance away it was a summer day. Goosebumps pricked from her skin. The path grew smaller and disappeared into a point. A frog sang somewhere to the left—its voice distorted and strange—and Julie figured that was where the pond was, so she rolled down her pant legs and stepped into the underbrush. She traipsed through until her feet sank into mud. Julie reached over and broke a few branches off a nearby tree and snapped them over her knee. Mosquitoes swarmed in a cloud around her ankles and neck. She laid the branch pieces in parallel lines in front of to use as a platform. The frog song was clearer now, and she could make out both the high-pitched creak of small ones and the low grinding tune of bullfrogs.

The pond appeared in front of her. The edges of the water used to reach farther back. A line of stones marked its former circumference. Every time she came here, it was a bit smaller. Evaporation was beating out rain. There were fewer frogs too. It used to be deafening.

A story popped into her head from *National Geographic*, that certain songbirds were near extinction in Italy, Egypt, Albania. Songbird hunting is a sport. Songbirds are like fish to some people, the article said. Here, we feel no emotion over killing fish. Though, people there were starting to notice the absence of birdsong. In some ways, Julie wished the songbirds would go extinct. And the frogs. And that the oceans would empty. So people could understand what they'd done. Regret would be so cathartic.

The pond hadn't been so brown before, either. The mud concentrated as the water shrank. A beam of sunlight broke through the foliage and lit up a spot in the centre. The branch of an oak tree reached across the pond and a ratty piece of rope dangled from it. It used to be a swing to drop into the water. The rope hung perfectly straight, with a few loose threads grazing the surface of the water. Several dead oak leaves floated on the surface, along with two bloated frog bodies. Julie took a deep breath and swatted at the mosquitoes. Her lungs tightened as she looked at the empty scene. She thought she might choke, so she screamed. "Marty!"

The frogs stopped singing, then started up again one by one. First the small and then the big.

"Mar-ty!"

Again they stopped. They took longer to get back into their rhythm.

"Marty! Fuck!"

This time, the frogs stayed silent.

Julie looked around and realized that nobody was coming. Not even JLL was going to walk over and tell her to stop being stupid.

She reached down and dipped a hand into the water. It was warm like a bath, at least compared to the rest of the forest. It reminded Julie of stove-heated milk and she wanted to be in it. The memory of being here with Marty—her eggbeater legs, his portable radio playing classic rock, the giant towel waiting, which he'd wrap around her like she was a burrito—felt distant. She could name the memory's parts, see the pieces one by one, but she craved to be inside of it, to experience the emotions the memory was supposed to supply.

She looked around and wiggled out of her jeans, shoes and underwear. She tied her shirt into a knot around her belly button and took a step into the water. She scooped out the dead frogs and tossed them aside, sure to avoid looking in their clouded eyes.

Mud engulfed her foot and pulled her in another step. She walked in further, having to yank each foot out as it got swallowed by mud and trapped by old roots. She got deep enough that the brown water touched her crotch and crept into her pubic hair. It tickled and Julie retreated a few steps into the patch of light that shone on the water. Here, she was the right temperature. The forest wafted cold air over her, but the sun and the water fought hard enough to keep her warm. Maybe there was hot spring water leaking into the pond. As soon as she left here, she knew, she would freeze again.

Julie stripped off her shirt, tossed it in the direction of her other clothes and sat in the water. The distinct smell of plant rot enveloped her. The pond water had a quality thicker than other water, and she enjoyed the feeling of it behind her knees, on her mosquito-bitten ankles, and seeping into her armpits. She floated on her back for a while and paddled from end to end. The muscles in her face relaxed and pushed Marty out of her mind.

But he hung there. With her eyes closed, her father lay in a pool that hovered above her head. There was a point somewhere above the pool that served as a rotation point, flipping the pool and the moss and the rocks above her head, and switching the person in the pool from being herself to Marty. Instead of cradling him, the water held him up. It gripped his wrists and neck and ankles, letting only his belly and face sink through into the air. His skin was pale. The water soaked into it and made it soft and pliable and algae-rich. Julie tried to open her eyes and couldn't.

She lost the concept of her own shape. Like Marty, she could have a hairy belly that stuck out of the water and a mouth that dropped open like a fish trying to snatch oxygen from the air.

If she could open her eyes, regain her own body, she would lose sight of the man hanging above her head, and she didn't want to lose sight of him yet. She concentrated on his features and tried to draw clues from them. Maybe her mind had clung onto details that she had previously missed.

Julie's body sank further into the thick water, and Marty's did the same above her head. Julie whisked the water with her hands, but her ass and legs sank downward and Marty was pulled into the black sky pool and then he was gone. Julie resurfaced after bouncing her feet off the soft bottom, but when she came back to the surface, Marty did not. The forest dripped with cold air and Julie stayed in the warm pool longer to see what else would come. She let the water seep back into her ears and pulse against her temples.

Sickness began to travel up her spine and folded her body. She flipped to her side and warm water covered her left eye. Her knees sank and pulled the rest of her so she was face down in the water. She closed her mouth, but could not open her eyes. Her limbs were stuck too. Frozen and facedown. Julie's lungs contracted and burned. She needed to breathe.

Other images entered through her temples. Like the feeling of the first moments of sleep. They had no outlines at first. Only flashes of colour and thickness trapped in nonsense plots. But eventually, they became trapped within their balloon forms.

Literal forms turned abstract and wove into one another, moving together. Spots of bright white and green speckled the insides of Julie's eyelids and a great pressure formed in the centre of her forehead. They melted into dirt and reformed, and she saw the whale and the crushed raccoons, broken down into colours and movement. Around this scene were other creatures. Things with wings and fins. Large sea animals, squid and whales, swam through clouds above their heads, their tentacles and tails pushing currents of air across continents. Instead of constricting now, it felt as if her lungs were expanding. She shrank in the pool to something the size of a tadpole.

Julie turned over, opened her eyes and gasped.

The air burned her chest. She wanted Marty to tell her it was okay.

It was an insult that the forest looked the same as before she closed her eyes. The leaves hung sad from the trees and the spot of sunlight on the water maintained the same position and diameter. The only difference, that she could tell, was that the outlines on the trees were sharper than before. The greens were greener. She lay there for a moment and let lungfuls of cold air swoop in.

When she climbed out of the pond, the mosquitos gathered around her, a magnet pulling them from all over the forest, nothing else edible here except frogs. She used her undies to towel herself off and to wipe her feet. She hung them in a tree, dressed, started commando back to the road. She passed the old car. JLL wasn't there anymore. She took a last look at the long vine arms that reached across the hood.

With the water evaporating off her skin she was left shivering. She jogged on the way back to keep herself warm and to outrun the mosquitos. Brambles tore at her shins. In front of her she could see larger patches of light where the road cut through the forest.

As soon as she stepped back onto the pavement, the afternoon heat slapped her. The heat penetrated her skin. The last of the water from the pond evaporated from her shoulders. It left a film behind.

JLL was asleep in the passenger seat. Bert rattled around in the back. Julie tapped to wake her.

Through squinting eyes, JLL looked her up and down, rolled down the window. "What in the fuck happened to you?"

Julie declined to answer. She got in the driver's seat and pulled the Cadillac onto the road. They didn't speak again until they were far from Port Braid, away from everything that went wrong.

twenty-three

CARIBOU

Jerry Lee Lewis is my raison d'être. Actually.

Lodge pine forest sidled up to the car, closing in on the vein-thin road. They had been driving northeast for two and a half days, stopping to camp when Julie wasn't able to concentrate on the road anymore. As of yet, JLL refused to tell Julie where they were headed, only that they'd probably find Marty at the end of it.

"Probably?" Julie had asked.

"Yeah, probably."

"Not definitely."

"No, definitely not."

They had to keep moving because a creeping wave of animal death trailed just behind. If they camped out in one spot too long, maybe if they found a nice quiet clearing, then it started to happen around them. First, it was the mice. Always the mice. Drowning in puddles, dropping from trees. The previous night, they'd found one in their camping pot. If they could stand the mice, the wave intensified and they had to deal with hares and raccoons with heads smashed against trees. There had been a lynx. That one was hard to handle. Face simply buried in the mud.

Pebbles clanked against wheel hub and added a musical note to their otherwise silent trip. Julie tapped her fingers against the steering wheel and felt a rising bubble of heat in her chest. "You could at least tell me how you know where to go."

"That would give everything away, wouldn't it? I gotta piss. Stop here."

Julie signalled and pulled over so that her side mirrors almost touched bark. The two of them peed side-by-side, didn't bother to duck behind trees. A truck drove by and honked. The Cadillac was getting a lot of honks.

After peeing, they worked together to scrape bloodied sparrow feathers from the grill. They'd hit three. Two at once and another one ten kilometres down the road. It didn't make much difference to scrape it off, but JLL insisted. But they left the tires. The guts of mice and martins would work themselves out on the pavement.

"Come on," Julie said. "Divulge. I'm not driving farther until you tell me how you know where to go."

"You don't like mystery, do you?" JLL cocked her head. She rummaged in the back seat until she found the dog rib, then climbed from the car and took up a position between two skinny pines.

"Julie, do you have fur robes?"

"Fur robes?"

"Yeah, you know, rabbit, mink, bear, whatever. It could even just be a fur coat."

"Why would I have any of those things?"

"Guess I'll have to do this in my own skin, then." She rolled up the sleeves of her T-shirt, then bowed in front of Julie. She raised the dog rib above her head and took a lunge stance. The rib balanced between her index and middle finger and wobbled with JLL's shifting weight. JLL closed her eyes and muttered some sort of a chant. It glided on a line of hard and sputtered consonants, the *p*'s and *t*'s and *b*'s making her face contract and the wrinkles by her eyes deepen.

Julie squatted on the earth and looked up at JLL in the throes of something beyond her realm. She wanted the desire to laugh to go away. The dog rib balanced, trying to make up its mind, and then JLL stomped her rear foot against the ground and a strong, warm breeze started up through the trees. A flutter of birdsong rose from somewhere within the pines, manic, more like a warning call than a healthy territorial song. The dog rib tilted to the northeast. It dropped suddenly in that direction and clattered to the ground. JLL opened her eyes. She released the lunge and shook out her shoulders before tossing the rib into the rear seat of the car. The birds' voices died down just as quickly as they'd picked up.

"That'a way," JLL said.

"What was that?"

"Just a little something."

"From where?"

JLL looked up at the sky, and Julie let her eyes follow. A small cloud the shape of a bulbous seal stood in front of the sun. She watched it morph and move away, allowing the light to pour down full strength again. The sound of laughter brought Julie back. JLL sat against the hood of the car with her face stretched out into a hyena's grin. "You're so serious."

"No. All bullshit?" Julie picked at her thumb cuticle.

JLL laughed again.

"You ass!" She ran over and punched JLL in the arm.

"I thought you weren't the gullible type. I was counting on that."

"You are such a shit."

JLL stared into Julie's eyes, and without breaking contact slowly moved into the magic bone pose again. "Are you really that angry?" She did a lunge in Julie's direction and turned her eyes back toward the bulbous seal in the sky, which had now reformed into a fat eel.

Julie stood with her arms crossed and watched the show. She did not feel mad. Perhaps for the first time in JLL's presence. She told JLL as much.

JLL dropped the act. "Really?"

"Really, really."

JLL grinned and grabbed Julie. Their sweat made the hug feel like she was a steamed hot dog in a bun, parts of JLL sticking to her skin. A wash of horror followed. She felt happy even with her Marty missing, with his disappearance still fresh. With each day that he was gone, his edges faded. What inhabited her mind were forced snapshots of moments, Photoshopping together a face out of disembodied cheeks and lips and eyelids. No, she would think, the bags under his eyes are darker than that, and she would drop them a few shades. Remembering a person that you met once is easy. They're static. Unchangeable. But her father, over Julie's life, had different weights, numbers of wrinkles, waxes and wanes of psoriasis. And for a year, he wore a toupee. What she was trying to remember was a collection. He was a pool of facial features, of different clothes, of moods and distances. She didn't really know what he looked like. When she saw him again, she swore, she would memorize him better. Spend an awkward day studying. She tried to think of him now, but it was imagination and not memory. And he kept turning up dead.

"We should get going," Julie said, and she separated herself from the embrace.

They got back in the car and drove farther east. JLL continued to give directions. Sometimes, it was an exit so that the two of them could get a sandwich. Sometimes, to get timely supplies like toilet paper and toothbrushes. Once or twice, it led to a field and they parked and JLL tied a rope around Bert's midriff so he could wander around for a while, and take a shit if he hadn't already done it in the back seat. Alan's leather seats were getting scratched to pieces. From his living conditions, Bert seemed to be a kidnapee in a bad hostage situation, abused and held for years, but Julie felt no sympathy after the living-in-the-walls ordeal.

"We're like Thelma and Louise," JLL told Julie, "except we thieved a raccoon from the wild instead of killing a man in a parking lot."

"And there's no one after us."

"No one, no." JLL looked behind them at the empty road.

Sometimes, JLL directed them onto a new road, and Julie scanned for signs to see if she could make sense of them.

"Seriously, JLL, where the fuck."

When nighttime came, instead of sleeping outdoors, they began to sleep in the car, occupying off-ramp shoulders or residential streets, sometimes lying parallel across the front seats like a couple of spooning lovers. Once or twice, a concerned RCMP officer shined a flashlight in the window and told them to move along, receiving an enthusiastic "yes, of course" from Julie and a conflicting middle finger from JLL. The officers hardly gave any facial response. If anything, they raised an eyebrow or tapped their notepad, followed by personal questions. Always personal questions.

Where are you girls headed? What's the purpose of your trip? Are you two alone?

Thankfully, none of them asked if they could look in the trunk.

"Just tell them you're sleeping here and that you have the right," JLL told her.

"Why bother? This gravel parking lot isn't where I want to make my stand."

"You're allowed to have more than one stand in a lifetime, you know."

"Thelma and Louise only made one."

"So this ends with us going over a cliff?"

Highways faded into roads faded into dirt. When there were street signs, Julie no longer recognized the names. She thought that she knew British Columbia well, but maybe they were no longer in BC. She couldn't recall a *Welcome to Alberta* or a *Welcome to the NWT* sign but, then again, maybe people didn't give a shit which province the government decided they belonged to.

Julie and JLL had passed a mine and an oil extraction site, and both were alien planets situated in an otherwise green universe. After a while, though, even the green left them. Lichen and moss became the only plant life. The car rattled along a dirt road, avoiding rocks that jutted out at angles and heights belying years of erosion or weeks of flood.

The space in the Cadillac with JLL became comfortable. Port Braid was blue and this place was cool grey. She hung her arm out the window. The air through the windows carried with it a reminder of frost even though the sun shone. They were six days away from that other place.

JLL took out a toiletry kit and removed a pair of nail clippers. She set to work on her toenails, tossing the remnants—those she caught—out the window.

"Let me get this straight," JLL said. She squinted at her toes, digging something out at the corner. "You googled the shit out of me, and you have never done this for your mother."

"No."

"Why the fuck not?"

Julie looked out the windshield at an approaching mountain.

Its base grew in the foreground as the view of the peak gradually shrunk away. The mountains here had wider bases and gentler slopes, like the Rockies pressed down by a thumb.

"She died before the internet," Julie said.

"That's not why, though."

"Oh, no?"

"Nope. It's one of two things. You're chicken shit." JLL tossed another nail into the wind. "Or. You don't believe she ever existed. Actually, let's make that one thing. I think you're chicken shit *and* you're afraid she never existed. Maybe your dad picked you up at the supermarket."

"Beside the frozen peas."

"Exactly."

"Why do you care about my mother now?"

"Conversating."

Coming up on the left-hand side of the road, Julie saw a line of signs approaching. They were placed about every fifty metres, bolted to the wooden fence posts that paraded along the shoulder.

IN TWO KILOMETRES
THE BEST COOKING
(THE ONLY COOKING)
FOR 200 KM! PLUS,
GROCERIES!
COFFEE!
WORMS AND AMMO!
IN ONE KILOMETRE!
LOOK FOR THE BIG BOOT!

"They forgot to say the name of the place," Julie said. "Should we stop in?"

"Only if the boot really is big."

Julie expected a sign shaped like a cowboy boot, or possibly even a building with a boot's likeness, Old Mother Hubbard style.

Instead, it was really just a large boot. A fence post stood by a gravel driveway, and on top of that, a green gumboot with a sole at least twenty inches long.

"It's not that big," Julie said.

"Yes it is."

"I'm going to keep going."

"No. Pull over. I'm hungry." They'd only eaten an hour ago. JLL reached toward the steering wheel. "Do it."

"Fine."

They parked a hundred metres down the road and walked back to the driveway to check the thing out. JLL wanted to put the boot on, but it was nailed to the post. She asked Julie to give her a leg up, which she did, and JLL managed to get her foot inside the giant boot and balance on the post.

"Get Bert! Take a photo!"

Julie used her phone, which had no reception for the last couple of days, and used it for the last thing it was good for. In the photo, JLL stood tall in the centre of the frame, her non-booted leg bent stork-like, and her arms above her head, holding Bert into the bright sunlight. Bert's face pointed down toward hers, and his legs reached out to the side like he expected to parachute himself down. His tail had grown so much longer, and it brushed against JLL's forehead. The bright light drowned out most of the background, but the sunken wood frame of the store showed up as a skeleton. It was a good vertical shot. Maybe a nice orange filter later. Or just let the bright white and blue live on.

JLL clambered down from her perch, and they went inside the shack.

The place was called The Big Boot, it turned out. That's what the woman behind the counter said. As they talked to the woman, JLL held Bert between his front legs, his head cradled in her hand. He hung there limp with his eyes closed. Totally content. He looked fat. Probably was eating better than them. Lots of carrion to harvest in the past days.

The woman seemed unsurprised by the presence of a pet raccoon. She noticed Bert, but her eyes kept moving over the two of them. She twisted and untwisted her hair over her shoulder while they talked. Her voice drifted out like fog. She described the day's menu.

"Hamburger or steak, caribou or moose, and you can have baked potato or French fries, plus we have Coke and ginger ale and Fanta, or coffee, or tea, and we've got pie and bread with butter."

JLL had moose steak, fries and a Fanta, and Julie had a hamburger, no drink, but bread and butter on the side, and the woman charged them ten dollars each. There was a small plastic table in the corner with two lawn chairs, and they sat themselves there. The air smelled of wood dust and there was a haze in the light that came through the high-up windows. After being in the town of whale rot, the dust smelled good.

Stands around the walls held up various goods, like chips and sad-looking fruit. A fridge hummed in the corner, filled with Styrofoam containers full of nightcrawlers. JLL said the place reminded her of her hometown.

As they were eating, the woman moved around the shop in an imitation of someone practising good customer service. But there was nothing to do. She straightened the chip bags and moved a pile of brochures to the other side of the cash register.

"Hey," JLL said to her, mouth full of moose. "This is really good." The woman turned back and nodded at her. "Question— can I pay to use your shower?"

The woman nodded again and told her it would be a toonie. Her age was hard to decipher. She could be twenty or forty. Maybe without a lot of human examples around, your body isn't sure how to age. She gestured to a door at the back of the shop.

"Come on," Julie said. "We can't stick around forever."

"Have *you* considered having a shower?" JLL left her plate and followed the woman through the door, taking Bert with her. The woman returned a few minutes later as Julie was finishing up her hamburger. She continued her rounds of the shop floor. Julie watched her for a while and listened to the sound of water moving through the pipes above their heads.

"Can I ask you something?" Julie asked.

The woman sat down opposite her.

"Have you seen a man come through here recently, on his own, bald."

"White guy?"

She nodded. "He's got one hand."

"Nope. No one-handed white guys. Some bald guys, though."

"Are there any other places to stop around here?"

"Gas station 50 kilometres back. That's it, though."

"They have any food?"

"Nope. Just pretzels. Who are you looking for?" The woman picked up Julie's empty plate.

"Just some one-handed white guy."

The woman smiled. She paused with the plate in her hand. "You can spend the night here if you want. Nowhere else for a while."

"Nah, we should probably keep going."

"How come?" The question was so blunt.

"I gotta find the old guy, I guess." Julie just gazed at those high-up windows covered in dust. The shower stopped. The woman started on their dishes.

Julie slouched down and put her head back against the lawn chair. "Actually," she said to the woman. "There's something else."

"Mmm?" Her focus stayed on the dishes.

"Has any wildlife been offing itself?"

The woman looked over her shoulder. "Offing itself?"

"Yeah, like, running into the road, drowning, nothing like that?"

She frowned. Shook her head. "Nothing like that, no. You're a funny one." She squeezed more soap into the dish bath in front of her.

"But if they did?"

"Hmm?"

"If they did start offing themselves?"

The woman inspected the ceiling. "I'd ask them what they'd do that for. You?"

"I don't know. Join in, maybe."

The woman shrugged and put a pie plate in the dish rack. "If everything got bad enough, sure. Who wants to live with only people?"

Even though these were the only chairs and the plastic dug into the base of her skull, the shack still felt comfortable, and she was feeling reluctant to leave. She asked for another piece of pie and resolved to stay the night regardless of JLL's opinion. They could lock themselves inside and sleep while it came down around them. She was tired.

The slaughter was coming here soon, either following them or spreading out of its own accord, their distance ahead of the curve only coincidence.

When JLL came out of the shower, Bert was with her, soaking wet. JLL said she'd just rinsed him in the sink, but Julie suspected that the two of them had soapy fun in the shower, and that JLL had massaged his fur with baby oil afterward. He smelled like a newborn.

With no resistance, JLL agreed to spend the night. The woman, rightly, decided that Bert wasn't allowed in the bedroom. She showed Julie an empty shed at the back of the yard where she could leave the animal.

When night fell, the woman retired to her living room, and the sound of the CBC evening news echoed through the house. JLL and Julie sat on the bed in the spare room. It was decorated like a kid's room, and Julie wondered who that kid was and how long they'd been gone. It was entirely possible that the woman in the next room used to be the child who slept here, and the adults had shuffled off.

JLL and Julie lay back on the double bed and stared at the chipped, water-stained ceiling. Their arms touched. Heat radiated out of JLL's like a fever. Her hair was fanned out like a rooster crest across the sunken pillow. Julie reached over and touched JLL's cheek. She recoiled.

"You're fucking burning," Julie said.

"You're arctic zombie cold."

"I'm always cold."

JLL tossed a floral-pattern blanket onto Julie. The smell of moss wafted out of it.

"I was using it to protect myself against your dead skin, but you should warm up."

"I'll just use you to warm up." Julie flipped herself on top of JLL and pinned her limbs down. JLL shrieked. Julie nestled her face into the nook of JLL's neck.

"Jesus Christ, get off of me!" She clawed at Julie's arm.

"Jesus isn't going to get off you without a fight." Julie lifted up both of their shirts and pressed their bellies together. "Feel the love!"

JLL screamed again and bit Julie on the shoulder. Hard. Now it was Julie's turn to scream. She rolled off. JLL rolled in the other direction off the bed. She landed with a thump.

A moment later, the Big Boot woman tapped on the door. "Everything OK in there?"

JLL peeked over the side of the bed. "Yeah. Still living."

"Don't wreck anything." Then, more quietly, "It's my house."
They heard the sound of her shuffling down the hall.

"That was like going from hot tub to snow pile," JLL said.

"I always hated that. Marty loved it."

They passed the night listening to the radio. Everything was
in waiting. The reception wasn't clear, but enough came through
the speakers that they could make out classical music on the CBC.
Julie didn't have an ear for classical, but it was better than listening
to silence. JLL's breathing was slow beside her. She watched her
chest rise and fall along with the rhythm of music. JLL seemed
to have a physical attachment to music that Julie wasn't able to
feel. The biorhythmic connection wasn't intentional, but Julie
guessed that if you left JLL locked in a room with a track of music,
over time her pulse, brainwaves, menstrual cycles, blinks and hair
growth would all eventually line up, like a series of metronomes
on an unsteady surface.

At 11 p.m., the woman knocked on the door again.

"Hey, you two awake? I want you to come out here. See something."

They emerged from the room with brains foggy from static
radio and followed the woman down the hallway to her crammed
living room. Bookshelves, coffee tables and chairs were joined by
overflowing books and blankets. They sat on either side of the
woman on her peeling leather loveseat.

The right side of the TV screen buzzed with snow like the
radio. Composed of black and white dots, a reporter in a trench
coat stood in front of Finnigan's, the grocery store in Port Braid.
So the mess had finally been found.

The footage cut to scenes from the town. Julie covered her
mouth as visions of wildlife corpses flooded her eyes. A pile of bats
against the wall of a red barn. A road slathered in the unravelled

intestines of raccoons, skunks and deer. A bald eagle and fledgling broken-winged on a rock below their nest.

JLL slid her arm around Julie's back, and the woman clicked off the television. She put the remote control on the coffee table. "I want you to go."

"It's late," JLL said. "We're staying the night."

"This is my house."

"We'll be gone in the morning."

The woman stood up. She leaned her body over them. "Go. This, on the news, this is what you were talking about."

JLL stood up too. She was shorter but just as solid. "Drop it."

They stood like that, face to face, while minutes passed. Finally, the woman's shoulders dropped an inch. JLL spoke.

"We'll just be here tonight." JLL took Julie by the arm and they went back to the bedroom.

The woman yelled after them. "First thing. No breakfast. Nothing."

When the bedroom door closed behind them, Julie asked, "What now?"

"What do you mean, 'what now'? Just like the lady says, we sleep here tonight and get going in the morning."

"And keep hunting forever."

"Until we find your dad." JLL hopped back on the bed and put her arms under her head.

"We won't find Marty," Julie said.

"Yes we will." JLL blinked.

"Come on, no we won't."

Julie joined JLL back on the bed.

The night ticked on and the weight of the house dipped Julie into a restless sleep.

Her dreams were circular ones about the woman coming into the room and shovelling them out the door and them finding ways to sneak back in the window to sleep among the mossy blankets. There were broken windows and pried open doors, hiding spots in closets and showers. Every time they were found, the woman's hands came in contact with their shoulders accompanied by a loud thump. This morphed into the woman slamming their heads into the carpet, or door, or tiles. *Thump.* You've been found. *Thump.* Get out of my house. *Thump.* She stirred in the bed.

Julie woke up what may have been hours later. A sheen of sweat covered her body.

"JLL?"

Julie looked over and waited for her eyes to adjust to the dark. She reached over to shake JLL awake, but the bed was empty.

"Jesus Christ."

She heard the thump sound from her dreams and looked toward the door, waiting for the woman to enter. The air held the wet chill of still-dark morning.

Another thump.

It came from above her head.

Thump. Thump.

One on the roof and a second just outside the window. Something else pinged against the window. Julie squinted to see a flurry of moths bouncing off the glass, though there was no light inside the room. There was only the red flash of the clock to draw them inside. The moths varied in size, but the ones that made the loudest ping were furry white things with bodies of barely evolved caterpillars. Fluffy maggots with wings.

As they thwacked against the window, their wings left powdery outlines on the glass. After three or four hits, individual moths would fall away.

Julie sat in the bed with the damp-penetrated blanket wrapped around herself. She listened for sounds from the bathroom, hoping for a flush of the toilet to indicate that JLL was on her way back.

But there was no sound from the bathroom, and Julie's heart beat so hard that she could feel it vibrate up her throat.

She crawled from the bed and slipped on a baby blue robe that she found behind the door. The pilly polar fleece reached just below her knees and a whoosh of floral perfume drifted out, the ghost of someone else's vanity rising from the fabric.

She creaked the door open and peered into the hall. A faint light emanated from the restaurant section of the house. She crept along the cold hardwood and felt semi-protruded nails dig into her feet. Cold sunk into her toes, and feeling in her pinky dropped away.

The room was empty. Julie borrowed a pair of galoshes from a rack. They were priced at $14.95.

She stood outside The Big Boot and waited for divine intervention. Light from the full moon created a black-light glow. Any white surfaces—the Ford pickup in the yard, the rocks in the front garden, the siding on the top half of the building—shone fluorescent.

Julie heard another thump and looked toward the roof. She squinted and saw a dark figure fall from the sky. It made the characteristic thump that had intruded on her dreams. Another dropped several yards away from where she stood. Julie approached it and saw the skeletal outline of a bat on the path. It squirmed and used a wing to flip onto its feet. It pushed with its back legs, reaching out, one side then the other, with its clawed wings. The fall had taken its toll. The bat dragged its head against the gravel. After a moment, it began to flap its wings and took off. It lopsidedly rose up, one wing working less effectively than the other, and then, after a dozen or so flaps, it plummeted again. This time, it hit the roof and didn't fly up again. Other shadows made the same rotation. Fly up, fall. Like the eagles, but without sharp rocks to finish them quickly.

It had caught up to them.

Julie heard a shriek from behind the house.

She rounded the corner and heard Bert thudding around the shed. When she got closer, she saw that a dead bat lay by the crack under the shed door. Bert's paws darted out, trying to catch the mangled flesh.

Julie opened the door and pulled Bert out. He scrambled in her arms. His claws caught in the polar fleece. A chunk of the fabric tore loose, and Bert tumbled to the ground. As soon as his paws hit grass, he took off in a sprint.

He ducked under the wire fence at the back of the yard. Julie fit her body between the strands. Past a few scrubby bushes, the landscape opened up. Bert's lead gained. Julie watched his lilted gait—front and back legs moving in separate but parallel lines—as he proceeded up a long moonlit slope, hunched and looking like a broken old man. The robe hung on as Julie sprinted, only the double-knotted tie stopping it from billowing off. The galoshes bounced on her feet. She was glad for them when she came to a shallow stream past the next hill. Bert scurried across a plank. Bert's gait lengthened over the next field, and Julie tasted blood as she struggled to keep up. Little bastard, no bigger than her head, somehow covered ground so easily.

The grass became longer and harder on the plain. It stuck out in barbs that caught her shins. Bert was only visible by the path he carved through the grass. Julie could feel something else beside the barbs. Every once in a while, her foot would come down on some-thing soft, something that gave under her weight and then slid out.

Moonlight bounced off an animal ahead. Its head pointed upward and its mouth gaped in a smile. Distance and size were difficult to distinguish in the dark, but it was smaller than a wolf. A coyote. Its back heaved in a pant. Bert's path lined up with the its stand.

"Bert!"

The raccoon ran on with no heed to the predator ahead. The

coyote's tongue lolled out. Between its parted teeth Julie could see the illuminated grass behind. When he tumbled out of the grass by the coyote's shoulder, Bert let out a squeal. The coyote remained still. The raccoon ducked in front of its face and stopped on the other side, stood on his hind legs. The coyote's face pointed toward some cold constellation.

Bert slowed to a lope and continued his journey, leaving the coyote to make its last stand. A cold wind travelled up Julie's thighs and ruffled the baby blue housecoat. As she chased after Bert, she shivered and pulled the robe tighter.

Another field-length away, the land seemed to drop away. Standing on the edge was a human figure with a puff of hair. Relief washed through Julie. Her instinct was to wave, but of course she was invisible. Bert took off in a run again, but Julie walked. She knew exactly where the little shit had been headed.

There was another soft pulse under her boot and she slipped it off to see what she'd been crushing. The soles were mostly clean, but there was a sheen to the rubber tread. A piece of something was caught. She angled the sole against the moonlight and saw a pinkish tail looped around the maze tread. Field mice.

Maybe the mice wound their way around the coyote's feet too, trying to push themselves under its claws, or scamper into its fur to insert themselves in its mouth, or created nose-to-tail chains to hold the coyote fast to the ground. Under this grass must be a sea of mice that heard her steps and lined themselves in her way. Julie bent down to reach for the mouse she'd just crushed. She ran her hands along the earth until she felt the wet silk of the mouse's fur. She lifted it by a paw and inspected it. The neck was snapped. She tossed it to the side and walked toward JLL.

The air rested on an interlude of calm. The moon emerged from the clouds as a flashlight. It hung ready.

She heard a sound coming from her left. On the other side of a short valley, a smoker's group of fifty or a hundred caribou huddled. Their collected breath rose moonward in a cloud. The sight made her stop. Even this far away, even as they stood still, the power inherent in the animals radiated.

When Julie got to JLL, JLL was already holding Bert in her arms. They stood atop a ridge that ran far into the moonlit night. The base of the ridge was a cheese grater of outcropped stone. Below, a black slash of road cut across the landscape.

Bert looked calm, with even breaths and half-closed eyes. JLL looked calm too. Her face was relaxed and her hand moved slowly over Bert's fur. Her face was a different shape with the muscles relaxed—the cheeks longer, the thin lines by the eyes gone.

The voice of a caribou—like the metal screech of a screen door—came from farther down the ridge. The animals wove between one another, a discontent mass of fur.

JLL caught her gaze. "He's not here."

Julie scanned the horizon in a panic.

"*Not* here," JLL said. Her eye muscles retightened and her age returned.

"What are you talking about?" Julie asked.

JLL lifted Bert to her mouth and yelled into his fur. Her voice bounced off the road below. Bert squealed and slipped from her grasp.

Faraway coyote yips agitated the air. Moths flitted against their skin. Being in front of JLL was sitting too close to a campfire. Julie, pleading for an answer, tried to pull JLL's gaze to her own.

"I bet everything on him being here," JLL said.

Julie looked at her surroundings. A road on its way to some-where else. A single scraggly bush clinging to the ridge and the layer of permafrost six inches below their soles.

"There's nothing here, JLL." The only thing that demarcated this section of the rock wall from the rest of the ridge was a loose pile of gravel.

JLL closed her eyes. She breathed in and out, looked over at the caribou. "They are fucking awesome, though, huh?"

She was standing like queen of the mountain, legs spread and head high. Bert sat at her feet. JLL grinned so wide that her molars caught the moonlight, but a meniscus of tears rode her lower lid.

Julie bit at the insides of her cheeks until the taste of metal coated her tongue. "Tell me why we're here."

JLL glanced at Julie. She rubbed her forehead and pulled a ball of newspaper from her pocket, compacted as though she had prepped it for swallowing whole.

The caribou herd pawed at the ground and shifted to find a stance that offered relief. Their breath shot upward.

JLL handed the newspaper ball to Julie, who picked at the edges, careful to preserve the yellowed paper. JLL took it back, pressed the paper flat against her thigh and handed it back ready to read. Julie worked her cheek between her teeth and looked at the article. Once it was open it was overly familiar to Julie. She recognized it from that rainy night when she was a teenager, when it was in his grasp as he leaned over the piano, and she stood hidden in the darkness outside, rain distorting the image.

Julie stood dumb with the newspaper in her hand. "Where did you get this?"

"His underwear drawer. But never mind."

In the photo, there were three smiling women. Two with short hair and one with long. The same three women she wondered about that night. JLL tapped the one with the handsome boy's cut. "That's your mom. I did your homework for you."

Julie shook her head, but not because she didn't believe her.

Under the flashlight moon the words jumped off the newspaper.

Brenda Bird, it seemed, drove off Highway 57 and struck a rocky ridge near a restaurant called The Big Boot. The words "Big Boot" were underlined over and over again with pen.

"That newspaper was unmarked when I first looked at it," JLL said. "I really thought this was where he'd go." She pointed down at the gravel. "I'm pretty sure that's where she hit."

Julie shook her head, gazed unfocused at the black scar of a road below holding its non-memory. JLL had inserted into her mind, without consent, sights and sounds for an event that had passed in her absence, and with this insertion there was no room for romantic notions of a piano bench left behind for her ass only. This road was a place of empty violence. A human removed and memorialized only in a dented section of a rock wall. Another violent scar on the Earth's surface rendered innocuous without the right context.

The caribou grew more restless, their minds infected by ideas that travelled from Port Braid, where a whale had once swum onto shore. They jostled off one another. The group began to walk, moving closer to the ridge. The caribou's snorts and hooves generated a drumming clamour even at this distance.

"Maybe he went home," Julie said. "Maybe you fucking drove us out to the middle of fucking nowhere when Marty's at home and I could be there by now. Drinking fucking tea."

Julie squeezed the newspaper back into a tight wad and pressed the article back into JLL's hand. She looked at their surroundings. The jostling caribou, the swaying northern grasses, the wire fence of a distant farm.

But if there was any chance he was here, she had to find him. The caribou kept moving toward the ridge. Julie looked to the spot they were headed and started toward it. Where they were going, that would be the place. She walked close to the edge. Triangular crags looked up at her from the bottom. JLL followed behind.

The change in the caribou was clear. They'd no longer stand on that ridge and lose their numbers year by year, losing their elders and youngest first and then advancing inward to prideful high-antlered members. Better to go out in a flash together. With each jostle, the caribou aligned tighter to face the cliff.

Shoulders brushed shoulders and antlers butted one another into action. As the antlers crashed together and locked at the joints, the mass moved forward in an amble.

Where the ridge and the road began to bend, there was a dark shadow on the shoulder. Julie's chest caved. She started to run. It had to be him. JLL yelled after her, but Julie couldn't hear her anymore. The shadow on the shoulder of the road sharpened and took the shape of a car. She thought she saw a person inside. She thought she might see movement. A tube from the exhaust of the vehicle ran through the back window. Her head pounded as she ran. She had to get in front of the herd. Pebbles of dirt kicked up by the galoshes bounced off her legs. A gluttonous hunter's trophy wall advanced toward her, a curated collection of antlers and overglossed glass eyes. The animals were close now. She smelled the mustiness of their fur. Saw their nostrils flaring as they trotted. She ran closer.

The space to duck in front of the oncoming herd grew thin. She felt the vibration of pounded earth under her steps. Marty could be in the car dead or alive. Soon she would know. She wondered if this was how Marty felt, craving to be cleansed in a bath of sharp hooves, or if it was only the afterward he wanted, to be pinned, dark and quiet. Soon she would know.

The hooves drummed the packed dirt and clinked off stone as the herd picked up speed, increased their power, moved up the last hill. The moonlight reflected off their antlers and caught the whites of eyes. Their breath a jet stream streaked along their route. The dark car was on the other side, invisible gas swirling inside. Maybe they would split their numbers, go around her like a tide. Her head thumped with the coming herd. The sound overwhelmed. The caribou developed individual faces.

She was yanked backward by the elbow, fell to the ground. JLL's sour breath close to her mouth.

"If it's him, he's gone. I haven't seen taillights since I got here. He's gone." Julie shook her head, but JLL insisted again and again. *He's gone.*

The train of caribou advanced, chugging in heavy breath. Pebbles of dirt bounced from the ground. The caribou loped faster and their antlers moved in an advancing wave. Time ticked down. Cold air whipped around her. It picked at the fringes of the blue robe and slapped them against her knees. The moths took a break from flitting against her ears and eyes, and the stars retreated to specks of dust, almost out of eyeshot. The caribou thundered through the last twenty metres.

JLL shoved her arms under Julie's and dragged her backward. A rush of heat came along with the leading front of the caribou. Julie and JLL scrambled back, gravel slipping under their steps, feet sliding on the loose ground, ending up on the precipice. They reached the margins of the caribou's route. The antlers clacked like the downing of branches in a windstorm.

Weight pressed on her eyelids. If Marty was gone, she wanted to sleep. Here in front of a galloping herd. This couldn't be Marty's death diorama—a tumbling herd, a romantic black scar of road, so contrary to his quiet existence in which he veiled himself from loud sounds, from crowds, from spectacle.

Julie was empty. She dropped to her knees as the caribou flowed in front of her. The stars were pinpricks of cold light and the moon a warm bath over the proceedings. All that was left was to stand on the ridge and watch. She wished she was being overtaken by the animals. Her trachea dried to a sticky surface that stung when she swallowed.

The first animal sailed over the ridge, legs flailing in air. The caribou's cannon bones snapped on impact. Its face was dragged along the runway of stone. Rocks pulled skin off its chin like a grater. The next animals glided over the ridge. The white of their bellies as they fell contrasted the stone. The sky buzzed with ship-abandoning flies. More caribou arced to the hard earth and skidded to a stop. Behind them the car sat silent and dark.

Two caribou collided mid-air over her left shoulder, and one of them tumbled directly down. Animals piled on top of others, pushing out the final breath they had retained. Some tried to rise, only to be pulled down by the relentless onslaught. The animals on the ground pedalled their legs in the air, trying to catch traction. They flipped to their sides and tried to rise on weak legs, only to be hit by another of their herd.

The caribous' grunts and screams echoed and still more of them piled from above. The animals poured over the ridge until it was no longer a ridge but a slope of muscle and skin. A few stragglers at the back of the herd, ones that looked very young or old, dropped their speed and plodded around distraught, no ridge over which to fling themselves.

The air stilled. The insects landed, finding their former hosts among the pile. Whatever had driven the caribou seemed to be gone.

Julie began clambering over the pile, grabbing handfuls of fur to steady herself as she climbed down to the road. The animals stank of musky piss. Their ribs contracted under her feet. Some of them still breathed, lifting her up.

Finally, she reached the road. The pavement was still warm. A few confused animals limped, swung their heads side to side, trying to make sense of their herd formation. Behind her, JLL crawled down the hill of caribou.

Julie walked to the car. The Milky Way bisected the sky. She tried to pick out the smallest individual point of light. Pins and needles travelled up her legs and reminded her she was alive. She recognized the shape of the bumper, the bent licence plate. The car was still running. She heard the engine turning.

The smell of the caribou's moss-rich fur mixed with the copper of blood. The trek to the vehicle was long, each step feeling like it might snap her legs.

Through the window was her father's bowed head. His forehead rested against the steering wheel, his face, slack, looking out as though to shoulder check. The smell of exhaust leaked out. JLL put a hand on her shoulder, pulled her back. Gently, JLL opened the car door. The radio was on, playing an unfamiliar garage rock song. She held Marty's body in position and undid his seatbelt, then guided his body to the road. The bandana over his scalp slipped to the pavement. He was pale. Julie watched with a hand over her mouth, knew he was gone even before JLL felt for a pulse and shook her head. JLL switched off the car. Julie knelt beside her father, took his hand, which was cool but still had dampness in the palm.

The lines of worry she was so used to seeing on her father's face had been absorbed back into his person. His forehead and cheeks were smooth, the red gone from the patches of psoriasis.

But that he looked calm was of course an illusion. Julie felt that she was choking. She was holding the hand of an inanimate object. His teeth, exposed through his parted lips, were only chips of calcium phosphate. His eyes, behind his closed lids, unseeing globules of water, salts and collagen.

It could have been a different ending, in which Marty was able to tell her that he'd tried, but that now he preferred to go. That he'd worked through his options. In this ending, Julie tells him that she understands. They'll miss each other. He's unashamed. They could be together as it happens.

It would now be her responsibility to carry the memories that his silent brain had released. He had left her a life of having to manically cling to details. In order to keep him alive she'd have to colour in the specifics of past birthdays and dinners, hikes along the shore. That's what it would cost to keep him.

"Life goes by really fast," she said.

JLL looked at her, kissed her temple. "Life crawls by. You just have a terrible memory. That's what it feels like when you have a bad memory. Skips and jumps. I wish I had a bad memory."

Julie looked at JLL, crouched by Marty's knees, her hair flopped over her eyes, a shadow cast across her face. JLL, who fought desperately to be remembered by the people she met. The performance of her life, the performance of death she sought. Using romanticism as a kind of anaesthesia.

Of course, clinging to details, his story, would never help Marty or make him feel better. He was gone. Julie breathed and let that thought settle. *Remembering could never be enough. In the scope of species and planets, all of this was forgotten already. We're all already forgotten, like those mice in the field, roiling under the earth then spat onto the surface, alive and seeing for only a moment before being churned back under, believing that what we see has significance, having time enough only to turn to the mouse behind us and describe what we observed.*

"We'll have to call for someone," JLL said. She told Julie she was going to walk back to The Big Boot. Julie could stay there.

A young caribou with stilt legs and molting fur trotted by, its hooves clapping against the road. The animal turned its head as it trotted, looking back at the pile of struggling animals. It circled back, snorted. Julie nearly turned to Marty to point out how the caribou seemed to coast over the pavement, its hooves resistant to slapping down. She dropped his hand when she realized what she'd done. Her father was gone.

She looked at him, the skin along the back of his neck, the backs of his arms, how they were becoming dark. *Humans are rememberers*, she thought. *Appreciators*. They take this job so the caribou, the dark gliding whales, the pallid bats, mean something, and so they themselves do too. Marty had gone from appreciator to one who needed appreciating.

She straightened her back. What was the point of loving these creatures? They were only the ones we happened to spot as we popped up for our turn on Earth. No one was mourning the ammonites and their reign of three hundred million years.

Julie looked at the area where her father had died. The temporary tableau. A silent rock face, a spatter of stars, animals already getting up and moving on, JLL disappeared over the hill. *Everyone is already forgotten*. She could relax. Even the mass extinction humans were creating, paring down the things worth remembering, trimming diversity into manicured homogeneity, running out of space while surrounded by an infinite vacuum, even this is forgotten as the galaxy moves to collide with its neighbour, as the stars accelerate out of eyeshot. In the end, Marty had left twenty years earlier than he might have. That was all.

Julie looked at her father's smooth pale face. He had donated a tiny space back to the world that could now be filled. He countered selfishness. Rejoined the dark, cold blindness of the universe. She looked at the few freckles by his elbow. The small crack at the corner of his lip. Remembering details was a panic, one she could let go of in the brief moment of fresh air between coming from the earth and returning to it.

Eventually an ambulance arrived. She heard the sirens cut the air for ten minutes before she saw its red and blue lights rebound off the ridge. Bert had found her by then and wove between her legs. She'd feel sad a long time. Maybe twenty years. She held onto Marty's hand until they lifted him on a stretcher.

twenty-four

HUMANS

Going back to town, JLL drove the Buick and Julie drove Alan's
Cadillac. Bert rode in the back seat of the Buick, an urn rode in the
front seat of the Cadillac. They arrived back in Port Braid early in
the morning, welcomed by the whale stench before they passed the
sign for the town limit.

At Marker 34, JLL pulled the Buick over. Julie kept driving. In
the rearview window, she watched her lift Bert from the vehicle
and set him by the edge of the woods. She left the raccoon with a
bag of potato chips. The animal stood for a moment watching the
Buick retreat, sniffed at a stain on the pavement, then ambled into
the bush.

The town was empty. Garbage filled the gutters along the
main road. Several street signs had been bent so they bowed to
the pavement. Before going to the bungalow, where the detritus

of a life lay waiting, Julie turned down the shaded road that led to Tallicurn Beach. She left the urn in the front seat with Midge's rib bone. Later she would have to figure out where to place them. She only knew she'd leave them together.

JLL backed the Buick in beside the Cadillac and they walked down the trail together, pinkies linked. They passed the groves of arbutus trees, their orange bark seeming to peel back in response to the sharp smell.

The beach was covered in a brown paste of aged blood and entrails. A flood of gulls had made this their home in the absence of humans. They passed the end of the whale's fin. While they walked, JLL talked about what she remembered about early Marty. He would fireman carry her and her best friend Rose when they didn't want to walk anymore. He told scary stories. JLL also asked Julie if she could stay for a while, just until she figured out where to go next. She could, Julie said.

They began to clean up the whale mess, something no one else had done. Their shoes slipped across the muck-covered sand as they carried manageable pieces into the water, so far out that waves lapped up their thighs. They dropped them with a splash. Turkey vultures shared air space with the gulls, their wings cutting sound like shrunken fighter planes.

Julie wiped her cheek and left a rusty smudge. She struggled to regain her breath on the shore. She and JLL found a clean rock to sit on.

The pieces of blubber floated on the surface and began drifting out. Julie turned back to the beach to shovel more whale blood back to the ocean.

ACKNOWLEDGEMENTS

There are a lot of people to thank for a first novel.

It starts, of course, with my family. My mom, Anne Braithwaite, who has my back in every way, and is my biggest promoter. My dad, Andy Neale, who was my first and hardest-working publisher. And my brother, Peter Neale, who provides much-needed comic relief.

Many thanks go to the team at ECW, including Michael Holmes, Rachel Ironstone and Jen Knoch. Editors deserve our undying love.

Thanks goes to my agent Chris Bucci, who was an early believer in this book, and helped get it where it needed to go.

Also, my professor Annabel Lyon, who encouraged me to pursue the strange, just when I needed to hear that. And all of those I met in the MFA program who helped workshop those strange fictions, including Janine Young, Chris Evans and Kevin Lee.

My bowling team, the Gutter Belles, also deserve thanks for commiserating and cheering with me during the publishing process.

The early readers of this book changed its shape and scope, so one of the biggest thanks goes to Jay Hosking, Chelsea Rooney and Kyle Shepherd. These are all writers and creators who I admire, and I feel very fortunate to have access to their minds.

But the biggest thank-you, of course, goes to Brendan Harrington, who, besides doing most of the above, having the best eye for continuity on the planet, and making me laugh, daily, until I might vomit, is the person that I love.

And Sulu, who slept at my side the whole time.

Jen Neale obtained her MFA in creative writing from the University of British Columbia. Her short fiction has appeared in *Maisonneuve*, *The Masters Review* and *Augur Magazine*. In 2012, she was the winner of the Bronwen Wallace Award for Emerging Writers. She lives in Vancouver with her partner and her dog, Sulu. *Land Mammals and Sea Creatures* is her first novel.

At ECW Press, we want you to enjoy this book in whatever format you like, whenever you like. Leave your print book at home and take the eBook to go! Purchase the print edition and receive the eBook free. Just send an email to ebook@ecwpress.com and include:

- the book title
- the name of the store where you purchased it
- your receipt number
- your preference of file type: PDF or ePub

A real person will respond to your email with your eBook attached. And thanks for supporting an independently owned Canadian publisher with your purchase!